"In this latest work from Rodrigo Fresán, the Argentine writer succeeds in offering us a book that closely resembles what he calls an 'orphan book.' These are books that come out of nowhere and that probably have no descendants, books like *Nightwood* by Djuana Barnes or *Oh What a Paradise It Seems* by John Cheever. They are books that feed on themselves, that are self-sufficient like autonomous machines, and that generally possess immense poetic force. In *The Bottom of the Sky*, Fresán writes the book that will come immediately after the era of apocalyptic books—the era that began with the Bible and the Aeneid, and culminated with postmodern books about the end of all possible worlds."—Enrique Vila-Matas

"*The Bottom of the Sky* shows us that reality *is* a kind of science fiction; science fiction *has become* reality. And while terrorism, invasions, and unending wars have led humans to treat one another like alien species, Fresán asks us to imagine that love, in its purest form, can survive and even triumph over chaos and brutality."
—Rachel Cordasco, *Speculative Fiction in Translation*

"Rodrigo Fresán is a marvelous writer, a direct descendent of Adolfo Bioy Casares and Jorge Luis Borges, but with his own voice and of his own time, with a fertile imagination, daring and gifted with a vision as entertaining as it is profound."—John Banville

"*The Bottom of the Sky* is an exuberant story transcending both space and time, shaded with hues paying homage to the sci-fi greats (with so many literary [and pop culture] nods along the way: Vonnegut, Dick, Cheever, Bioy Casares, Chabon's *The Amazing Adventures of Kavalier & Clay*, et al.). Fresán's ambitious tale is, at once, a love story, an enigmatic eschatological puzzle, a book rooted firmly in the present while simultaneously orbiting in a far-off realm, and a genre-transcending work unbound by formulaic construct or conceit. [. . .] Read Fresán. And then tell everyone you know to read him, too."—Jeremy Garber, Powell's Books

"A vast Argentinean bildungsroman of reading and writing, Rodrigo Fresán's *The Invented Part* . . . offers one form of resistance to encroaching fascism: style."—Adam Thirlwell

"A kaleidoscopic, open-hearted, shamelessly polymathic storyteller, the kind who brings a blast of oxygen into the room."—Jonathan Lethem

"I've read few novels this exciting in recent years. *Mantra* is the novel I've laughed with the most, the one that has seemed the most virtuosic and at the same time the most disruptive."—Roberto Bolaño

"[*The Invented* Part is] a tour de force. . . . Invented, and deeply inventive as well, an exemplary postmodern novel that is both literature and entertainment."—*Kirkus Reviews* (starred)

"The question of whether *The Invented Part* is a novel was a rhetorical exercise meant to draw out certain aspects of this text. Of course, it is a novel. It is, however, something much more: a resounding refutation of the assertion that the novel is dead, and a statement of how omnivorous and adaptable the form is."—George Henson, *Quarterly Conversation*

"Rodrigo Fresán elegantly balances the strange with the common, the experimental with the traditional, and the result is one of the most satisfying postmodern novels in recent memory."—Benjamin Woodard, *Numero Cinq*

"If Borges and Pynchon fell off a boat, Fresán would be the one to come out of the water."—Gilles Heuré, *Télérama*

The Bottom of the Sky

Rodrigo Fresán

The Bottom of the Sky

Translated from
the Spanish by
Will Vanderhyden

OPEN LETTER
LITERARY TRANSLATIONS FROM THE UNIVERSITY OF ROCHESTER

Library of Congress Cataloging-in-Publication Data: Available.
ISBN-13: 978-1-940953-78-6 / ISBN-10: 1-940953-78-2

*This project is supported in part by an award from the New York State Council on the Arts
with the support of Governor Andrew M. Cuomo and the New York State Legislature*

Printed on acid-free paper in the United States of America.

Text set in Caslon, a family of serif typefaces based on
the designs of William Caslon (1692–1766).

Design by N. J. Furl

Open Letter is the University of Rochester's nonprofit, literary translation press:
Dewey Hall 1-219, Box 278968, Rochester, NY 14627

www.openletterbooks.org

For Daniel,
in Ana's arms
pointing up at the stars

The Bottom of the Sky

Reality (like big cities) has been extended and ramified
in recent years. This has influenced time.
—Adolfo Bioy Casares

One can be a lover of Space and its possibilities [. . .] I am also
aware that Time is a fluid medium for the culture of metaphors [. . .]
Space is a swarming in the eyes; and time a singing in the ears.
—Vladimir Nabokov

Distances are only the relation of space to time and vary with
that relation [. . .] There are optical errors in time as well as space
[. . .] The only real journey, the only Fountain of Youth, would be
to travel not towards new landscapes, but with new eyes, to see the
universe through the eyes of another, of a hundred others, to see
the hundred universes that each of them can see, or can be. . . .
—Marcel Proust

I don't think you can stand outside the universe.
—Kurt Vonnegut

This notion about each creature viewing the world differently from
all other creatures—not everyone would agree with me [. . .]
We have a fictitious world; that is the first step.
—Philip K. Dick

Sometimes I think our presence here is due to a cosmic blunder, that
we were meant for another planet altogether, with other arrangements,
and other laws, and other, grimmer skies. I try to imagine it, our
true place, off on the far side of the galaxy, whirling and whirling.
—John Banville

Oh, let us rush to see this world!
—John Cheever

I

This Planet

Find yourself wherever you find yourself, near or far, if you can read what I now write, please, remember, remember me, remember us, like this.

Remember us, remember me, remember that in those days the inhabitants of our planet, of our tiny universe, were divided into interstellar travelers and creatures from other worlds.

The rest were just secondary characters.

The anonymous builders of the rocket.

Or men and women enslaved by distant creatures of impossible anatomy that, nevertheless, a great mystery, always spoke our language perfectly.

Or humans who practiced an extraterrestrial tongue that, an even greater mystery, was so similar to the English spoken by a foreigner of a not-too-distant country.

And *astronaut* or *alien* weren't yet terms of common use.

They weren't, like today, present equally in the mouths of children and the elderly. Those words, like a familiar flavor, easy to identify at first bite for teeth both young and new or old and fake.

It wasn't like now (think of technological jargon as a new form of pornography, of the production of military and domestic gadgets of all size and utility, of faces and bodies modified by laser procedures, of a life after life, and of alternate realities tangled in a web of small computer screens), when there are days that I'm invaded by the suspicion that all the inhabitants of this planet are, without being aware of it, science-fiction writers.

Or, at least, characters created by science-fiction writers.

Back then, in the beginning, it was different.

Back then, in that now-old New Age, space was truly dark and, at the same time, a blank page to be filled with the flashes of our prayers and promises and supplications.

Back then we were paid to imagine the unimaginable and the future was always so remote, at a distance of centuries, of millennia.

And there were those who liked to write about earthlings climbing aboard rockets to climb ever higher.

And there were others who opted for the inverse approach, preferring to write about extraterrestrials who come here to lay waste to everything, sparing a lone witness to put it all in writing. Thus, the ending of their story superimposing and anticipating itself in the beginning of our story, its pages left behind to instruct those who, with luck, would come after and start over. A new tribe of individuals of scientific aspect—lab coats and glasses and always-lit pipes under spacesuits and helmets—building amid the rubble and ruins and trying to understand who all those armless, headless statues of onetime heroes or villains were. Future men, amnesiac from centuries of walking through immortal ruins, unable to specify what took place, but imagining so much about what might have happened to the ancient denizens of those palaces and mausoleums and thereby creating, without wanting to but maybe with an inkling, a new form of reverse science fiction. A science fiction that would be nothing less than the myths, the events, and, finally, History. Because the History of what was—every new theory, every historical essay—is also a science-fiction novel.

What has happened is as fantastic as what is to come.

The past never stops moving though it appears motionless.

Like snow.

And yes, there was snow and there were snowmen, men made of snow.

And there we were—Ezra and I—in the snow.

And our planet is never more another planet—never does it feel more alien and distant, never so new and so different—than after a long and heavy snowfall.

And that year—remember it, remember us, like this—it snowed like never before.

And the two of us there, in the snow, standing in front of all those snowmen and that huge sphere. And it was as if we—Ezra and I—were ascending through the snow, motionless but alive in the pale light of the new day. And it was as if each snowflake—distinct from all the others—were a singular star. And snow—see the snow, feel the snow—makes everyone more poetic and makes me a bad poet.

And a gust of wind and you in the window.

And it was as if the wind had been invented to blow through your hair and proclaim that, though invisible, it too had a shape: the shape of your hair in disarray, in the air of that dark daybreak, was the shape of the wind.

And the snowflakes moved, pushed by a rush of energy, and the two of us, there, like the inhabitants of one of those glass and plastic globes that a higher power, or a giant, shakes to create a white and imprisoning storm.

A storm that fits in the palm of the hand that summons and sustains it.

And the two of us—Ezra and I—there inside, happily trapped, in your hands.

We, the two of us, who called ourselves The Faraways and who began and ended in ourselves.

And yet, true enough, there were others who considered themselves Faraways—in the vicinity of our barely plural singularity, a singularity of only two—simply out of proximity. Orbiting around us until, inevitably, they grew tired of it and of our indifference, and went off in search of more interesting attractions and bigger groups of friends.

And it was because the two of us—Ezra and I—felt we were so different.

And we liked to consider ourselves distant beings, of a familiar configuration but driven by a decidedly alien will. The will to know ourselves intruders and subjects of a private mandate to travel great distances, to cross space, to arrive at the bottom of the sky, and, once there, to turn around and go back to the point of departure. And, only then, return to a home we didn't recognize and that didn't recognize us.

Then we would wander aimlessly through streets and parks.

Our bloodline would be dissipated and impossible to detect in the mix of new bloods.

We would have become foreigners whose only comfort would be to write about precisely *that*: about belonging nowhere after seeing everything.

And we would be happy.

Someone once said that behind every science-fiction writer (at least behind the first, the *original,* science-fiction writers) there was, always, a frustrated scientist.

I am not entirely sure this is true; then there's Ezra: first a successful scientist, then an agent of *classified* documents, and—when the future only interested him as a launch pad to a past in need of modification—forever a frustrated science-fiction writer.

Ezra, who—when you disappeared without logical explanation, after the night of the great snowstorm, without even leaving a goodbye note, an *amazing story* or *weird tale* or *astonishing travel*—decided to give it all up in the name of exactitude.

But I'm getting ahead of myself without clarifying the trajectory of this story: where its head is and where its tail—bleeding from so many wounds inflicted by its own fangs—ends.

The Faraways, on the other hand, maintained that behind every physicist and astronomer there lay the inert but not dead—just in suspended animation—body of a storyteller who'd succumbed to the cosmic temptation of calculations and formulas. And yet, beneath all of that, barely hidden, *top-secret,* the true possibility of a writer waiting to be activated by a nervous password not on the tip of the tongue, but in the tips of the fingers. Someone who, impotent and unable to attain the ecstasy of limitless speculation, ends up settling for—simulating that tentative pride of those who want to believe themselves special— the stainless steel walls of a controlled-climate laboratory.

A code. A combination of numbers and letters. A formula. A heavy metal door that opens like a book onto facilities whose core can only be accessed via the repeated use of successive passwords implanted in the magnetic bands of steel cards that guide you down white corridors watched over by unblinking soldiers and sleepless cameras. The eyes of both rigidly fixed on a pure present, fed by the paranoia that a more evolved and efficient Apocalypse is being invented and set in motion in some other laboratory or in a cave where a special button is being pushed to kick off the end of everything in this world.

And the challenge always lies in knowing who will be first to begin the end.

But my story, the story of The Faraways, is just beginning or, better, I am, here and now, beginning to begin it. Forgive all these preliminary words. I justify them saying they are the cautious whispers of someone who doesn't dare flip certain switches known to activate certain memories.

Memory like that inexplicable time-machine and the past like a fourth dimension and an alternate planet containing life slightly more intelligent than the life inhabiting the present.

For in the past (arriving there so much later—the horrifying thing about the past—because we can only see it from the future) we're all wiser.

Traveling to what already was, we comprehend effortlessly and contemplate with clarity, errors that, in truth, we cannot and won't ever be able to correct. But at least we get the consolation prize or the agonizing punishment of knowing exactly how we could've done better, how we could've changed to improve the results, altering certain factors or making different decisions. Looking back, there are many who, before using and, maybe, getting hooked on the powerful drug that is the past, opt instead for another drug: oblivion.

And then, I suppose, they inhabit an eternity of sunsets, always new and unique.

Thus, life lasts but a day and then starts over.

That isn't, hasn't been, and won't be my case.

The acute perceptions of memory's disruptions, of irregularities of the heart—the palpitations of time that now crawl, then run, and later fly—have always been my pleasure, my privilege, and my condemnation.

Memory is an astronaut struggling to establish lasting connections between the stars, many of which are dead; but the act of remembering them lights up points in a space that, though distant and out of reach, still form part of the proximal yet elusive nebulas of our thoughts. To remember is to discover without ceasing to search. We don't know if a memory is something we give up for lost just as we remember it, or, if it's something lost that we suddenly recover.

And perhaps the oddest part of all (or maybe most normal, because distortions of space-time are one of the genre's most recurrent clichés) is that now, when my memory aches with the acute, throbbing pain of its own loss, I am trying to remember through writing what I no longer remember unless I use my hands.

And I don't do it with the utilitarian and almost telegraphic language of science fiction.

I am referring to that style that is really an absence of style, where what actually matters is plot, a good idea, a new prophecy. Perpetual interest in the future but such primitive writing.

No: my lines are long and sinuous (parenthesis functioning like the pincers of crustaceans made hubristic and swollen by Epsilon Rays), more like those of an experimental yet inexperienced nineteenth-century gentleman at the turn of a new century.

Once again, the past.

How they wrote in the past when books could count on all their reader's time and all the time in the world fit inside those books that were so difficult to escape from; because so much more took place inside them than outside them. Books for a reader from an era that was ending so another era, ready to establish the idea and the theory of a distant future, could begin.

And, so, a new and paradoxical conviction that, by prolonging our lives, the future would not only stay far away, but we would be able to arrive there.

So, a mutating reader, suspended between two phases.

A removed reader with access to everything.

Someone who would soon discover—amid the explosions of a Great War, supposedly unique and final—not only that the future was expanding, but that time was accelerating.

Someone who—despite never having had the right tools to imagine complicated teletransportors or galactic highways wrecked by black holes—was soon flung onto the *continuum* of an age of gears and levers and inventions, ready to do what's necessary in reality in order to disobey and rebel in fiction.

Back then, I imagine, the air was flammable and sparks flew when lover's lips touched, for kisses were historic and electric. Static electricity moving everywhere and suddenly anything could trigger combustions both external and internal.

But I must insist: why do I write these long, serpentine sentences, these blurry images laden with adjectives, why do I think that this, that all of this happened, that all of this happened to me, and yet . . .

Patience, be patient, is it all right to ask for patience the way one asks for mercy, swearing you'll put everything in order soon or die trying?

Here and now—maybe that's it, maybe that's why I write this way—I am also *like this*: the long lines and brief thoughts of someone who has surrendered to the reign of machines, not understanding them, but using them. Using them, but never quite forgetting that he won't ever fully understand exactly what electricity is (animal or vegetal or mineral?) or how the simplest motor works. Someone for whom airplanes will always be elevators without cables. A man on the edge, a frontiersman, someone who's not exactly anywhere, but who sees everything from a perspective more shifting than privileged, and yet . . .

I write all of this amid the inaudible din of a secret battle I know is already lost.

I write this in an attempt to overcome the forgetfulness that washes over me like a black tide, like something blotting out the stars. Stars going out one by one, like worn out names that have been used and repeated so many times that their corresponding faces have faded. A blackness that hangs over me and drowns me and at first I try to stay afloat, but before long, I understand that there's no sense in resisting the call of the depths and oblivion and I let myself go, I sink, liquid air bubbles escaping from my lips and out through my scuba suit.

I write so that all of this functions like the debris of a shipwreck readying to come up to the surface while, on the other side of the river, a column of black smoke rises, dancing to the music of red sirens in a city where, tonight, no one will sleep.

Diffuse fragments, yes, but pieces of the same hull and from the same head that can maybe offer some idea of what it was that sank or, at least, serve to indicate the more or less exact spot where there lies, motionless, everything that once sailed, guided by charts, compasses, and constellations.

I write to leave something behind, not to clarify what happened, not to help me remember (I can almost see myself here after a time, as if I'd decided not to go but to stay, reading these pages, understanding nothing of the little they contain and only a little of the nothing they attempt to explain).

I write like someone saying goodbye.

I write all of this that I never planned to write. A good part of it I don't even write, but just think, that elusive and pure form of writing that is unadulterated memory, rare nostalgic energy, its workings incomprehensible until it's put down in writing, reduced to disconnected words. I write propelled by the reactive fuel of an unexpected visitor.

I write, opening and closing parenthesis (maybe, borrowing those parenthesis that embrace numbers and letters but not words, to approximate my uncertain language with mathematic precision, with the exactitude that Ezra has surrendered to in order to define the contours of the diffuse), the way I closed my roll top desk when I heard someone knocking.

And I got up and went down to open the door.

A young journalist.

Though I call him a "young journalist," the truth is I don't believe he was a journalist in the strictest and most professional sense of the term.

I don't believe, as he stated, that he worked for a "specialty" magazine because, as far as I know, magazines "specializing" in science fiction no longer exist and, if one had survived it wouldn't devote its limited pages to interviewing antiques, but to featuring the exchange of opinions between fans more interested in the special affect produced by the special effects—all that erotic, digitalized technology to dig their fingers into—of the next big, frigid blockbuster of the hot summer.

I didn't believe him when he showed up at my home without calling ahead; so I made him swallow the bitter pill of convincing me of the veracity of his alleged credentials.

I preferred to think of him, simply, as someone who *needed* to imperiously ask many questions (questions he'd asked himself many times, silent and alone), in order to, if possible, hear the perfect answers in the voice of a stranger he knew—without ever having spoken to him—all too well.

A young journalist (I don't think he was exactly "young" either; but it's also true that I've reached an age when nearly all living beings are, or appear to be, quite young compared to me) paid me a visit today and asked many questions about things that happened long, long ago.

At first I imagined his small notepad contained, written in an illegible hand, words cut in half, more disjointed than abbreviated, a long list of questions revolving—as so often happened back then, on the rare occasions I let myself be cornered and caught—around the figure of Warren Wilbur Zack. His life so different from mine. An opposite life. An anti-life. Everything that happened to him—reading aloud by the light of his last wish—like everything that *never* happened to me and . . .

Here, I believe, a pause is in order.

A pause, like these other empty parenthesis where—paragraph after paragraph—I think I glimpse the true texture of time. Pauses like the antimatter matter between one space-time leap and the next, like the moment when the pieces rotate into place and slide into the grooves of the complicated mechanism of what we decide to remember or what decides to be remembered.

One more pause before I allow myself to think about Zack . . .

. . . like taking a deep breath before diving into that memory and descending into its depths.

Zack, who was crazy, who became a science-fiction writer as soon as he realized that nobody was going to publish his odd, realistic novels about couples who fight all the time.

Zack, who conjured an almost immediate future where nothing functioned properly apart from the invisible yet oh so solid device of paranoia.

Zack (Zack's always-moist eyes, like those of a sad dog, his docile and canine smile, his face covered in fur, fits of snapping and barking at the most unexpected moments), who survived on canned dog food during his most difficult and impoverished days and who could no doubt recommend for you the best and tastiest brands.

Zack, who married and divorced so many times and Zack's many children dressed in brilliant rags, filing behind him through the streets.

Zach, who in public would say things like "we science-fiction writers are pathetic beings: We can't talk about science because our knowledge of it is limited and unofficial, and usually our fiction is dreadful" or "there is nothing stranger than to write something believing it is untrue, only to find out later that it was actually true."

Zack, who never stopped dreaming about his telepathic, twin brother who died at birth (and from whom he swore he received messages and commands), Zack, who was sure he was the reincarnation of an ancient Christian saint, lost in a "false reality" that in truth, he asserted, was nothing but a secret wrinkle ("a kind of elaborate curtain") behind which still pulsed the invulnerable grandeur of the Roman Empire.

Zack, who was involved with West Coast militant groups like the Black Drummers and who reported that his files had been raided "by the CIA and the FBI and a governmental organization so secret that it has no name" because "in one of my books, without realizing it, I revealed the nature of the most absolute and definitive experiment that is being carried out by the most acclaimed and qualified scientists on the planet . . . I ask myself which book of mine it might be."

Zack, who didn't believe in other planets or in rockets and whose flight crews always ended up pushing the wrong button while distractedly thinking about some random thing, about Barbie dolls or psychotronic drugs of high voltage and density.

Zack, who died descending a ladder at the most ascendant moment of his career, when headlines and the stories on the evening news were beginning to look a lot like his fantasies.

Zack, who, at one of the only meetings or conventions we attended, smiled politely in response to my call for a return to the classic galaxies of science fiction.

And, yes, Zack was better than I was (Zack was better than almost all of us) and I laughed at Zack. I resented his acknowledged opportunism and the speed with which he wrote novels, novels that, it's true, I didn't like and didn't understand; but they were novels unlike any others.

Zack knew of my resentment and got his revenge in the most elegant and perfect way: at the reading of his will, it was revealed that he'd named me his literary executor and—those were hard times, I had no choice but to accept—stipulated that I receive a generous percentage of the profits any future adaptations of his work might earn. Just a few years prior, that designation would've been nothing but a bad joke and an uncomfortable and inopportune ordeal: much of his work was never catalogued and would have impressed no one but his underground followers. But just before he died, Zack's stock had been on the rise. His works were being rereleased in prestigious collections and his name was beginning to be heard, repeated more and more by the voices of "serious" writers who considered him "a secret prophet" or "someone who dared to look beyond" or "the philosopher who came from the future to help us understand our incomprehensible present." And what was most intriguing about Zack's novels wasn't their plots (difficult to adapt, strange, like a different language that was actually just an exotic variant of our own), but their *ideas*. Ideas that producers, screenwriters, and directors could distill into movies flooded with digital effects, popular and, on more than one occasion, critical successes.

The first that premiered—the one that turned on the engine of his posthumous mythos—was a noir mutation featuring sentient androids. I was hired in the capacity of creative supervisor and advisor and "specialist" in Zack's visions, and when the director offered to let me write the final monologue of a dying robot under the acid rain of a retro-futuristic Los Angeles, I thought I'd be able to take revenge against his ghost. I put words in his mouth that, I thought, Zack would despise: elegiac phrases honoring the memory of galaxies, where Zack's characters—more preoccupied with their place on Earth, or, at most, in a decadent Martian colony too similar to an industrial suburb—would never have dreamed of venturing, because there was nothing that interested them less than traveling far away. The speech overflowed with poetic lines easy to remember and immediately place. Many people found them moving and, I'm sure, there were some who cried during the filming of the scene. I felt that, with that, I'd done right, I'd managed to slip in a particle of restraint and nobility. A call to return to that future that we'd believed in so fervently in the past. My idea of science fiction contaminating Zack's idea of science fiction.

And yet, it's true, ghosts can never be beaten.

And my gesture was lost and swallowed up by the blinding light of a dead star named Warren Wilbur Zack: everyone thought he had written that humanoid machine's farewell under the rain, that it had been extracted from one of his many notebooks and unpublished manuscripts, which were no longer unpublished, but were being bought for astronomical sums that, like I said, I benefited from and that today are my only stable source of income, my means of survival.

The movie premiered, it wasn't a great popular success, but with time, it became a cult classic, almost a religion, an incessant maker of money and prestige, a masterpiece—there's nothing more marvelous than a cult artist who also makes money—admired by the young, who soon occupied important positions in the industry and declared themselves fans of Zack and his visions.

So it goes: I'm kept afloat by Warren Wilbur Zack, he pays my bills, my health insurance, he's turned me into an expert on his life and work, and I even wrote the first of his various biographies and annotated a volume of his eccentric letters and a collection of his "meta-philosophical-religious essays."

And it is regarding Warren Wilbur Zack that I get invited to speak, to answer questions, to lie.

But no.

Not this time. To my surprise, my young visitor doesn't want to talk about Zack and the legend of Zack and the array of rumors orbiting around the persona of Zack, the type of thing one hears at conventions or reads in fanzines. "Zack . . . Overrated," he says with a twisted smile that I can't help but silently appreciate.

My young visitor isn't seeking to elucidate some mystery about Zack, but to discuss The Faraways and the rumors circulating about the modern-day Ezra Leventhal and about *Evasion*. (Indeed, Zack was one of the few, if not the only person, who ever thought I might be the author in the shadow of *Evasion*. Zack explained to me, with that tone of voice that never sounded like an insult, but like a strange form of respect or, at least, like the interest of someone confronted with a rare species: "Your imagination is so imaginative . . . Your imagination has a logic and an order that I envy. You don't know what it's like to live with an imagination like mine. Inside my head, all the ideas yell and raise their hands at the same time, fighting to get to the front of the line and say their piece. In a way, I write so that I'm able to stop thinking a little.")

To my amazement, my young visitor wasn't there to find out about what I'd witnessed, but about something that I'd lived through and taken part in; something that today feels so far away, more shadow years than light years, but descending now at full speed, rolling toward me down the stairs from the attic of the past.

And, at the same time, his questions seemed like veils, concealing answers to other questions he dared not ask or didn't really know how to formulate.

And yet, I answered all of them.

Why did I answer him?

Why answer?

Because he reminded me so much of myself?

Because of his glasses with thick, black plastic frames (glasses that now, apparently, are in style and that, when he took them off every so often, didn't reveal the steely-eyed gaze of a superhero, but the fragile, naked eyes of one of those fish for whom the brilliance of the sun and the blue of the sea are nothing but an impossible-to-confirm rumor)?

Because of his crooked teeth (back then all *authentic* cultivators of sci-fi had bad teeth)?

Because of the impossible-to-hide pockmarks on his cheeks, wreckage of a difficult and still painful adolescence (those lunar, epidermal craters, dead skin where only with great difficulty might there have landed the extraterrestrial visit of a young kiss)?

Why did I feel he was like a ghostly vision of Christmas past, like fugitive spores seeping through a crack in the wall, leaving the damp stains of a distant galaxy?

Why the perturbing sensation that—at times—the same questions were repeated in different words to insure that he not produce a single inaccuracy?

Why when he left did he leave me with the gift of a supernova-intensity migraine?

Why didn't I resist, why did it feel like I'd succumbed to his sharp and persistent voice, like the buzzing of certain ancient insects?

Why . . . ?

To put it another way—if asked to explain my submissive and voluntary conduct—I was moved by his enthusiasm and respect for me, a person who, for him, wasn't really a person, but more like a symbol. Someone considered a living souvenir of a dead age that he sensed, or needed to believe, had been glorious and, I thought at the time, I bestowed on him that particular and solemn joy that one only experiences when facing a great ruin. Facing a monument from another age. Facing something you dig up first and decode later, to convince yourself that you understand absolutely everything without knowing practically anything.

His hypotheses, I suppose, were fuel for my vanity, immobile after so long.

For him I was a kind of deity.

One of The Faraways.

The alleged but never confessed co-author (and not mere editor and sincere prologuer, who claimed not to know or even suspect the true identity of the author) of *Evasion*. The faithful guardian of a thousand pages of a legendary science-fiction novel that'd been coming to me in the mail for several years (without the sender's name on the envelope, always sent from different offices), which nobody had read in its entirety (because it'd never been finished or it was so open-ended that it failed to meet the protocols of the genre), but about which many had written and theorized, drawing on the various fragments circulating in a way as underground as it was airborne. A science-fiction novel that wasn't a science-fiction novel and possibly, not even a novel. A science-fiction novel in which—unlike typical science-fiction novels where things happen all the time—almost nothing happened. Just a succession of sunsets—their many differences described in minute detail—contemplated by the last inhabitant of another planet. Little more than loose fragments and scattered extraterrestrial thoughts, which I finally collected and organized under a classical and typographical cover. Yellow background and black letters, dispensing with the illustrations characteristic of the genre that, generally, had little to do with what was said and told inside. A few handmade copies published with my own money (I want to emphasize this, I don't want there to be doubts about this: not with Zack's money) so long ago, in another century, in another millennium.

You might also say—I don't mean it as an alibi or an excuse—that in that moment, faced with the young journalist and his questions, I was still shaken, or more precisely, frightened, by everything that'd happened to me the day before. Which, lacking a better name but needing so badly to be named (because unnamed things produce the most fear) I (availing myself of the conspiratorial language so in vogue, *Expedients Z* and all that) had come to call *The Incident*.

But I didn't talk to the young journalist about The Incident and told him, even better, that I was depressed, but that being depressed didn't worry me too much: a recent psychological study had proven that the majority of writers had depressive personalities or came from melancholic bloodlines. So I qualified under both conditions, no problem.

I answered him how and as best I could.

I was honest but also partial, incomplete (*to be continued . . .*).

I kept to myself—as I've been doing for years, you should know, wherever you are—the antimatter of your name, or what you told us your name was, and now it slips through my fingers, as if I were chasing a firefly through a forest full of fireflies.

And yet, I believe, I was both generous and selfish: I remembered for him, but also for myself.

I told and answered and, I suppose, filled in or improved or invented some dark zones while simultaneously activating numerous protective shields of varying force and intensity.

Every question, it is known, hides too many possible answers.

And, in a way, all of them are accurate though maybe not correct.

The truth is fractal. It breaks into pieces and scatters in infinite directions. So, how to catch it.

Ah, yes . . .

I know . . .

By being progressively regressive.

Memory like the launch tower for the rocket of the past.

It's no coincidence, I think, that the countdown required to initiate a rocket launch is exactly the same as the one used by a hypnotist to make his subject, who has volunteered to come up on stage, surrender his will and fall into a trance.

Like this:

10 . . . 9 . . . 8 . . . 7 . . . 6 . . . 5 . . . 4 . . . 3 . . . 2 . . . 1 . . .

. . . 0

Zero.

Childhood is the zero.

Childhood is another dimension.

Childhood is the atmosphere-zero where, looking back, we feel we breathed deepest and best. But maybe this is a distorted impression, a result of too many years of insufficient oxygen and then, of course, there are some adults who are suddenly certain they remember being used in satanic rituals and secret orgies by their loving and, until that moment, perfect parents.

Childhood is pure radiation that refuses to disappear, making the needles of our Geiger counter jump at the most unexpected moments with a glowing, fluorescent green. That unmistakable science-fiction green. Alien green. The color of a particular moment that we thought had vanished but that was actually pulsing, wrapped in an artificial dream, electrodes attached to its head, lying on a stainless steel gurney. There, like I said: in a subterranean bunker only accessible by a magic word or, all at once, with the aid of a fortuitous and capricious stimulus that provokes failures in the previously inviolate and fortified security of our mind.

Childhood is that longed-for other planet that we travel from toward this planet. Toward our so-called maturity, which, we know now, will never be like that other early world where we dreamed of growing up, of stimulating our bodies' protons, of defying the heavy gravitational laws imposed by our elders, and flying off, breaking the barrier of their warning sounds, overcoming the speed of their lights, which invariably, with scientific punctuality and at a fixed hour, go out. Nine or ten tolls and then the key moment when at first we'd pretend to be asleep (all of a sudden I'm transformed into something else, I pluralize, I'm not just talking about me, but about so many others who were like me, clones fascinated by the same feeling and same longing for the future) and then turn on our flashlights under the covers and keep reading. Reading there, in a cave, living inside the adventures of some galactic guardians, our mouths full of difficult words and a gun bursting with lightning and thunder. And, of course, maybe most important of all, along with the voluptuous anatomy of Martian princesses that they wrapped themselves around, were the green tentacles of beings with thousands of revolving pupils that never tired of devouring those princesses with their eyes, which weren't, but at the same time were, our eyes. Their scaly skin a metaphor for our acne. Because, even though we never dared consider it even in the lowest of voices, it's possible that they were what enticed us, the illusion that, on some distant horizon unfit for human life, albeit by the most drastic means, someday someone might end up in our arms. A place where nobody had ever been: cyanide in place of oxygen, too many suns in the sky, and days as long as years. And maybe *there* women *like that* would notice us, notice people like the young journalist who has come to pay me a visit and ask me questions.

The young journalist has gone, but his presence and questions have radically altered the atmosphere of my world. His arrival has had an effect similar to that of a nearly undetectable but critical tear in an astronaut's spacesuit. Little by little the oxygen is escaping and thoughts flow and the sound of the memories is exactly the same as the sound of air seeping out through a tiny opening.

A hypnotic hiss.

A growing delirium.

And I float.

There's no above or below in space.

And I travel back to the past and, yes, it's a hazardous voyage. Because any intrusion into the process of transmutation (or whatever you want to call it) by a mosquito-sized quantity of foreign matter, or just stepping on a butterfly, is enough to make you arrive on the other side of the dematerializer (or whatever you want to call it), radically and definitively transformed or in a world that's no longer ours and that's been changed forever.

Memories are sensitive material, volatile.

Memories are particles in constant and increasing acceleration.

Memories have made neurons burn.

Memories can make you to forget everything.

So I must handle them with great care. Hermetically seal them in the command room and review the coordinates and controls again and again before deploying them. Touch them with robotic pincers connected to my brain with wires. Move them telekinetically and bring them near my optic sensors and my heavy breathing of a spaceship admiral, almost a ghost, while I wander around the orbit of my memory.

Now I am a machine.

I feel—I feel I am—like a machine.

And I've been feeling like this ever since The Incident, since a few days ago when they put me in a machine to try to find out what was going wrong with my machinery.

And, when I came out, everything had changed.

People were screaming and running in the streets.

Buildings were coming down.

Everyone was looking up at the sky or taking pictures of the sky with their little phones.

And there I was, I who've not yet gotten used to the fact that phones have won the streets and that people go around by themselves but talking to someone far away, like sane lunatics, plugged into a world where technology has been miniaturizing knowledge into something increasingly small and simultaneously more inclusive and more exclusive. Multiple functions in devices that fit in the palm of your hand. Devices impossible for me. For someone who grew up convinced that computers would be as big as buildings and only operated by wise grownups and not, like it is now, by children who barely know how to talk and who carry them around in their pockets and use them to travel far away, with faraway eyes, with the minute but all-powerful power of their fingers.

Now I'm armored (though stories where computers or robots suddenly humanize have become almost a subgenre in the genre) and I make myself impenetrable and logical and unfeeling.

Or at least that's what I strive for.

It's the only way, I think, that I'll be able to report what happened with any kind of objective indifference, before it's too late and the hour of *my mind is going* arrives . . .

To try to separate myself as much as possible from my species: transient and fragile beings and, unlike what we know about other animals, oh so variable and unstable. Men, happy and sad and foolish and wise and yet, maybe for that reason, without the ability to arrive at the collective agreements and accords that other living organisms enjoy. Men who decide to smile or commit suicide, all together, perfectly interconnected, beyond any doubt and men for whom nothing could matter less than the hypothetical existence of an authority embodied in a god who has fled the scene or in an advanced intellect with a more-than-a-little disturbing sense of humor.

I refer here to a scientific god.

A god who sucked down the half-toxic half-ecstatic air of the synagogue for which not even the greatest interstellar traveler was prepared.

A god my father ended up believing in and the god who ended him and everything he'd theretofore believed in.

A god who silenced the Hebrew in my father's voice, sounding oh so like the guttural, sinuous languages of Martians and Venusians in those early and exceedingly cheap science fiction movies.

A god who destroyed my father with his faith and his love for the expansive wave of an all-powerful memory.

A memory that grew and devoured everything until that memory was all that was left.

The memory of a woman who was his wife and who, for a short time, was my mother.

I don't remember my mother.

My mother—known as "Fair Sarah"—died during the great influenza epidemic, when I was less than a year old. I got sick too. And against all prognoses, condemned by the doctors, I survived, and no one dared call it miracle: there had been so many victims that my modest resistance was more an unrepeatable statistical anomaly than a singular divine gesture.

My name was Isaac, which means *laughter* in ancient Hebrew; but I wouldn't say I laughed a lot as a child; there weren't many things to laugh about in my childhood.

And I can't remember what my father was like before my mother's death either. But I do remember how he was after she died. And how my mother seemed to have replaced his shadow, sewing herself to his heels and accompanying my father, Rabbi Solomon Goldman, at all times, everywhere.

I remember my father crying, reading right to left, looking for explanations in the paper and ink voices of ancient prophets. Words filling his throat that only housed pained groans, hushed screams: the sound of one catastrophe produced by the echo of another catastrophe.

Hear it now as I still hear it.

My father chasing an explanation for the end of his world in the forms of the world's beginning.

Before long, my father begins to detest the false comfort of other religions (the multitude of Eastern gods and Western saints and that oh so *sci-fi* notion of Paradise, that other utopian "planet" that comes after this planet, I think now) and to rage in front of churches fuller all the time with the Great Depression. Dumps run by fake-orgasmic priests swearing, with a regularity beyond irritating, to have been "touched by God," as if God were some kind of specially endowed, all-powerful playboy. And so, all of sudden, everyone is claiming they've witnessed something or someone and my father ceaselessly condemns this socialization of miracles. Visions like a plague, for someone who thinks that miracles shouldn't be massive and popular, but individual and occasional and capable of carefully selecting the site and eyes and body where they come to rest.

That clamor of lies and the incontrovertible truth of the Jehovah's absence. It's then that he reads what the Spanish cabalist Abraham Abulafia wrote about something called *Tikkun Ra*, or "the reappearance of the world," and disclaimer: I'm not entirely sure about the meaning of this term or of the other cabalistic ideas I refer to here. I cite things from memory that I don't remember precisely but won't ever be able to forget.

I remember perfectly, yes, my father studying those symbols. The furious intensity of my father staring at a book. The energy that seemed to enter through his eyes and shake his entire figure, which a *pulp* illustrator of the day would've drawn as a mad scientist with sparks and lightning bolts emanating from his burning brain.

I remember my father telling me what the books told him.

I remember my father explaining to me that the mystics believed that in the beginning, the Divine Light of God, keeper of all things good, was preserved inside one or multiple sacred vessels. But, as the glimmers and cracks of evil had also already appeared in the world, the vessels couldn't contain that splendor and they shattered. And the beneficent Divine Light broke into countless fragments that fell like crystal rain across the world. And, as they spread, swept by the winds and the slow but inexorable inertia of the planet's rotations, those divine fragments changed sign and transformed into all the horrible and monstrous things that have happened ever since. Diseases and wars and cataclysms. The mystics, my father tells me, maintain that the task of mankind is to reunite all those malignant fragments by doing good deeds. Transforming them back into benevolent material and reassembling them, like restoring a broken statue to its original whole. The perfect good. The indivisible splendor of the creator.

Tikkun Ra, thought my father.

And it's then, I believe, that my father decided that I'd be one of those small, lost pieces: something evil only in appearance (because he was unable to avoid associating my arrival with my mother's departure), but in whose fate and origin lived, barely hidden for those who knew how to look, part of the original and absolute root of the best and first good news.

My father also read (and only then did he feel he'd grasped its true significance and importance) about *Tzimtzum*. That constriction—the Kabbalah explains—experienced voluntarily by God. God contracting and compressing himself and renouncing his own infinite essence to allow for the existence of a conceptual place: *chalal panui*, a space where a world could exist independent of Him. In a way, God made Himself into the perfect reader so that we'd be imperfect yet fertile writers.

Tzimtzum means, I believe, "to conceal Himself from the beings He created, to let them exist as tangible creatures, instead of overwhelming them with His perpetual and infinite presence." So God limits Himself—puts boundaries on His divinity—withdrawing without disappearing so that there might be something outside of Him. What Solomon Goldman was never able to fully understand was if God's diminished size implied a relative reduction of His power or, to the contrary, turned it into a far more potent concentrate. If God's self-limiting weakened Him, then maybe man's corresponding role was to occupy that *chalal panui* and attempt to resemble God. Or, perhaps, to the contrary, to commit human errors over and over to emphasize the imperfection resulting from the partial yet decisive withdrawal of the Lord and Master of all things and thereby provoke Him to come back to make order of the chaos. Solomon Goldman didn't know what to think. Both possibilities seemed logical. That's the problem with the Kabbalah: unlike other sacred texts, it doesn't offer answers, just pieces with which to assemble an answer. It's not a compendium of infallible instructions. In the end, the true manual is mankind, the reader, the interpreter and assembler of all the loose pieces. Man approaches God through reading. And God—this god— is a man with deep faith in mankind. That's why He's left them alone and only in certain moments does He reappear, proud, to punish some blunder He deems incomprehensible. Some ignorance unjustifiable in creatures as magnificent as His, in beings artificially designed in His image and semblance. At times, the reason for His presence is easy to comprehend. Floods, commandments, and sharp shadows that cut off the lives of firstborn children and sacrifices that, sometimes, at the last second, are halted or neutralized. Events and marvels woven with the transparent texture of legends or fables.

But Solomon Goldman felt that he was the protagonist of something else, something far more complex. Something only accessed, or suffered, by the enlightened. Because God didn't halt the rhythm of Fair Sarah's death. God allowed Fair Sarah to cease existing and allowed him to survive her.

So would his mission be to reunite the pieces of the broken vessel, to reunite the lost exhalations of the Divine Light?, my father wondered. One night, after explaining all of this, he asked me that terrible question, and I really didn't get it. I didn't even realize that my father was in trouble, that his was another kind of illness. But I intuited how all of that would seem curiously similar to what I'd read later in science fiction magazines.

Religions are, all of them, early forms of science fiction: sudden flashes, flying, above and below, visitors from galaxies on the other side of infinity, appearing and disappearing. It doesn't matter which planet: the story is always the same and it's powered by the volatile fuels of love and death and an inferior faith in something superior: man creates God so that God creates man. And then they discover they cannot deactivate each other and that both, in a way, have turned into each other's Frankenstein's monster. Thus, man believes in God so he can do as he pleases in His name and God believes in man so He can blame him for all His mistakes.

At some point (I realize now that I refer to him, indistinctly, as *my father* or as *Solomon Goldman*, as if I were trying to divide him in two without having to break him into pieces more dark than light; as if in the one or the other I might find, barely hidden, the explanation for his madness) my father Solomon Goldman begins to talk to me about "aerial beings," about "stellar powers," about "portals," and about "dimensions." And about how I—having been on the threshold of death without being wounded too deeply, having almost come back from the other side—was the key that'd open the cell where he'd find my mother, Fair Sarah, a prisoner.

And it's not that I believe him, but some part of me wants to believe him. Some part of me needs to believe him, because his visions are so much brighter and livelier than reality's faded hue. And because, for the first time, in his delirium, in the magical properties he confers on me, I feel that my father loves me as a son, that he's proud of me.

So, one night I clearly hear the whirr of a machine outside my window and believe I see them, just landed, with fierce smiles and tracing symbols in the garden soil with swords of light. Timeless angels held aloft by the wind of other "planes of existence," their wings exuding a strange, immaculate glow. The next morning I wake up possessed by terrified happiness. Thinking I'd come to believe in what my father believed, convinced that from that moment on a new life would begin for me.

A life of true lies.

A false existence where I'd find myself forced to remember everything I said because—if I were to tell someone what I was almost certain I'd seen the night before—I'd be instantly written off as a liar. And liars have the terrible obligation of remembering everything they've said. Each and every lie. And that's how they wind up arriving at that crystalline instant where the lies are enough to completely cover the surface of the planet of their true lives. The lies cover everything like a deadly virus imported from the far reaches of the universe, and for which there's no cure or comfort. And when there's nothing left to infect, when everything has been devoured, the lies begin to devour each other.

My lies, I realize, will be *very* different from the lies of other children. Children who lie to cover up a naughty deed.

I, on the other hand, will lie because, for me, all truth will seem far worse than any falsity.

For me, all truth will be unbearable.

I'm not at home when they come looking for my father and find him and take him away.

When I get home from school, they tell me that Solomon Goldman climbed up on the roof of the synagogue, that he was naked or dressed (there didn't seem to be an agreement on this particular point) in a strange silver uniform or with his body covered in gold paint.

And that my father howled alchemical formulas and cabalistic prescriptions and desperate curses at the heavens.

And that he waved his arms, over his head, repeating again and again the gesture of someone drawing the blinds or opening the curtains.

Months later, a letter informed me that my father had died when he jumped from a terrace at the Bellevue Hospital Center.

The specialists' final verdict was of sudden, unpremeditated suicide: they explained that my father was a "model patient," whatever that means.

Years later, during a book signing at Andromeda Books—a specialty bookstore on Bleecker Street where one of my novels was being launched—a stranger with shrunken pupils approached me. Pupils the size of pills. He told me he'd been institutionalized with my father, but now was "completely cured and probably saner than you." And he told me—presenting a copy of *Remote Universe* for me to sign—that my father hadn't committed suicide, that that was a sham.

He told me that my father "had finally comprehended the secret language of the clouds . . . Clouds, immense and complex like ice cream sundaes in the summer, clouds as powerful as castle armies."

He told me too that my father had attempted to fly and that, for few meters, he'd succeeded. He told me that he saw it, that he witnessed the deed, but that "the nurses' cries made him lose focus and the poor and saintly Solomon ended up falling into the void."

And he concluded: "Believe me: your father, Solomon Goldman, died happy—knowing he was right."

And he handed me a notebook.

All the pages were blank except the last one. There, in Solomon Goldman's familiar handwriting—but shrunk to microscopic size; I needed the help of a magnifying glass to read it—I made out words that I was quick to memorize because, despite their complexity and scope, I understood them to be my father's last words. The final destination of his last voyage and, consequently, something worth preserving. In a way, I thought, these words were my inheritance, a legacy that had finally come to me:

"The only true essence of magic resides in the ability to exist in a state of consciousness where the past and the future long to trade places. Classical Hebrew, without going any further, has two verbal tenses: the present and another barely discernible time between the past and the future. Thus, to denote something that already happened, it's enough to say *I went*. To refer to the future, however, one only need add the participle *already* as in *I already went*, which is understood as an *I will go* in a perpetual motion of coming and going. Thus, it suggests a kind of primitive understanding of existence. An understanding that would transgress our mode of separating, in actuality, the real from the imaginary. But in that ancient grammar, facts are not seen as facts that have already occurred, but as instructions from tomorrow. That is to say, as premonitions that visit us in dreams and nightmares. In the primitive world, yesterday's facts mingled with the wonders and adventures of last night's dreams. So saying that you have done something that you didn't do is the initial and essential step to take in shaping what will be the future. Facts arise from premonitions. It's as if the future couldn't exist without the existence of its a priori delineation. A pencil sketch of what someday will become an oil landscape. The childish exercise that grows into the wise and mature symphony. God (or whatever you want to call Him; I know His true name, but I'm not allowed to put it in writing or say it or even think it) conceives of the world first and only then creates it. Thus, the cabalistic perception of this kind of miracle passes not through the magnitude of the enterprise, but through the fact that, in the act of imagining how the world will be, God has already created it before making it."

Yes: my father *had been* and *had already been* and *would already be*. Something like that.

But years before all of this (and just after they took Solomon Goldman away, tightly wrapped in a straight jacket) a man and a woman belonging to one of those organizations charged with the protection of minors told me to pack up what few belongings I had in my small suitcase.

My magazines, my notebooks, my books, some clothes, two or three photographs. I didn't have any toys, I never did, they never interested me.

I made the short but transcendent journey from Brooklyn to Manhattan where I was taken to the house of an aunt and uncle—my mother's brother—whom I'd never met before.

And there, in a house on 7th Street, where I thought I'd be cured of my evil secrets, I met my cousin Ezra Leventhal.

I remember that moment perfectly.

I remember it as if it were happening again right now.

A thing that had been and had already been, but that would already be and will be again: Ezra shakes my hand, he shows me our room which until then was "just *my* room," he explains to me, arching an eyebrow while—feigning a reflexive pose, hand on chin, thinking I won't notice—squeezing a pimple. And, raising his voice to make himself heard over the relentless clamor of the sewing machines in the shop downstairs, Ezra tells me, in a serious tone of voice, suddenly broken by uncontrolled, high-pitched adolescent hormones, that my father "has probably been kidnapped by beings from a planet called Omikron."

And with a conspiratorial gesture—almost nonexistent in its efficiency, as if it were a secret embodied in an object, in something palpable and true—Ezra hands me a notebook with a black oilcloth jacket and a cover where, on a white label, in precise caps, it reads: Manual of a Young Space Traveler/Instructions for how to Operate, Interact, and Prosper on This and Other Planets According to the Precepts of Ezra Leventhal (Rex Arcana of the Milky Way).

Then Ezra points dramatically upward, toward the room's ceiling, toward something beyond the sky, toward the other side of everything and the end of everything on this side.

He looks at me, smiling.

And looks up again.

And I look exactly in the same direction that he's looking and pointing.

And I see.

What I remember most about my first days in Manhattan are the nights. So different from those of Brooklyn. So much noisier. More alive. Nights that walk and talk in their sleep. It wasn't like Brooklyn was rural, but compared to the incessant and aggressive electric pulse of the metropolis, Brooklyn's voice was much closer to a whisper, acoustic and loving.

And the sky of the great city—because it's at night that we're most aware of the immensity of space, of its infinite possibilities, as during the day the sun's blinding presence blots out everything—seemed, to me, to have shaken loose the stars so they fell across an always burning skyline. A city in flames, phosphorescent and trembling with subterranean gasps of subways and moans of elevated trains.

I remember that I could barely sleep, that I heard the voices of nearby skyscrapers as if they were talking to each other in that language of steel and cement that buildings communicate with. There they were, all of a sudden, all those immense skyscrapers, like rockets condemned never to fly, having to settle for being signposts of girders and windows indicating the path to follow. Thinking about it now, from here, from this present, for me, at that time, Manhattan was the future. A science-fiction city. A tomorrow and—once again—an *and already was* in the present. And there I was—recently landed in Manhattan—like a caveman lost in that space where for me everything was new and at the same time as ancient and primitive as matters of family tend to be. "Family" understood as that thousand-headed organism where stories—situations—repeat themselves over and over with slight variations and dissonances that are surprising at first, but find their original aria before too long. Because inside a family—though it goes unsaid, a deafening silence—nobody hesitates to pinpoint the exact situation of that original and now-dead star whose sickly light still reaches us.

In other words: my father wasn't the first Goldman—nor will he be the last Leventhal—to go mad. But it was clear that, for me, neither the certainty of a past lunatic nor the possibility of a future madman was any comfort at all.

They stuck my father in a straight jacket, inside a room with padded walls, cursing a nameless creator. And I was alone, far from home, sharing a room with a cousin of exceedingly peculiar habits, who was convinced that our world, as we know it and as it is shown in the history books, wasn't really *ours*.

But really—I realized almost right away—Ezra's ideas, his histrionic poses, the borrowing of revelations written, in letters that looked more printed than handwritten, all the same height, repeating the same curves and straight lines, in the pages of his MANUAL OF A YOUNG SPACE TRAVELER/INSTRUCTIONS FOR HOW TO OPERATE, INTERACT, AND PROSPER ON THIS AND OTHER PLANETS ACCORDING TO THE PRECEPTS OF EZRA LEVENTHAL (REX ARCANA OF THE MILKY WAY), were just my cousin's way of welcoming me. His way of helping me feel less alone. A way of telling me that he and I belonged to the same rare and privileged species. Because Ezra would say to me the day after my arrival, in the morning following that first terrible night, looking me in the eyes, his hands on my shoulders: "To be an extraterrestrial it is enough, cousin Isaac, to feel that you're an extraterrestrial."

And I knew right then that Ezra would never lie to me, that he'd always tell me the truth, and that he'd devote the rest of his life to searching for and discovering new truths. Truths that could only come from the new order of a still-faraway future, yes; but one that was approaching faster and faster all the time. Running toward our shadow years, huffing and puffing—as if they were the little candles on a birthday cake—the ageless light of light years.

I write this as if it were a science-fiction story suspended in space with little chance of ever coming home.

A science-fiction story that wants to be something else—speaking a language not of the genre—but can't stop being what it is.

I can't help it.

Dubious automatic reflex.

Something that is, I fear, more existential degeneration than occupational compulsion.

Entertainment of a writernaut, sitting, fixed to desk and chair.

Static centrifugal force but his face still deformed by the acceleration of paragraphs in whose lines nothing ages and everything seems new.

There's a moment in any life (maybe the moments that we start to sense as our last moments, after looking at and not recognizing ourselves in the morning's first reflection, because you always think of yourself as younger than you really are) when the past becomes something paradoxically futuristic.

So, as I've said, the act of remembering has something about it that's as technologically inexplicable as any of those miracles of extraterrestrial cultures so advanced they end up unattainable.

And so, pretty soon, we find ourselves wondering what happened, what took place, what is truth and what is lie in everything we see again when we go back in time.

Memory is a reverse time machine that's as powerful as—always moving forward or in multiple alternate directions—that other time machine: imagination.

And so—in the same way that all realist and contemporary novels would be science fiction for a reader in ancient times—the novel of our current and past existence, viewed mechanically and organized artificially, always strikes us as fantastical. Something that—to keep from getting depressed or feeling like a device on the verge of breaking down beyond all repair—we prefer to conceive of as happening in another galaxy. Foreign customs. Exotic vistas, often in black and white or sepia. Words whose meaning we don't know. Cleaner air and a simpler life that, also, we like to think of as more civilized or at least more peaceful.

And—beyond certain fixed dates and common coordinates—this implies that each person's past constitutes, in and of itself, a different world. And so, every time I went to one of those now-bygone conventions of science-fiction writers, someone would ask me a question that nobody asks anymore (because no one is interested in the answer to this question, it's passed its expiration date): "Do you believe in the existence of intelligent life on other planets?" And I answer: "Yes of course, just look back and think about what was and reflect on everything that's been. That's also the explanation for why, inevitably, day after day, life is extinguished on several thousand *other* planets that are on *this* planet: people prefer not to remember and to not draw useful conclusions with respect to why it was that this or that catastrophe occurred. People prefer to live on a planet called Present without realizing that that is the planet whose civilizations have the briefest history and least posterity. People prefer not to think."

I write this and I do so by hand, slowly, not trusting machines and knowing that none of these pages will degenerate into that supposed and rapidly failed novelty of electronic books. Knowing, as well, that its writing and its reading are already futuristic in their own right:

when mankind hadn't yet set in motion the mysteries of cables and keys, we were already functioning—and already reading and writing—on the basis of that internal and mysterious electricity leaping from neuron to neuron and bouncing off the more or less well-painted and well-appointed walls of the caverns of our brains.

I write exactly *like this*: outside time and space, weightless, beyond any communication from the control center.

I'm a solitary cosmonaut of my own life, lacking sufficient oxygen to return home, somewhat disturbed by what's happening to me, but without that meaning that I'm upset that I don't entirely understanding *something* that's just happened.

Or that always has been and won't stop happening.

The Incident and all of that.

I write this like a shipwrecked writer of messages in bottles, who casts them into the sea with the naïve hope that maybe *she* will find one of them. And that she'll break it open and remove the glowing and sacred green crystals of these pages, and *Tzimtzum*, she'll unfold them and read them. And I hope that she feels something like pity, or, maybe, a trace of tenderness, and that she comes back to me, not to love me, but—because I don't believe there exists a more noble and sublime way of loving someone—to explain everything to me.

To explain everything to me as my cousin Ezra Leventhal once explained everything to me.

And friendship is a strange force that strengthens us while simultaneously negating us with the need to feel ourselves as close and as similar to the other as possible. When this friendship also involves the unifying and homogenizing force of blood, then the whole thing becomes far more powerful.

But, of course, the final result is that of a false similitude; because there was nothing more different, between me and Ezra, than our reasons for being interested in science fiction.

While Ezra sought the comfort of other worlds to try to escape a future that would force him to carry on the family tradition amid rolls of fabric and mannequins, I, for my part, needed to travel to planets that were as far away from my past and my family's past as possible.

Ezra was a rebel who had to overthrow a galactic tyranny that turned men into androids, defeated and subjugated by sewing machines. Beings who only rebelled, within the labyrinth of the tailor shop, by organizing clandestine poker games, cards dropping from their hands onto the same long tables where by day they trimmed fabrics with the irrevocable slowness of the autumn leaves at Central Park and Fifth Avenue. That almost-forbidden territory where the most exclusive women walked about, wearing the heavy winter coats they had sewn, and where they—the coats' anonymous and servile creators—sometimes ventured with their families, braving the the city above to point out to their wives and children, with a mix of pride and sadness: "I made that coat . . . And that one . . . And that one over there."

For Ezra, I belonged to an even stranger yet equally tormented race: I was the orphan of a mother annihilated by forces from another dimension and a father who had lost his mind and—getting too close to the absolute and radioactive truth of the universe—his life.

For Ezra, in a way, we were all victims of higher powers, of despotic cultures, of galactic tyrannies to be overthrown.

For Ezra, science fiction was an escape hatch, a door opening onto a better world, a shadow he had to illuminate so it would come to life and he could see it.

For me, on the other hand, science fiction was something to believe in: the only way I had to understand my life and the planet where my life had landed. It gave me the power to see myself from outside, to feel foreign, alien, and, yes, Faraway.

Science fiction—unlike the uses Ezra gave it—not as something to attack with, but something to hide behind and defend yourself with.

For Ezra, science fiction was a weapon.

For me, science fiction was a shield.

And so, there we are again. Ezra and I. And there we'll stay.

After telling me the interplanetary whereabouts of my ill-fated father and pointing up at the sky of his—suddenly our—room, Ezra sat down on one of the beds, rolled up his pants and showed me, with a fiercely proud smile, two abnormally skinny legs wrapped in harnesses of metal and leather, he stood and said something in a strange accent, punctuating each of the two words with a little pant. In that moment, the first thing that occurs to me is that Ezra has a speech impediment, a disability or, perhaps, some other metal apparatus wrapped around his teeth. Or asthma. Or tuberculosis. But then I realize what he's trying to do: Ezra wants to *sound* like a stranger from somewhere very far away. Ezra—the imperfect youngest child, arriving on the heels of six perfect sisters who are constantly plotting with their mother to undermine a father who never put up a fight—needed to think of himself as alien to all of that. A spy, an infiltrator in the controlled and toxic atmosphere of planet Leventhal. An extraterrestrial who speaks perfect English but can't ever—or doesn't really want to—entirely forget the accent of his home planet.

"SCIENCE FICTION!" was what Ezra said.

And I, of course, knew of the celestial vicissitudes of gods and mortals in ancient religions. I'd stumbled across the odd crackpot satires of philosophers and patriots. And I'd read novels with heroes who traveled to the center and the bottom and the highest places of the world and self-styled "scientific romances," with wise laboratory men driven mad by their own messianic genius. Or with creators of immortality elixirs. Or with adventurers discovering lost continents inhabited by dinosaurs. Or with warriors battling invaders from an exotic ocean Empire. And all of them, always, written by men who had never really traveled anywhere, for whom the simple act of standing up from their desks was a struggle. Men who invented perpetual-motion adventures for young readers who couldn't easily escape from the orbits of home and parents. Science-fiction writers, on the other hand, made no attempt at illusion or deception: we knew and they knew that they never went and would never go where they said and wrote that they had gone, but they trusted that, yes, we *would* go. So, all of that—those invisible men and those human animals and those bellicose visitors from the red planet and those flying rockets and those voyages into the future via Victorian apparatuses or hypnotic trances—was, in reality, a collection of instruction manuals, barely hidden inside novels and stories. Instruction manuals to set the future in motion.

"SCIENCE FICTION!" Ezra repeated.

And it was then, for the first time, that I heard those two words that at first, to me, seemed impossible to bring together in the same environment. *Science* and *Fiction* struck me as irreconcilable and contradictory terms, like polar opposites.

Two of the greatest novels in the history of literature (two novels not considered part of any genre, instead, each of them a genre that began and ended in itself; the same would occur years later with the polemical *Damitax*, which follows, throughout the cosmos, the amorous obsession of an old astronautics professor with a manipulative Venusian adolescent whom he clones over and over, hoping that one of the versions will, finally, love him) were, indeed, fantastical and spatial. But more than anything, they were classics. *Krakhma-Zarr*, Ezra's favorite, tells of the madness of a captain who pursues a mythical cosmic creature from star to star. And *Times Without Time*, my favorite, was the obsessive tale of the last Martian, Mars-El: a traveler who, after ingesting a strange drink distilled from the dust suspended in the melancholic rings of Saturn, goes back in time to the confines of his childhood and, from there, passes through his entire life all over again as if contemplating it from outside, as if he were reading it, as if it were a book composed of many books.

In a way we were defined by one or the other novel (titles that now I can't find anywhere on my bookshelves and that seem not to appear in the card catalogues of any library), and by dividing us they made us perfectly complementary: Ezra was a man of action and I a man of reaction.

Or something like that.

And my reaction to those two magic words—*Science* and *Fiction*, suddenly like one word with two heads and a single brain—was instantaneous and perfect.

It was as if Ezra were a magician—someone who'd just finished announcing that "For my next trick I'll need a volunteer"—and I, a more than willing spectator, ready to climb up on the stage and submit myself to anything: to be cut in half, to be the body stuck full of swords, to disappear in a cloud of colorful smoke or inside a magic cabinet decorated with oriental characters and dragons with almond eyes, to float and ascend and lose myself forever in the rafters of a vaudeville theater.

I was—I knew then—someone who had waited for years to succumb to this illusion that soon came to seem truer and solider and stronger than everything I'd experienced previously.

It's easy for others—I have no command of that language—to write, and even write well, about the highs and lows of the tides of love. Much more difficult to pinpoint are the ripples on that apparently placid lake that is friendship, at whose center, every now and then, circular and secret storms explode, just for the pleasure of, in turn, being eclipsed by a sudden blue sky.

Of one thing I'm certain: with the arrival of Ezra in my life (and until his recent and possibly final departure, just a few days ago, again, The Incident) everything seemed to accelerate.

And, looking back on it, everything I've said up until now (all my false starts, repetitions, clumsy statements about the genre, and all my absurd attempts to translate the elusive texture of time and space into writing) changes sign and language.

Because when Ezra enters my life, I arrive at last, to another planet.

I say and write *Science Fiction* and everything accelerates. Walking the way Ezra walked after they removed his metal harnesses: side-to-side but moving forward and, if you watched his legs, producing the curious impression of receding and advancing, laterally, feet barely moving, like he was suspended over phantom wheels a few centimeters off the floor.

Like he was floating.

Like the dance moves of that singer of indeterminate color (I don't remember his name, why'd I think of him right now?) who ended up throwing himself off the spiked crown of the Statue of Liberty.

Like that interplanetary spaceship on that television show I wrote for called *Star Bound* (today considered a classic, today almost everything is a classic of something or for someone), that attained absurd velocities when a captain in an absurdly tight uniform gave the order, sitting in an armchair on the command bridge, surrounded by women with short skirts and impossible hairdos, and counseled by logical, unfeeling extraterrestrials who, of course, like I've said, spoke perfect English, the universal language of the universe, apparently, and I wanted to be like that: to be from that far away and to feel that small.

And so the rhythm of what I write accelerates and I accelerate.

The years pass and run over each other and before long everything shocks me (and I decide I shouldn't be shocked, one of the many consequences of The Incident, I suppose) and everything happens so fast and there's so much that happened that I don't remember and will never write down here.

The unsettling sensation that the same event happens multiple times, with minimal or massive variations, as if someone were making adjustments, correcting and comparing different versions of the same event without ever picking one. Hundreds, thousands of details that end up defining the fabric of a life, and the unsettling sensation that I'm not the one who determines its direction and deviations, confusing dates, superimposing epochs, until it becomes so difficult for me to pinpoint how old I am, knowing that I'm too old, that there is not much left for me to tell.

Better like this, I think.

Better to let go.

Better to think—better to surrender to the dictates of an unknown entity—that it is someone else who writes me writing all of this.

There is a photograph of the way we were back then.

A photograph taken in that kind of black and white that seems more faithful somehow and to reveal more than all the colors in the world.

I have it here, I didn't imagine it.

It brings me peace that something of what I think I remember—something that happened—can offer physical and incontrovertible evidence of its existence.

It's one of the two photographs I would include in this hypothetical dossier regarding The Incident and its circumstances.

The other photograph is also of me and Ezra; but what makes that photograph special is that she is in it too, and since it's *her photograph* (I have it here as well, Ezra gave it to me a few days ago, and it seems to be vibrating ever so slightly, wavering like a nightlight with a bulb so small it serves more to obscure than to illuminate), it is much more difficult to *narrate*, but soon I won't be able to avoid the risk of attempting to describe it.

In this one, the first photograph, Ezra and I pose together, shaking hands—with the solemnity of the small who must believe themselves big—as if ratifying a transcendent and indissoluble society. It's an old photograph and its age is evidenced not just by its date, but above all, by the attitude of its subjects. It is a photograph from a time when getting a photograph taken was a big deal: you had to make an appointment at a professional studio, dress up in your best clothes, select the backdrop motif, leave home to have it taken, and never stick out your tongue at the moment of the flash. A photograph was a serious thing. Photographs weren't yet *instant*, easy to correct and retouch. Photographs were slow and permanent and I don't know if they were stealing our souls, but, yes, they definitely captured an instant forever. Back then, all photographs were historic.

The photographer—Abraham, one of the Kowalski brothers, specialists in bar mitzvahs and weddings and funerals; his brother had died in the war, his children and grandchildren would die in conflicts yet to come—did not, of course, have any futuristic or interplanetary motif that we could stand in front of. So Ezra and I ended up picking an enlarged engraving of Greek and Roman temples, the closest thing, we agreed, that mankind had to civilizations far away in time and space.

"Now we've got our picture. Now we are somebody. Now we can be who we want to be," Ezra says and we steal two sewing machines from his father's workshop (they're black, heavy, antiques, we slip them out a window at night) and trade them in for a small Kelsey hand press, and within a week we publish the first edition of our magazine.

We call it *Planet*—we like the cleanness of its name, no adjective to contaminate it, we like to think that the planet it referred to could be any planet—and it includes a story of Ezra's whose subject I don't recall, and one of mine that I'd rather not remember and—almost out of pity—an advertisement for the Leventhal Tailors.

But *Planet* puts our names on the map.

We distribute a few poorly printed issues, slip them under the doors of bookstores and libraries, and before long we get a visitor. And it is then we realize that we're not alone in the universe, that there are others—too many—like us: kids for whom the present is intolerable, and so they escape to the future, to many futures, because the idea that only one future exists is insufficient, insufferable. Thus, the future as Christmases and birthdays. The future as anticipation of a party of possibilities, of gifts and presents and wishes. But a party where, before being allowed in, you must know how to decipher the invitation.

If the past is a foreign country, then the future is a distant star. And in those days there were so many of us who longed to get there and to plant the flag of our name. The way others competed outdoors in grunting contact sports, or in student debates, words burning up oxygen until the classroom air was almost unbreathable; we opted to combine action and words, fantasy and logic, and to play our game inside imaginary spaceships bigger than stadiums and amphitheaters. We were bad athletes and got cripplingly nervous in public, so, instead, we flew with our minds.

And soon, we were marked: our fingers permanently stained with purple ink. The purple ink characteristic of small printing presses, of hectographs and mimeographs, of machines with names like Speed-O-Print or Multi-Printex or Typekto. Simple machines, but so complex to keep running without the paper jamming or the wax tablet cracking or the rollers twisting before copy number fifty, when everything appears to melt down and come to a stop.

And the kind of ink that never fully dries on the fresh copies, forcing you to handle those few pages with the same care required for the most ancient and noble scrolls.

And the slow vertigo of pages emerging one after another, with that adolescent velocity that's neither fast nor slow, but seems to drag along with the slow vertigo of something that needs to go everywhere but has no idea how to get there.

But *Planet* is powerful enough to reach nearby colonies.

And one afternoon a group of kids comes calling. They stare at us and—as a sort of universal greeting requiring no words—reach out their hands and show them to us. And their fingertips are stained too with what the mother of normal children would probably identify, erroneously, as raspberry juice. And with reverential silence, they pass us copies of *Phantom Universe* and *Time Traveling* and *X-Rays* and suddenly Ezra and I are trapped in the tribal orbit of boys who meet in basements or on school stairways or in rooms reserved for "recreational activities," to discuss whether or not it all began with the gothic fantasies of that drunk from Baltimore; or whether that radio-broadcast false alarm announcing the invasion of those exceptionally exhibitionistic Martians might not have been, in reality, a clever tactic designed to distract us from a real and much subtler invasion of Martians who "are just like us . . . And maybe our weird Latin teacher is one of them!" We read comics about interplanetary and immortal superheroes whose only vulnerability was to colorful fragments of their home planet and we build rockets with materials stolen, little by little to avoid attracting attention, from Physics and Chemistry labs. And—one of our principal "experts" would wind up working in the space industry and another, after combining flammable elements with satanic invocations, would end up getting killed in an explosion in Pasadena that was never entirely explained—we launch them with mixed results: some blow up on the ground, some fire off on furious horizontal trajectories and start small fires, in the best cases they go up some twenty or thirty meters and we celebrate as if they'd attained cosmic heights above the vacant lots and fallow fields of the Bowery.

Before long, almost without realizing it, we were a group, a generation. And one of our principal activities—as so often happens—was dividing into smaller groups, unleashing small and clandestine but exceedingly bloody battles, uniting with one faction for a few days only to double-cross them and join another. All in the name of the future and of outer space: two things—the yet to come and the great beyond—that we had no access to but thought about nonstop, because, if we thought about them all the time, it was like they were ours, like they were holding on to never let go.

Soon, fully aware of it, Ezra and I start to feel outside all of that, distant from everyone. Far away, yes. We become a two-person movement. The Faraways. We move stealthily between the different factions, we listen and gather information. And pretty much all of it seems absurd and childish to us. And when night falls we walk home under the falling snow. I remember us so much better in winter, wrapped in heavy jackets, vapor spilling from the volcanoes of our mouths, the eruption of conversations where we can't stop cracking up at what we've seen and making fun of what we've heard. We go up to our room and we write, and it's like sledding down the slope of a fever that leaves us delirious with happiness, reading our pages aloud to each other almost as we write them. We're happy and we're unique and we're the best and we need the others only and exclusively so that, with their unconscious and voluntary and oh so proximal mediocrity, they confirm our mastery and our unattainable distance. A distance so great that it's not even necessary for us to act cruel or proud with all of them. It's more than enough for us to be invisible.

We are, yes, The Faraways.

And we're different.

Our stories aren't made public. We don't read them aloud with tremulous voices at meetings. Our stories have little or nothing to do those of the others: space is there, yes, but Earth doesn't figure into our plots and when it does, on occasion, get mentioned, it's only as an impossible-to-confirm rumor, a space legend no one is all that interested in verifying. Our magazine, *Planet*, soon goes out of circulation and is printed only for private consumption. We don't want to be just more faces in the crowd, amid so much space trash floating in the atmosphere.

Ezra and I observed all of this as if through a telescope but with microscopic malice, as if it were a virus or bacteria. The abundance of fanzines, the dreadful but enthusiastic stories, the absurd and impassioned theories, our sects' epithets: The Futurists, The Cosmics, The Futuristics, The Dimensionals, The Astronomics, The Futurexics. Each of them corresponding to the different Manhattan boroughs we were from and organized according to a ranking system more complex than those of many armies and businesses and families where everyone despises everyone else with cordiality and courtesy. And, soon, the different political stances: those who understood that being devoted to the future should inevitably be linked to the birth of a better and more just world, where science would be of everyone and for everyone; and those who thought that what was to come should be privileged material, that a chosen race would have to write better and better what they imagined, turning themselves into laser beams for the never servile but always obedient masses. Some time later, several of the former were accused of anti-American activities by devout patriotic organizations. And, from the newspapers, I learned about suicides in hotel rooms in Miami, about small-town jails and alleyway beatings, about those who emptied bottles to try to feel full, and about a man with a worn-out face whom I saw later behind a supermarket cash register and who pretended not to recognize me in hopes that please, please, I'd pretend not to recognize him.

Meanwhile and in the meantime, editors with good noses (previously dedicated to printing noir detective novels and disheartened romances) had descended on us, aware almost immediately that—it didn't matter if we were good writers or not—we symbolized the reader of the future, so they bought our clumsy first stories for almost nothing and collected them in magazines with long names full of adjectives with big letters and absurd but captivating illustrations.

I've read a couple of books written about those days (Ezra and I barely appear in them; we were barely a blip on the radar screens, few invoked our last names along with their own) and I remember the combination of boredom and astonishment I felt reliving all of that, arranged and narrated like transcendent historical events that changed the face of the planet, like all of it meant *something*.

Sure: some of those who marched in the streets and raised their fists or made insane proposals ended up titans of the genre: writers admired by hundreds of thousands of readers, into visionaries, into guests appearing on late shows every time a satellite was launched or the success of a formula made public. Satisfied men smiling at cameras with the all-knowing smiles of those who are convinced they were the first to think or predict something. Because, soon, in an age when everything seemed to accelerate—when progress *progressed* faster than ever—science fiction had become a combination of meteorological forecast and horoscope and hundred-meter dash. The important thing wasn't to write well, but to get there faster and before everyone else. The imagination didn't need to be reflective, but boundless.

I could write out their particular features here in a long and black list. I could accuse them and list the charges against them. I could point out the one who sold out to Hollywood. Or the one who surrendered to the orgy of writing books of scientific revelation on commission at an astounding speed. Or that other one who ended up a "future consultant" for a conglomerate of companies developing home electronics. Or the one who ended up working on a robotic theme-park honoring the memory of a messianic cartoonist who made a fortune off the primary material of old fairytales.

But it would be a waste of time and I've got no time to waste and, I discover now, I get the faces and aliases confused and, for an instant, I see them and I hear them clearly only to lose them again in a storm of vertical and horizontal lines and white noise, like ghosts on haunted television sets. I can't—even if I wanted to—tell them apart. They appear to me now, moving through my memory with the weary, martial steps of a crowd of extras in a movie that's gone on way too long.

But there is one who stands out among them.

His features come into focus, suddenly unforgettable after so many decades.

And with him and his name—a ridiculous name for an absurd man—we get back to the unforgettable part of this story. The story that so long ago and with so much effort I promised myself to never remember, and that now, all of a sudden, in the wake of The Incident, I begin to recall as if I were reading it as I write it.

A name and a face and a body. All at once. Once again. Materializing without warning. Like the crew of the S. S. *Endeavour* in the science fiction series I worked on in the 60s, *Star Bound*. Teletransporting.

Here it is, here it comes.

His face like that of an angel bored of hanging in temple rafters, blonde curls crowning a big and too-round head, eyes small and disturbingly blue, pert nose barely peeking out between his cheeks, mouth always fixed in a grimace of disgust or reproach. His body big and tall and oval, the legs and arms short, the feet small, and the hands minuscule.

Jefferson Franklin Washington Darlingskill.

The only son of the owner of a prestigious department store. Descendant of a patriarchy so patriotic that their son was condemned to grow up crushed by an avalanche of heroes, a Mount Rushmore of surnames.

Jefferson Franklin Washington Darlingskill is heir apparent to a father—a mere James Darlingskill, but far more powerful than his son—who dreams that his firstborn will become president and believes that the road to the White House begins with the absurd impetus of famed historical surnames that help you make history.

"Please, call me Jeff," Darlingskill would almost moan.

"Or, if you prefer, J. F. W.," he added, rubbing his baby-doll hands together in a nervous and frantic gesture that somehow recalled the latent, combustible dangerousness of an obese emperor like Nero preparing to devour a banquet or incinerate a city.

And how was it that Ezra and I—already Faraways with no chance of going back and joining a different club or association, considered "untrustworthy" by the others—welcomed Jeff? What was it that led us to accept him as the third Faraway?

The answer is simple: convenience.

Jeff has money, he comes from a rich family (he makes us swear not to tell anyone), he buys us books and magazines, and takes us to movies as if making us offerings in exchange for our mechanical respect—never affection, much less friendship—for his person.

Jeff seeks us out because he feels we are—like him—pariahs of a system incapable of understanding its own grandeur.

But what fascinates Jeff most is that Ezra and I have voluntarily chosen to be pariahs, while he wants so badly to belong, to be included, to be part of something . . . But this has not gone well for him. To his father, it's clear that Jeff isn't going to measure up: he's not the triumphal dolphin, but a kind of slow walrus who, at his best moments (that constant and desperate smile of a dense, unctuous doll, the hair black and moist with pomade as if painted on his skull, the elastic smile of the almost-androgynous stars of silent films, the quasi-reflexive propensity to look at himself in any reflective surface), barely manages to arouse the occasional sympathy in the oldest clients and shareholders. And it's not like it goes much better for him with the sidereal youth: the few times that Jeff was allowed to read his pages at a meeting of one of those clubs that changed acronym and password every week, the results were nothing short of disastrous. Or, in his own words, hoping to glaze over the truly epic terror of public embarrassment, "apocalyptically noteworthy." And it's not just that the poor kid isn't a good writer: he's an awful imaginer. His fantasias are febrile, childish, absurd, combining monarchs of Atlantis with mad scientists. His heroes are nothing but masses of muscles shining from the application of exotic oils who always speak with exclamation points. Time and again his ideas insist on the need for world domination via telepathy. His descriptions demonstrate a pathetic lack of familiarity with female anatomy (without this preventing embarrassing descriptions of what a dress ripped to shreds by a superman reveals) and provide a glimpse of a distressing tendency toward racism and revenge. In Jeff's stories, I recall, there is always someone getting revenge, or about to get revenge.

And maybe most important of all, beyond the professionalism of his bumbling, what makes Jeff fascinating: Jeff is the nephew of Phineas Elsinore Darlingskill, Ezra's favorite writer.

Phineas Elsinore Darlingskill was something like the black sheep of Jeff's family. A sheep that, on full moon nights, turns into a wolf. Another pariah. He lives a few hours outside Manhattan, near a river of waters so still they look painted. In a nearly ruined Victorian mansion granted to him by his relatives on the condition that he never visit them and that he always stay far away from the businesses and celebrations of the family. Jeff's father refers to his brother as "The Other" and explains away his eccentricities as the result of a rare form of syphilis combined with numerous psychosomatic disorders he'd suffered since childhood, which had gotten him expelled from school at the age of eight. And, from then on, long nights of ravenous reading, insomniac night terrors, and—translating into a sort of circular scar around his right eye, like a reddish tattoo recalling a monocle—the constant exploration of the heavens with a telescopic device he built in their parents' attic.

Darlingskill—it was Ezra who made me aware of his work—wasn't exactly a science-fiction writer. Darlingskill was something different. Something else. A mutant version of a science-fiction writer. The missing link between the rocket and the catacomb. And so the young aficionados of the genre read him with a mixture of fear and contempt and distrust. His stories and short novels—which Ezra sought out with patience and desperation in old publications; one of the gifts that Jeff gave him was a custom made, beautifully bound volume containing the complete works of Darlingskill—combined ancient Greek and Arab myths with stellar cosmogony, where primordial, amorphous, tentacular gods danced frenetically, blinded by the fatigue of having too many eyes, worn out by the weariness of long and unpronounceable names, pure consonants, names more screams than names. Gods that know themselves slaves of a fierce and touristic need to visit our dimension to strike up short but impassioned relationships with mortals who've made the mistake—with the help of an ancient and dangerous *grimoire*—of invoking them, without it being entirely clear why and to what end. The only thing that matters is to bring them here, to unleash them, and only later to find out what happens and what has to be done to make them go home.

Darlingskill's prose is baroque and antiquated and, often, incomprehensible. But there's something in it that fascinates Ezra: the reality of an irreal world coexisting alongside ours and slowly growing, little by little, like a demented, damp stain on the walls of our sanity.

Jeff, on the other hand, was more interested in—considering them "my principal influence"—the classist and racial aspects of Darlingskill's delirium: constant allusions to superior and inferior orders, the threat and danger of Orientals, the degeneration of bloodlines. Jeff—when Ezra, almost on his knees, begs him to arrange a trip to visit his uncle—warns him that Darlingskill isn't crazy about "Semites, Africanoids, and those sub-humans living south of the Rio Grande." On the other hand, Jeff agrees to show him the extensive correspondence that he maintains, in secret, with his uncle. Long letters full of diagrams and instructions and diatribes against "that dangerous Jewish physicist who's altering the mental composition of our universe with his theories" and containing paragraphs like "the savage descendant of the ape runs through the jungle with mating as his sole objective; but those chosen by the creators must look upward and consider their relation to the cosmos." Letters dated, always, two hundred years in the past because, Darlingskill explains to his nephew, "that was the best time in my life."

Shortly after we met him, Jeff tells us that they've discovered his uncle has terminal cancer, which Darlingskill insists on referring to as "not a cancer, but a scorpio: a unique sidereal variant of earthly evil; nothing as banal and commonplace as cancer could finish me off." Jeff tells us that his family has brought his uncle back to the city after his long exile and that now he is dying in a hospital in the city.

With great effort we convince Jeff (Jeff is one of those people who seems especially sensitive, always primed to see catastrophic possibilities even in the most inoffensive gesture) to take us and bring us up to Darlingskill's room. We threaten him with expulsion from The Faraways, with turning him over to The Futurists. Or, worse, to The Futuristics. Denouncing him. Revealing the truth of him as a decadent, old-moneyed rich kid. Jeff agrees and trembles and rubs his hands together. We walk down half-lit corridors (it's the time of day when hospitals sleep) and arrive at a private room rife with the overpowering smell of incense. Standing next to the door, a group of pale kids in black coats and ankh cross bracelets are talking in reverential whispers, as if praying. A few of them have their heads completely shaved. Ezra and I peer in through the half-open door and we see him. Sitting up in bed, supported by several pillows. A transparent man who reminds me of an elaborate sand castle at sunset on a deserted beach. Its moment of maximum glory and splendor came a few hours ago, under the vertical midday sun. And now the onlookers have gone home and the wind and the stray dogs and the foam flying off waves, coming ever closer, have been erasing its details and softening its angles. Almost nothing left in that vacant façade. Just the hole of a mouth that opens and lets out a shriek making the glass vibrate and bringing nurses and doctors running. Then Phineas Elsinore Darlingskill passes on to another "spiritual plane in the vast geometry of the universe," and his adoring fans bow their heads in reverence and perform a complex salute with their hands when the gurney carrying their master's body passes by on its way to the morgue.

And among the young acolytes—Ezra and Jeff and I see her at the same time—is a girl our own age.

And we're so young, so many years left to live we almost think we're immortal, but we all feel ourselves weaken a little.

Suddenly, here, in the hospital where a cursed writer has just died, his body already cooling so the engines of his legend can start firing up, Jeff and Ezra and I experience another far subtler, yet equally powerful form of the finite.

A death that's not the little death of orgasm, but the limitless death of ecstasy.

And none of us say a word; but I'm sure that all three of us, each in our own way, thinks precisely the same thing: you can survive the certainty that a particular woman is the most beautiful woman you've ever seen; but it's a lot harder to go on living after experiencing the absolute certainty that that woman is, also, the most beautiful you will ever see.

Her face—the face of her—is the light that illuminates and lays waste to everything.

Years later, watching footage of atomic tests in the desert, observing with delighted terror the way that phosphorescent wind leveled entire towns always populated by smiling mannequins, I said to myself that I'd already experienced something similar, but couldn't remember where or when.

And a few days ago, in the middle of The Incident—Ezra, handing me that photograph where the three of us appear together, the two of us serious, and a burst of laughter moving and blurring her face—it all came back to me.

All of it but her name.

Or maybe it's not that I've forgotten or can't remember it.

Maybe, what happens is that I don't want to think it, much less speak it for fear that all of it would disappear again, that the light would go out again, and I'd return to the darkness where I've been living, surviving, for far too long.

I suppose that here (to distract myself from her reappearance, to resist the impulse to fill pages upon pages with her smile or her voice or her eyes or the way she seemed to be elsewhere when thinking about things we didn't dare to think about for fear of discovering we weren't part of her thoughts) a short but necessary parenthetical is required addressing the role that young women occupied in the nascent science fiction of that time.

The role that young women occupied in the science fiction of that time was no role at all.

Science fiction, in its beginnings, was a masculine enclave, and women were no more than veiled princesses, lab assistants, girlfriends there to let out the perfect scream when the creature from beyond the stars appeared.

And in reality, the truth is there weren't many girls at the meetings of our galactic clubs and associations. They had nothing to do there and there were so many other, better planets than ours. Because—above and beyond the more or less controlled atmosphere and the toxic and exhilarating battles we unleashed among ourselves to resolve whether Venusians would necessarily be more intelligent than Martians or things of that nature—in the dark of our nights, when there was nothing left to read or write, we knew that we were very much alone. That ours was a cold, sad world where the light of the sun barely arrived from the world where the athletes, cheerleaders, and class presidents lived: those popular and perfect kids who spent their weekends spinning the latest cool dance moves and not orbiting around dead stars.

So—without wanting to offend anybody—the girls who hung out with us were, obviously, not the most attractive. They were "nice" and "interesting" and "smart." And possibly a little crazy, as their theories were, always, so much more hallucinatory and hallucinated than our own.

For some of them, the space fever soon abated. They attributed it to a brief hormonal imbalance and returned, without understanding entirely what had happened, to Home Economics classes and to wondering who'd be brave enough to ask them to prom.

Some turned into girlfriends and, later, writers of strange pages always penned under absurd masculine aliases.

Others—the few—as the years passed left behind the chrysalis of their false male names and became feminist writers who at conventions condemned the proliferation of female robots destined for domestic tasks or denounced those early transgressive narratives where an earthling coupled with a giant, sweet-voiced insect or succumbed to the charms of an alien maiden who, weary of the mega-power of her brain, realized that she only wanted to love and be loved by the man who told her about his ranch in Nebraska.

None of them looked like her.

She began and ended in herself.

She—the sound of her laugh, the way she widened her eyes when you told her something, the way she grabbed your arm when she had something to tell you—drove me and Ezra crazy. And, of course, Jeff too; but Jeff was so easy to drive crazy that I don't consider him a victim of the expansive wave of her joyful explosion in the theretofore indivisible nucleus of our lives.

And I wonder if there is anything more *sci-fi* than the sudden outbreak of the virus of love in the hospital of youth, of that extraterrestrial presence that suddenly and without warning seizes you and turns you into a hypnotized cosmonaut.

That first love that will forever be the first. And that found a way to perpetuate itself in future loves, like a voice at the bottom of the black hole of a well in whose waters, sinking, drown the reflections of the stars, high in the sky.

That love that initiates everything and brings you down just so you can ascend, enveloped in the spiraling and invisible revolutions of a ray that makes all the needles of the strange-energy detectors jump.

That love that makes you suddenly so fragilely invincible, so delicately immortal.

And then time starts to pass in a different way, in sudden and unpredictable spasms. At the beginning of love there are days that go by in a minute, there are insomniac nights that seem to occupy the space previously reserved for entire geological periods where bygone fantasies (that once we confused or wanted to confuse with true love, all the while wondering if it really was *like this*, if you really feel so little when you think you've *fallen in love*) were suddenly just dull fossils whose only interest resided in informing us how erroneous and primitive the romantic sentiments of our prehistory—of everything that happened (without which nothing would ever have happened) before her—had been.

And her arrival makes Ezra and me (and Jeff too, because Jeff felt a version of the same thing, because he was always around, satisfied with being a kind of satellite, orbiting us, waiting to sate our most absurd needs with the green combustible of crisp bills) even more Faraway.

She arrives and looks at us and says hello and we don't see her again until a week later, when she shows up at one of the meetings we almost never attend anymore but fortunately happened to attend that time. And she asks to speak and reads a strange story. A story that takes place on another planet where neither the notion of "another planet" nor that of the future exist. It was, in a way, a realist story—a day in the life of someone who knew nothing of us, earthlings, and didn't really care to. The daily routine of a being who didn't seem all that different from a human (there was, yes, a single mention of silver pupil-less eyes that "like a mirror, reflected not what they saw but what they thought about what they saw; as if the eyes were a keyhole to the mind"), and who, at the end of the story, fell asleep saying: "Tomorrow will be another millennium."

And she finished reading and nobody said a word and she arranged her pages and took off her jacket and put it back on and walked out, and Ezra and I (and Jeff) got up and followed her.

And reaching this point, attempting to suspend this torrent of memory in the air for a few seconds, I can't help but wonder how it is that now, after so many years, I suddenly remember so many things that I'd forgotten or didn't want to remember.

I can say—and almost be convinced—that the wheels have once again been set in motion by The Incident.

By my reunion with Ezra.

By the photograph that Ezra gave me a few (I guess, I'm not sure of anything anymore) days ago.

By what happened (or didn't happen) on that morning of sun and fire.

I can marvel at my never-suspected ability to, at the very least, attempt to understand and describe the workings of love, love being one of the most infrequent emotions in classic science fiction, because love takes up too much space inside spacesuits and cargo holds of spaceships. There is sex in science fiction, yes, and even passion, but love rarely survives long voyages to far-flung solar systems or alternate dimensions. One of the obligations of the genre—like in detective novels, especially early detective novels, where crime is more a hobby and an intellectual art than the result of a brief yet definitive instant when the rational lights of the brain turn off—is that of explaining everything, of not leaving anything out or any loose threads untied.

And love upsets all of that.

Better to toss it out the hatch.

To watch it drift away, floating in space where there's neither above nor below, no vertigos of the body or depressions of the soul, and love cannot survive.

And yet, every so often, I remember now, there was the rare miracle. That thing that forever altered the paradoxically rigorous discipline of a genre that liked to think of itself as free, without limits of frontiers.

And I remember an afternoon more than thirty years ago when I went to see a movie everyone was talking about. At that time (Zack hadn't died and turned me into the well-to-do guardian of his memory and legacy yet) I was writing screenplays for the series *Star Bound* and it was considered part of my job to stay up to date on all things future. Science fiction had become, for me, the most earthly of jobs: looking up at the sky knowing that nothing interested me less than ever getting my feet off the ground.

So I bought my ticket, paused for a few seconds in front of the posters that depicted a space station with Earth in the background. "Winner of ALL this year's Oscars," I read under the title. And I went in and sat down in the darkness and understood once again why so many fugitives—that gangster riddled with bullets at the exit to a movie called *Manhattan Comedy* or that presidential assassin hiding in the half-light of a double feature of *Battle in Hell* and *Cry of War*—always choose to disappear for a while in a movie theater, to pass time, to float in limbo, to escape reality, to try to trap themselves in that magical moment when we're not entirely sure if the lights have begun to come down so the show can start up.

The air in the theater was rank with a mixture of rancid butter and popcorn and the vegetal smoke of marijuana and the perfumes of the Orient. Most of the seats were empty, but the people there seemed to have been camped out for months. One flashed me the peace sign, another was dressed in camouflage, a freckled girl watched everything from the floor, her legs twisted in a seemingly impossible position.

The movie opened on a timeless African landscape with apes that were no longer apes, but weren't yet humans, then an ominous black monolith materialized and a bone transformed into spaceship that danced the mighty blue waltz of weightlessness and then there was Jupiter and the madness of a supercomputer far more sentient than the men who had built it and, in the end, a kind of hotel at the far reaches of the universe and the return home, transformed and better and, definitely, without remorse.

And the eloquent silence of space.

And the emptiness of that space so full.

And the music of yesterday like the sound of tomorrow.

And the heavy breathing of astronauts sealed in the void.

And a new being, floating inside a placenta of galaxies and, again, the inner space that so closely resembles outer space: the same dark light, the same luminous darkness, the same weighty weightlessness.

I'd be lying if I said I understood all of it. Later I read interviews with the director (who said very strange things) and the writer (who was *one of us* and with whom I'd crossed paths at some convention; he'd never seemed very friendly, I'd never been interested in his compulsive futurologist zeal, always announcing new inventions and discoveries and, later, the dates elapsed, explaining why and whose fault it was that they hadn't come to fruition) and I don't know if I understood better, but I knew there was nothing more to know. All I knew was that, when the projection finished and the lights came up in the theater, my eyes were wet with tears. I knew that what I'd just seen was a rare wonder: a science-fiction movie where the future wasn't *acting* like the future. For once, there was no emphasis on it: the future was normal, the future was the present, a present we could feel as it floated off into the past, waving goodbye. Nobody seemed particularly excited—and almost avoiding the temptation to look at the camera, to look at us and give a wink—when they ate synthetic foods or spoke to their little daughter via videophone from the space station. There weren't any explanations either. You didn't have to understand everything. Science fiction, at last, freed itself from obligations of detective mysteries. Because, though the explanations were implausible, in science fiction there was always the responsibility to give them, to justify what'd happened with what would someday happen. Not here. Here, everything we'd previously known came to an end. Here, was the beginning of the end. Goodbye to the future as promised land, the total and artificial memory of a machine as something far more sentient than the minimal and cold recollections of an astronaut, and the welcome return trip—and not the departure—as the definitive form of transcendence. What in the movie was described as, yes, a *historic moment* waving to us as it drifted off into the distance so that, soon thereafter, it could come back changed forever.

I left the theater missing Ezra like I'd not missed him in a long time. I suddenly needed to ask him if he'd seen that movie and if it hadn't reminded him of *something*. Now I remember, I remember what made me remember that movie named for a year, the name of the same year in which, now, I remember seeing it and realizing the painful paradox that the most forever-young futuristic work suffers the stigma of the most ageable title of all time.

And now I know that what made me remember it was that story that she read in that meeting of kids dreaming of a better future, not for humanity but for themselves. A future that would look nothing like their present. A future in which the future had stopped being important.

And above and beyond all of that, that simultaneously young and old ambition and frustration—of knowing that none of them would travel into space, none of those young and zealous mental cosmonauts would be the right age when the time came to climb aboard the rockets, and that the glory of walking on new worlds or, written off for reasons of space, of leaving behind this planet minutes before the Apocalypse, wouldn't be theirs—her voice shaping each and every one of those words as if she were saying them for the first time, as if they'd just been created and their meanings were still fresh and fragrant.

I saw myself young again. Old fashioned but bursting with future. I watched myself listen to her read again. Standing, in the middle of a little room. Not having taken off her jacket or scarf, which covered part of her mouth and made her voice kind of strange. If we didn't love her before (if we hadn't started to love her the night Darlingskill screamed his last scream or stopped screaming the scream he'd been screaming for so long), it was then that Ezra and I (and Jeff, condemned more and more to being a docile and mimetic parenthesis alongside our names) knew we loved her. And maybe most important of all: we knew that it was okay that both of us loved her, because the love of only one of us would've been insufficient, almost an offense in the face of what she generated. We knew that we both loved her and the joy of that reencounter, of growing even closer loving the same person, made us so happy for we were certain that she couldn't help but love both of us. And that through her love the two of us would be together forever.

With her.

But no.

Then something happened.

One of those inexplicable phenomena of which I only remember disparate fragments because of the explosion: me and Ezra and her, Jeff getting up and reading and screaming and running out of one of those meetings, and, of course, swearing to get his revenge on everyone and everything.

And the night of the men of snow.

Something like those photographs sent from deep space telescopes, images of cold sidereal bodies in combustion, new colors, unprecedented shapes that scientists give a name. Whatever name. Fooling themselves into thinking that, by christening them, they have some idea what they are, what they do, how they came into being.

Have you seen them? I'm sure you have. They often appear in the Sunday paper. Dispatches not from faraway lands but from distant skies. And, below, captions like "Quintet of Stephan" or "The meeting of NGC7318A and Be, producing bursts of stellar formation" or "Panorama of the galactic nucleus in X-Ray" or "Proto-planetary disc of Alfa Piscis Austrini."

Things like that.

You read the name and look at the photograph again and—like what happens with certain names given to certain people, like the name she claimed was hers and, I get it now, I don't say or remember it here because it adds nothing, because it doesn't define or explain her at all—you don't get how something like that could be given that name.

You don't get how there could be something like that out there.

You really don't get the certainty of living in the center of something that, from the outside, looks like that.

You suspect that all of that—shapes and colors—was put there for but a moment, for the blink of an eye, by someone who knows that we're taking photographs a place where there is nothing, where there's only emptiness, and they don't want to deprive us of the joy and the wonder of seeing and thinking "Oooooh" and "Aaaaah."

Oh.

Ah.

Then we were separated.

She disappeared.

(Jeff disappeared too, probably crushed by his parenthesis.)

I stayed, but I suppose that, for the others, by staying, it was like I disappeared.

Life went on like in those old movies where, to give the impression of time's passing in just a few seconds, calendar pages turn, seasons change, newspapers spin out from the center of the screen and stop in front of the spectator to reveal big headlines, the news that makes an age.

Ezra and I communicated every so often.

To tell the truth, it was always Ezra who found me. Always. I guess I was easy to find.

I went back to Brooklyn like someone returning to his home planet.

I adapted quickly.

I became a simple being, easy to categorize. My species was so numerous it ran no risk of extinction. And so, for that reason, no one was all that worried about it.

As for Ezra, I knew nothing of his whereabouts apart from increasingly bizarre rumors regarding his life and career. And so, every so often, a telephone ringing in the middle of the night, a package containing an assortment of objects, a postcard like the one I found slipped under my apartment door that evening when, my eyes full of stars, I came home from seeing that movie.

The postcard, bearing a stamp of the Eiffel Tower, was a still from a different film (a French film) in which two boys ran across a bridge after a girl.

The postcard demonstrated, once again, Ezra's strange ability to understand everything I was doing or feeling irrespective of time and distance. On the back of the postcard, in the microscopic and precise handwriting acquired, perhaps, by those who write more numbers and initials than words, it read: "Cher Isaac, the French change the name of everything. Fortunately, they've kept the number. But here HAL is called CARL: *Cerveau Analytique de Recherche et de Liaison*. You have to see this movie. See what it makes you remember. Your space brother of blood and oxygen, floating, always. Ezra."

Now, looking back, I get it: I'm but a humble astronaut, descendent of an ape, dreaming of evolving; Ezra is a disorganized and confused computer trying to comprehend the secrets of the universe.

She is our monolith.

I said it already, I'll say it again: my space brother of blood and oxygen disappears.

And Jeff disappears.

And she disappears.

And everything seems to indicate that I'm the only one left to tell of their disappearances. To tell what happened and where they went.

But my role isn't that simple.

All of a sudden, I'm an actor whose cast members have left him all alone on the stage with no lines to recite, no prompters to tell him what to say, and yet . . .

A few days ago it was the reappeared Ezra—during The Incident, on the top floor of a tower of steel and glass and wind—who asked me, pleased with himself, his twisted smile that hadn't straightened with the years, whether I didn't find it a little strange that I'd forgotten . . . no, not forgotten, but that I didn't remember "because no one forgets the exact moment that innocence ends and they realize that, from then on, life will be a succession of more or less well administered transgressions."

I looked at him without understanding and understood, suddenly, that I'd never understood anything.

And then his strange voice and his strange explanations.

The roar of thunder ever nearer.

And the flash of the impact and the fire and the nothingness and home again—and I'll be getting to that part of my story very soon.

Before, long before, right before he disappeared, an Ezra, so young, crying with fury, not understanding why she'd gone and left us behind.

An Ezra that is a new Ezra.

An Ezra who was always there, waiting in the shadows, for the right moment, the perfect reason, to unleash his fury. His wrath so long held in check. The bestial eruption of a long-contained rage at not being able to run like everyone else, trapped in resentment, hidden under a thin veneer of irony, of knowing he was different and, according to many, inferior. The need to seek justice, to demand explanations. For Ezra, mentally fleeing to far-away planets was no longer sufficient. Now Ezra would focus on the destruction of the world that surrounded and constrained him. What's the point of dreaming of other worlds when you have at hand the possibility of turning this world into a nightmare?

I see and hear Ezra again and it's like hearing the invisible moment when the wheels of a tornado start to spin.

"Enough fiction; now science will be all," Ezra tells me. And then he explains that he's enlisting in the army, "where true power lies."

I can't help it, almost reflexively my eyes are drawn to his metal wrapped legs. Ezra catches my glance and, for a second, I perceive and appreciate the enormous effort he makes not to hate me forever (though it's clear that there is a before and an after to that glance). And Ezra says to me with words that barely escape his mouth through the small gaps between the two rows of tightly clenched teeth: "Isaac: they won't care how my body marches or files. What they'll care about is the vertiginous velocity at which my mind runs and flies."

Then Ezra shuts himself in the basement and reads books and discovers formulas and barely speaks to anyone and, a few months later, mails out an envelope crammed with his notes to some branch of the military. And a few days later they come for him. And they tell him that he doesn't even have to pack, that everything will be provided in the place he'll be living from now on. His parents and sisters don't really understand what's going on, but say nothing. Over and over they read a letter signed by the president. A letter they have to give back after reading it so many times in so few minutes. And, with difficulty, Ezra gets in a big black car. And, with an odd smile, he waves to us through the window.

A few years later, the phone in my house rings and I answer it and, there in the receiver, is the voice of Ezra:

"Don't say anything. Just listen," he instructs.

And what I heard then was a new sound, something I'd never heard before. The sound of something that, until then, had been kept behind a door for whose lock nobody had found the key. The sound of light and shadow, of a thousand suns proclaiming the arrival of darkness.

"If you could see what I'm seeing, Isaac," Ezra said then, and his voice seemed to come from very far away. It was a long distance call—I clearly heard the crackle and echo of successive switchboards passing along the voice of my friend, one to the next, like a ball, across hundreds of miles—but also a call that arrived from the far side of history, from a future suddenly lassoed by the present. And then, all of a sudden, the connection was cut.

Later I learned that Ezra had called me from Alamogordo, Los Alamos National Laboratory, Trinity Camp, Manhattan Project, New Mexico, at the exact time on the precise day when the first atomic bomb was detonated.

Soon the rest of the mortals—suddenly so mortal; so defenseless and at the same time so capable of bringing about the end of everything in the world and of the world itself—found out about that thing of which someone said, "I am become Shiva, the destroyer of worlds" to which someone else added "Now we all have become sons of bitches."

But I knew about it before all of them.

And days after the first explosion, another explosion, and I received in the mail—the first eternal sunsets of a faraway planet that couldn't stop watching our planet—the first pages of a novel called *Evasion*.

And yes: the dates don't line up, the locations are imprecise, the faces are confused one to the next, and I appear and disappear in multiple places at the same time.

You'll forgive, I hope, these exact inexactitudes.

The small print on that certificate, its pages so wrinkled it has almost made me a centenarian, I suppose.

Into a man old as the century.

Into a part of history.

Into the footnote that, nevertheless, is still on its feet for so many events. It wasn't my plan; but it's clear that someone has planned and decided it for me.

Someone or something must be responsible for this inexplicable vitality, this lack of ailments, for the fact that sometimes, in the mirror, I look the same as I used to, so long ago.

Something or someone has arranged it like this. So that Ezra—and I've known it for a few days now—and I survive and live to tell the tale.

So—trying in vain to put it all in a particular order more for me than for him—I answered almost every question the "young journalist" posed as best I could, and, a few times, did not answer as best I could what I couldn't and didn't want to answer.

At times, I opted to answer just to myself, in the low yet deafening voice of my thoughts. At times, it terrified me to discover that I didn't have an answer to his questions and that, in a way, I'd lived tranquilly, never wondering how it was possible to have lived like that.

True, I must admit: I was touched and flattered that his photocopied version of *Evasion* was underlined as if it were a bible (I offered and he accepted one of my copies, one of the originals, moved like a crusader before the Holy Grail). I was excited (and I felt a spark of jealousy at having been so quickly ruled out) by his questions about the theory that Ezra Leventhal was the mysterious and anonymous author behind those pages. Then I was made uncomfortable by his insistence regarding the dark rumors circulating about Ezra's participation in even darker episodes of recent military history.

Ezra—the first admired and later disgraced Colonel Ezra Leventhal—participating not in great world wars but in small planetary conflicts with the rank and occupation of "guest." Ezra—they say—uniformed under multiple aliases in China, in Korea, in Moscow, in Vietnam, in Africa, in Latin America. Ezra as one of the Office of War Information ideologues and as the principal designer of the Operation Planning and Intelligence Board. Ezra as the author of an admired and—I'm led to believe—still operational manual for uses and applications of "psychological warfare." I saw a copy once, I recognized his prose, his particular sense of humor, and clear echoes of the Manual of a Young Space Traveler/Instructions for how to Operate, Interact, and Prosper on This and Other Planets According to the Precepts of Ezra Leventhal (Rex Arcana of the Milky Way) when he recommended "a) convince the prisoner he's on different planet, b) tell him that if he doesn't cooperate with the interrogators, he'll never return home, c) explain to him that here he'll inhabit a world very similar to Earth, that he'll be set free to live with perfect replicas of his friends and relatives but that d) none of them will ever truly love him."

Stories about Ezra that weren't entirely reliable but immediately plausible.

Ezra helping to oust presidents in devastated nations.

Ezra who—I ended up reading it somewhere or someone told me—was a key figure in deescalating (or, according to some, active in activating, as a double or triple agent) the Cuban missile crisis.

Ezra drinking drinks and chewing shellfish with absurd names (that he orders from the waiters in a robotically perfect Spanish) on South America terraces with views of the Pacific while, behind him, columns of black smoke rise and rivers of red screams overflow their banks.

A photograph of Ezra on the front page of a newspaper. Blurry, out of focus, almost impossible to make out. Afghanistan, it says. The upper part of his body obscured by the shadow of a tent. An Arabic name misidentifying the blurry man in a caption at his feet: "The Master of War in the heat of battle in the Panshir Valley." And yet I recognize the shape of that head that seems to levitate without the help of a neck, the strange legs once wrapped in metal and now, in the photo, inside a pair of aerodynamic boots full of cables.

But, maybe, everything I describe here, all these different sightings of Ezra were nothing but the expression of a desire, a need to see him and to be reunited with him.

Because I thought I saw Ezra everywhere.

In the video of that terrible morning in Dallas, 1963 (Ezra watching from one side of the street as that car passed by), or, in the black and white of my television set, my face frozen in a proud, childish smile, watching those men in short-sleeved button downs and loosened knots of identical ties (was Ezra the one with the thick-framed glasses and the buzz cut?) applauding the words of an advance in the heavens arriving, light and weightless, from the surface of the moon. Words so rehearsed. The first great space slogan. Everyone celebrates that "small step and giant leap" and overlooks what came next. A spontaneous comment, almost childish and, for me, moving, because it reminds me of that boy I once was, so many lives ago, staring at the sky: "It's different, but it's very beautiful out here," says the astronaut.

I told myself no, it couldn't be, Ezra couldn't be everywhere, involved in every historical moment. But then, a few weeks later, someone knocked on my door with a special delivery, a box with my address written in Ezra's unmistakable handwriting and, there inside, a handful of gray rocks and a card that read "Guess where these are from, Isaac. Yeah, you guessed it."

My life, I insist, has not been what you'd call entertaining. Little has happened, and most of it's been banal and predictable. A life that didn't shrink in on itself like in that classic *The Shrinking Man* because it couldn't: it couldn't shrink any smaller than what it already was: small, miniscule, almost invisible.

A few nights ago, I saw again that mediocre movie adaptation of a classic of the genre: the story of a traveler projecting himself into a distant future without ever having to leave his laboratory. You know the one: the place was always the same, it was time that changed. And, amid lame special effects and nothing-to-write-home-about performances there was, yes, an ingenious detail, I don't remember if it appeared in the novel that inspired the film: the protagonist—sitting in a time machine of elegant Victorian lines that'd been converted into something like a super-chrono-armchair—assimilated the passing decades, contemplating the successive metamorphoses of a mannequin in a boutique storefront facing his house. The mutations of clothes and hats on the cold skin of a mannequin that remained immutable, not aging, maintaining the same pose, only changing in how it was dressed. That was all, and it was better than trees losing leaves and calendars turning pages and newspapers adding words.

That's kind of how my life has been. The life of a mannequin for whom the passing of the years has been like a leisurely stroll, with many high-velocity things flying vertiginously by.

I look at myself and I see a writer who published a few decent, forgettable books, who edited several anthologies more or less well received by his colleagues (would I be committing the sin of vanity if I attributed to myself the discovery of a young English doctor who later ended up enjoying a certain fame, first as an imaginer of environmental catastrophes and later as a narrator of terminal landscapes and dried up swimming pools and wild social choreographies where, all of a sudden, everyone discovers that there are no longer any rational reasons to not lose their minds?). Someone who—with the arrival of television—became one of the most respected screenwriters on the now legendary series *The Gray Area* ("You are the greatest adapter I know, Isaac," the host of the show said over and over; and I never could tell if this was cold praise or a hot insult; I kept reading fantasy and science fiction stories and I suggested candidates and even signed on one little-remembered screenplay: "The Traveler," something about a sick man who travels back to the final days of the Aztec Empire) and who later assembled the team of writers for *Star Bound* (I, though nobody acknowledges it, had the idea to create the cold and logical Lok, the most interesting member of the crew of tight-pajama-clad space officers; I'm also the verifiable author of one of the most admired episodes of *Star Bound*: "A Message from Urkh 24," a title that—is there anybody out there?—is a mischievous wink at the author of *Evasion*) and, it's true, I must confess: I was also involved in some of those teen movies, featuring young actors with aerodynamic hairdos and young actresses with tight sweaters and even more aerodynamic breasts, whose opening scenes always took place inside an automobile with the silhouette of a spaceship parked along the side of the road, amid kisses and caresses and panting, all of a sudden, a glow in the sky and a meteor crashing into a nearby forest and the rest, you already know it, you've seen it all so many times . . .

I look at myself the way you look at a relic and I realize that I was a lousy tourist (I stared at a colossal pre-Columbian calendar, a steel tower, a fresco where God reached out His hand not quite touching the hand of man with the same eyes) and a lover who never wanted to love (the names of some women, including that of the one who accompanied me during a very brief marriage—a minor actress who played an "ambassador from Epsilon" on *Star Bound* and who, before long, told me that she had "mistaken your deep silences for intelligence, but now I realize that really you've got nothing interesting to say"—are less important to me and just as distant as the names of nebulous constellations).

Maybe, now that I think of it, I was a man who—consciously or unconsciously, today, after The Incident, I realize this with a mix of relief and sorrow—decided not to live or to feel all that much, but to spend his time trying to recall the most transcendent days of his life. A man who, every so often, at the most unexpected moments and in a not-entirely-clear way, received intermittent news and irrefutable proof of intelligent life from a remote and—I can feel it, the ping of its echo already resounding on the radar screen, I almost see it now—fast-approaching planet called the Past.

But before descending to its surface, blooming with wrinkles and craters and catacombs, here come the initial sightings, the diffuse transmissions, the imprecise yet revelatory photographs of an undeniable presence, of a body floating in the dark.

And what our communications—contact between me and Ezra—were like over time.

How to *see* an invisible man who, in his undeniable absence, always seems to be right there, breathing over our shoulder, reading what we're writing.

Technology that advanced doesn't exist.

So the means we used to communicate with each other were quite primitive.

Ezra had given me a PO box address where I, every so often, sent messages of varying length and intensity. Pages that ranged from midnight insomniac confessions to costumbrist sketches, updating him on the battles and truces of the shrinking and moribund planet of science fiction, as well as the inevitable, but ever more infrequent, noteworthy event.

Like what happened one day when a renowned and troublesome magnate had, without warning, stormed a convention of fantasy writers in Milford, Pennsylvania, and had walked up on stage and delivered, with delusional passion, a speech as heartfelt as it was terrifying; because suddenly for us there was nothing worse than learning that someone who might have been our most devout follower was possibly insane. His words, though unhinged, were probably far more evocative and powerful than any of our own pronouncements, ever more weightless and apathetic in those days. We gathered together, our faces embalmed in yawns, in university amphitheaters too large for the audiences we managed to draw. Our voices reverberating off walls of immense rooms that sent back the sad echoes of our own despondency. Many attendants showed up dressed as their favorite character from their preferred television series: pointy ears and eyes on the foreheads of desperate beings who needed to believe for a while that they were extraterrestrials in order to tolerate their excess days here on earth. Beings with no interest in writing but who, nevertheless, desperately needed someone to *read* them. And, in the meantime, no hurry, they were pacifying their insatiable addiction to merchandise and spending their savings on toys that they never even removed from their packaging so they wouldn't "lose value." They fought clumsy duels with buzzing light sabers. And almost wept in front of duplicates of those two annoying robots, you know the ones, I can never remember the digits of their names—better that way.

And worst of all weren't our absurd followers (endowed with a patheticness that in no way resembled the patheticness of our beginnings, a patheticness that to us seemed epic, because we were children of the Great Depression and our love for the future came from an absolute absence of a present and not, as was the case decades later, from the presence of a now, seemingly invulnerable and eternal in its stillness and permanence), but the new writers who came to the conventions. Strange individuals. Fourth generation Darlingskill cultists and addicts of novels that anticipated, swept away with the excitement, the arrival of a Fourth Reich that would exterminate "all the sub-races" as well as the coming and ascension of a new psychedelic messiah. Things like that. Science fiction as pollution and catharsis. Science fiction as a space that would include and dignify them, many of whom, I thought, as I watched them, would end up killers or killing themselves trying to follow the partially- or totally-eclipsed brains of people like Zack—already beginning to be deified in France—once again present at our conventions, babbling about the present as a fleeting gleam in the deforming mirror of the Roman Empire, which never ended, which was still here, standing, watching over us with that combination of admiration and respect accorded weary gladiators in the increasingly blood-soaked arena.

Yes, we gathered together, almost out of inertia, to discuss solar systems and distant races while the youth raged outside, refusing to fight in exotic, foreign wars. Many of us, on the other hand, were veterans of more intimate battles and it made us uncomfortable to find ourselves, after so many years without seeing each other, in those rooms plastered with posters for the latest movie about invaders, like something abducted from inside our own bodies. Bodies that to us were old and familiar, but newly eroded to those who remembered us differently and how we once were and how we would never be again and—suddenly I understood—how they would never be again either.

The words of the millionaire with the rose-scented family name had been faithfully recorded by multiple recorders and I transcribed them and sent them to Ezra preceded by the words: "All is not lost: the extraterrestrials appear to love us." And this is what the crazy philanthropist—who, I soon learned, was about to be declared insane by a law firm interested in assuming control of his fortune—had said:

"I love you sons of bitches. You're all I read anymore. They're my nourishment and my raison d'être. My destiny. You're the only ones who will talk about the *really* terrific changes going on, the only ones crazy enough to know that life is a space voyage. And not a short one either, but one that will last for billions of years. You're the only ones with guts enough to *really* care about the future, who *really* notice what machines do to us, what wars do to us, what cities do to us, what big simple ideas do to us, what tremendous misunderstandings, mistakes, accidents, and catastrophes do to us. You're the only ones zany enough to agonize over time and distances without limit, over mysteries that will never die, over the fact that we are right now determining whether the space voyage for the next billion years or so is going to be heaven or hell."

I transcribed all of this and, yes, I felt shame and pain that I couldn't recognize myself in these words. For me, the future had turned into a profession, a way of life. That's all. Nothing interested me less than the future, which was increasingly small compared to my increasingly large past.

Communiqués from Ezra, on the other hand, didn't come in writing, but at the speed of sound and usually in the middle of the night, via telephone. I heard the ringing in the dark and answered and there, undeniably far away, crackling with interference and the sound of electronic bugs with their stingers stuck in the line, was his voice:

"Don't say anything. Don't ask anything. Just listen . . . The date and place don't matter. The names and context don't either. It's all classified. All *top secret*. That's how it is, that's what it's become, my life. So I'll limit myself to telling you that it'll all happen on a small island in the great atoll of the Pacific. Or, if you prefer, in Washington, DC. In one place and the other, the radioactivity is the same. High levels of radiation, sometimes physical, sometimes mental, equally contaminating. Did you know, Isaac, that the creators of the atomic bomb never thought about its residual effects, about what would happen *after* and *beyond* the explosion? They only thought about the instant of detonation and not about the consequences of its expansive energy. And maybe that's the problem: real scientists rarely read science fiction. In any case, the protagonist of this conversation, which I know, I apologize, is a monologue, answers to the code-name of Doctor C. The initial of this surname that I'm concealing is, really, an Anglicized version of his true Italian surname which begins with the letter B. Doctor C. is now being interrogated by a special committee and, when they ask him about changing his surname, he responds: 'I changed my name for a variety of reasons. It was difficult to spell, it was difficult to pronounce, and difficult to identify myself efficiently. I also changed my name because there are some parts of this country and some people who still suspect anything foreign. A foreign name is inefficient. I changed my name as in going from one country to another one changes one's currency.' A few days ago Doctor C. told me he was sure that, every morning, a bird alighted next to his window and melodiously intoned his name. Doctor C. is being questioned by a committee of specialists concerned with his increasingly impassioned opposition to any program related to exploration beyond our solar system. Of course the committee members, who aren't scientists, but bureaucrats or government employees, actually *do* read science fiction and reveal themselves as more-than-a-little concerned about the advances of foreign nations in these areas. They're fearful people. Doctor C. explains to them that all of this is foolishness, but he admits that it'd be premature to assume that we're the only more or less intelligent civilization in the universe. Doctor C. presents various relevant theories. Irrelevant technical jargon that I won't expand on here to avoid putting you to sleep. 'Interesting' signals in Tau Ceti, Planck Constant, optic masses, magnetic storms, things that sound much better when left unexplained and allowed to conserve the pure mystery of the letters that make up their words. One of the interrogating officers decided to reverse the polarity of the questions, referring to Doctor C.'s 'ungovernable temper' and to many episodes that demonstrated his explosive temperament. Doctor C. has torn down Venetian blinds, slapped his subordinates, used obscene language with stewardesses on Pan Am Airlines, gone into a church shouting that he knew the exact spot Jesus has been hidden all these years, thrown a heavy glass ashtray at a colleague during a symposium postulating the most appropriate anatomy for a rocket destined to carry human colonists to a star whose name I can't reveal to you, either, though it doesn't really matter: there are few things,

I think, less revealing than the names of stars. The names of stars are, almost always, like the names of the most expensive medications. Then another officer opens an attaché case and begins listing figures corresponding to governmental funds that Doctor C. hasn't managed as he should, devoting them exclusively to the development of remote-controlled weapons and, reading from a file, 'a computer program that will enable us to always defeat the soviet chess players.' Someone else made reference to an epidemic at the base under Doctor C.'s command caused, supposedly, by microbes—'a fungus of the genus Loremendrum'—that breed in mid- and long-range missile fuel. Doctor C. smiles and doesn't object and, when they ask him if he believes in the inevitability of an atomic conflict, he says, yes, and when they ask if, in the event of defeat, he would be in favor of destroying the planet, he answers: 'Yes, I would. If we cannot survive, then we are entitled to destroy the planet.' And this is when what I'm most interested in telling you happens, what amounts to a kind of mirrored and codified response to your anecdote about the supposedly crazy millionaire. What happens then is that an old man on the committee raises a shaking hand and asks to speak, his voice is feeble but at the same time seems to reach the farthest corner of the room with intimidating intensity, and he begins to talk about the sunrises in the small town of his childhood, about the five wars that he's lived through in his long life, and about the irresponsibility of misusing 'Promethean powers,' ending with a sob 'Oh, please, please, don't destroy our earth.' The silence that follows this outburst is broken by a new series of somewhat strange questions. Doctor C. admits to only reading short *Western Romances* and claims to know how to play the violin and, to prove it, takes the instrument in question out of a case and awkwardly plays a very simple Bach air; which excites the old man who goes off on an epiphanic and allegorical spiel aimed at the inhabitants of other galaxies and concludes, before breaking down in tears, with 'Oh, let us rush to see this world! They have invented instruments to stir the finest aspirations. They have invented games to catch the hearts of the young. They have invented ceremonies to exalt the love of men and women. Oh, let us rush to see this world!' Then, after an uncomfortable silence, someone asks Doctor C. if he has a son and, his voice cold, he says, yes, and that he's been hospitalized. And then a housekeeper gets to her feet and offers testimony of the cruelty Doctor C. treated his son with, locking him in closets without food or water for entire days and, all of a sudden, a door opens and a grown man with white hair and mongoloid features comes in yelling 'Daddy . . . oh Daddy . . . It's raining,' and then something seems to snap inside Doctor C., something that'll never be fixed, and his son says 'It's raining, Daddy. Stay with me. Don't go out in the rain. Stay with me just the once . . . I write you all the time, Daddy, but you never answer my letters. Why don't you answer my letters, Daddy? Why don't you ever answer my letters?' Doctor C. looks straight ahead, not looking at his son, he looks like someone looking at a firing squad or at the sand of a beach after too many weeks at high sea, and says: 'I don't answer your letters because I'm ashamed of them. I send you everything you need. I sent you some nice stationery and envelopes, you write me on wrapping paper, you write me on laundry lists, you even write me on toilet paper . . . I'm ashamed to receive them, I'm ashamed to see them. They remind me of everything in life I detest.' This said, the boy is taken away and the father, Doctor C., sits down and shuts his eyes. And when he opens them it's as if nothing happened, as if by force of will alone Doctor C. has immediately erased all of it from his memory, as if he'd ordered the dishes cleared away after a long and heavy dinner. Then, after the cries of Doctor C.'s son moving off down the corridors fade away, someone proposes stripping Doctor C. of all his powers, credentials, and security clearance, and the motion is unanimously approved. And this is all I have to tell you today, my friend. Homework: Who is Doctor C.? Goodnight and sweet dreams."

A month later, the telephone—a heavy, black Bakelite phone that's been with me most of my life and which I refuse to abandon—rings again around midnight. It's December and a thick snow is falling outside and, in living rooms and dining rooms of houses, on the other side of windows, the intermittent glow of Christmas trees makes it seem like the street has transformed into a landing and launch strip for sleighs or something else.

Ezra's voice—more distant than usual, in the background I can make out a conversation in a language I'm unable to identify and booms and screams of birds and beasts—says only: "Hello, Isaac. I'm calling now to tell you I won't be calling again."

And this is the last I hear from him until many years later, until a few nights ago, when what I've come to call The Incident begins.

Of all the forms of fear, human beings have produced few as effective as a telephone ringing in the middle of the night.

There's no special effect more effective than that: a man alone, in a dark house, not expecting anyone to call because he knows he's the last living being in his story. And, suddenly, a sound that becomes a noise. So he gets up and walks, almost weightless with sleep, moving through the corridors of a dead spaceship that will never return home because it has become home. When he reaches the phone he waits a few more seconds. Two more noises. Like I said: it's one of those old and heavy models whose ring sounds more organic than electronic, like the howl of an animal trained to raise the alarm. And he stares at it, as if not entirely believing that it functions.

It's been a long time since it rang (every so often the man lifts it to his ear, checking that it still works and, as such, the absurdity of its existence in that place) and now it rings again and finally he picks it up and hears a voice that is close now and sounds even closer.

"It's Ezra," the voice says, "I need to see you."

I didn't go back to bed after Ezra's call. It wouldn't have made any sense: his voice on the phone had shaken the sleep out of me (I've always been proud of being an old man who sleeps like a baby), and I made a pot of coffee and sat down to look through some old documents, as if I were preparing for an exam, worried I'd forget some important detail or be unable to answer a decisive question. I was surprised by how little I had. Just a few objects and documents capable of provoking an echo, of bringing back something from so far away.

Inside a box I found a notebook on whose cover was written MANUAL OF A YOUNG SPACE TRAVELER/INSTRUCTIONS FOR HOW TO OPERATE, INTERACT, AND PROSPER ON THIS AND OTHER PLANETS ACCORDING TO THE PRECEPTS OF EZRA LEVENTHAL (REX ARCANA OF THE MILKY WAY) and when I turned its pages, they crumbled between my fingers. I felt dizzy and decided the best thing to do was to stay still, to sit by a window. But before long, the almost sadistic slowness of the rising sun made me feel the weight of each minute of the hours remaining before my meeting with Ezra.

There's nothing more unbearable than the sudden proximity of something we've been waiting for a long time: we can accept its remoteness, but its sudden proximity is unbearable.

I went to my library and decided that the best thing to do was to read something. I looked for my copy of *Times Without Time*, but couldn't find it. The same thing happened with *Damitax* and *Krakhma-Zarr*. They weren't in their places, in the places I was sure

I'd seen them and flipped through them a few days before. None of my books were there. All of a sudden my library was full of books by authors I had no memory of reading. They were—it was easy to tell from their covers adorned with rockets and robots—science fiction books. But who were these authors? Asimov, Clarke, Lovecraft, Bradbury, Sturgeon . . . Where had they come from? What were they doing there?

Something strange was happening and I preferred not to think that something strange was happening to *me*. All of this, I thought, must just be the effect of the emotion of hearing from Ezra again, of knowing that soon I'd see Ezra again.

I decided not to think about it anymore, I attributed the episode to sleep's final spasm, I left the unfamiliar books where the familiar books should have been, I told myself everything would return to normal and, without being interested in confirming this, trembling, I walked to the bathroom, took a shower, went out into the street, and started walking toward the subway stop.

It was that time of day when the air is full of flying newspapers.

Then, the thrilling fright of seeing someone you haven't seen in a long time. Seeing someone we haven't seen for years is like *seeing* time. The time that passed, the time that never stops passing.

The same impression you get when you see, for the first time, the credible miracle of an open clock. I'm talking, of course, about classic clocks—far more *expressive* than the cold red and electric light of digital devices—whose hands are pins that end up fixing you with an epitaph that, if you're lucky, will mark you for posterity. There, all those miniscule pieces, those gears and springs and turning screws, inside such a small and fragile space, the solid immensity of the centuries.

So, seeing someone after so many years is like looking at another part of that same mechanism. A part that's invisible, but there, that wasn't there to start with but that never stopped growing: the part that shows what time has done to that mechanism. The brutal erosion of the caress of the years, a caress that ceaselessly caresses a face and a smile.

Ezra smiles.

I've crossed a bridge and I've returned to this city and I've ascended to the heights of this tower and the elevator doors opened and I walked to the door with the number Ezra indicated and I knocked and nobody answered. So I turned the knob and entered an immense, empty room, a room occupying the entire floor, that opened to the full circumference of the building. An empty room with views of the city and a clear blue sky. Then I saw him. At one end of the space, on a red rug whose brightness produced an immediate irritation in my eyes, there was a desk and two chairs and in one of them sat Ezra. And Ezra seemed to possess that quality between liquid and gaseous that you see on the most distant point of a highway or at the end of airport runways. Ezra as something not entirely solid. Ezra as if painted in the aquarelles and colors of a mirage.

I walk over to him and those few meters feel like kilometers. I tremble. I haven't stopped trembling since I left my house this morning without really understanding why I was trembling. Now, at least, I know that I'm trembling with the excitement and fear of understanding how something known can also be unknown.

I look at Ezra and I recognize him, but as I get closer, I see him, and I'm no longer entirely sure that it's the same Ezra I used to know. And my surprise isn't just due to the years that have passed, to the distance of decades suddenly reduced to the seconds that now separate me from Ezra. Ezra stands up and walks toward me, not with the difficulty that encumbered him as a child, but with a strange grace.

Like before, he seems unable to move in a straight line, still weaving back and forth. Like before, again, the impression is still that he's moving on wheels, as if he were suspended a couple centimeters above the floor. But now the effect is more convincing because it no longer depends on the considerable muscular exertion that deformed the muscles of young Ezra's face. Now—a mechanical whirr coming from his legs—Ezra moves immutably forward, his smile perfect. I open my arms and go to him and Ezra pulls back and says: "Careful, Isaac! I'm not really sure it's a good idea for us to hug . . . Our interdimensional compositions might be incompatible and contact could cause a cosmic cataclysm . . . And, yes, this terminology sounds a little absurd, like something taken from something Jeff wrote, if you can call that writing . . ." Then, seeing my confusion, Ezra smiles again and looks at me, tilting his head slightly. I would rather not imagine what he was thinking when he looks at me. My good health hasn't been accompanied by—paraphrasing in *lingua sci-fi*, no other way to think of it or say it occurs to me—"an adequate conservation of facial tissues" or something like that. I suppose that a weather-beaten traveler from the past might recognize, in the now devastated panorama of my face, something of the meticulously designed gardens of yesteryear. Good luck and thanks for trying. I can't do it anymore.

What had happened to Ezra, on the other hand, was even stranger. Ezra had not aged. What had happened to him recalled something more like the process of fossilization. Everything—his skin had that perpetual tan of someone who's flown too close to the sun too many times without taking precautions—was the same as before but, at the same time, desiccated somehow, as if reduced or distilled to its minimal and most expressive expression. I'd seen faces like Ezra's in museums, in the immortal remains of pharaohs and emperors. Skin stretched over bones, taut as a canvas where for years everything in the world has been painted and, when there's nothing left to paint, all that's left to do is apply a final coat of white that fails to conceal or contain what lies underneath. Like this, close up, Ezra appears to be all ages at once. His features do not seem to want to sit still and flow back and forth, and give the unsettling sensation of watching an insecure skull unable to decide what clothes to go out in. More than Ezra himself, I realize, what I'm seeing is a projection of Ezra. Something that gives off a crackling hum of energy: the ghost of electricity howling in the bones of your face. Ezra smiles and it's one of those smiles that bites.

I want to say something—Ezra raises his hand—and I discover that I cannot speak, that I don't have anything to say, someone has decided to turn down the volume of my voice.

Ezra speaks.

Ezra speaks, and when he speaks I'm reminded of one of those foreign films that's been poorly dubbed into English: the movement of his lips out of sync with the sound of his words. Ezra speaks and I don't understand everything he says, at times waves of static drown out his words. But I listen to him as if reading him, subtitles at the level of his chest, and memorizing as I go, the first time, not having to go back and reread a single line. I'm his best possible student. More than hearing, I see his words and write them down across the suddenly hospitable surface of my memory.

Ezra speaks and at first his sentences are short but, as he goes on they get longer and longer.

Ezra speaks:

"Very strange things have been happening."

"Welcome to the Age of Strange Things, Isaac."

"The cold."

"How could she leave us?"

"A world without her is a destroyable world."

"*Evasion.*"

"All times at the same time, Isaac."

"Do you remember her?"

"A few days—or a few years—ago I saw her again."

"In the desert."

"How could she leave us? How could [*incomprehensible*] do that to us?"

"The palace of memory . . . My memory is no palace. My memory is a space shuttle spinning in dead orbit around the past. There I am, from there I broadcast, in a trance, like a midnight DJ."

"All those pages. All those sunsets. I don't know how, but they came to me wherever I was, everywhere I was. In embassies and bunkers and underground laboratories, and before long I realized that, just as I thought at the beginning, you couldn't be the author of all of that. You were never that good of a writer. And neither was I. Before long I realized that [*incomprehensible*] her way of explaining to us the unexplainable."

"I've seen so much. I've seen so many things that the sensation is no longer that of seeing but of uploading. Every new landscape is one more object submitted and deposited at the edge of my eyes and instantly uploaded to my brain and stored in an archive alongside so many other things. Every night I pray, because the space is filling up and soon nothing else will fit."

"The really naïve idea of building machines, computers, that increasingly resemble man when, in reality, what is desired, what they want me to find, is just the opposite: for men to be more and more like machines. For them to think in sequential, linear fashion, and about just one thing. For them not to get distracted thinking about what they've been ordered to do, but to simply obey orders . . . And it's obvious that for many of my superiors the results I obtained seemed to them somewhat [*incomprehensible*] so they claimed [*incomprehensible*] and I had to look for new . . . let's call them . . . sponsors, and [*incomprehensible*] here I am."

"Freedom of choice? Free will? What for? Where has that kind of thinking ever gotten us? The ability to choose the best way to destroy ourselves. To kill each other. But always partially, with little efficiency [*incomprehensible*] putting off the inevitable. So why not make things easy, facilitate the endeavor, and [*incomprehensible*] once and for all."

"Going to the brain and breaking in, smashing everything they find on their way to the memory's core [*incomprehensible*] until none of those annoying neurotransmitters—which only distract us from the definitive and absolute objective—functions anymore."

"Without feelings. Without distractions. Without doubts. Without fears. Without memories."

"Every time I manage to forget her, I don't know how, she finds a way to come back, to make me remember her."

"Remember. You remember so many things I cannot allow myself to remember because [*incomprehensible*] inappropriate."

"Remember. Now I forget all of it perfectly: you and I, working together under the light of the Moon. The storm has passed and it's not cold. Or maybe it's the heat of our enthusiasm that keeps us warm and [*incomprehensible*] to face the [*incomprehensible*]. We're the heroes of our own favorite legend. We are, suddenly, thanks to her, legendary."

"Remember. You and me in the snow and her watching us from the window. It's a very romantic image: the beautiful prisoner in the highest tower of the castle and the devoted knights who dare not rescue her. They don't know how. They're too young and inexperienced. And the novelty of shared love—brothers of blood and sect who are now, also, brothers of love—makes them feel invulnerable, yes, but they don't know how to use that strength. There are times they think they might burst. Spontaneous combustion. Detonated by the passion their bodies and minds generate."

"Her. The snow. Her hair in the wind. Watching us."

"Remember. A few hours have passed since the great quorum. Everyone against everyone. The Futurians, The Cosmics, The Futuristics, The Dimensionals, The Astronomics, The Futurexics. Political debates. Those who believe science fiction should be a tool for the new man, for the heroes of the working class. Fictions of the revolution. The machines working for great change. And those who want to feel like cosmic aristocrats and preserve the stars for the use of an exclusive elite. And then there is us. You and me. And Jeff. Who takes the floor to read something he considers 'essential and illuminating.' And the laughter. The laughter."

"'You'll see! You'll see!' he screams."

"Remember. That's when everything began. Since then we've lived an eternal ending."

"Remember. It's a night like no other. It's a night like you see in certain paintings. Her. And you and me. The two of us building snowmen. One after the other. And not typical snowmen, that stupid pyramidal accumulation of snowballs. No. We used branches and a handrail we stole from a neighboring house. Our snowmen are *men* of snow: shaped like men. One and another and another until we lose count, and the whole time she watches us from the window. It's dark and we can't tell if she's crying or smiling. Probably both. At the same time. I already told you, Isaac: all times at the same time. And when we finish with the men of snow, without exchanging a single word, because suddenly it's as if we knew exactly what the other was thinking, we start to shape a huge snowball. A planet. A planet for her. Suddenly it's daybreak, the metallic light of daybreak, and there we are. Standing next to our men of snow. We feel so small, so small. We feel insufficient and unworthy of all that love we feel for her. And so, like small and humble gods, we created and made others. A legion to help her understand that we did it all for her. That we felt that [*incomprehensible*] together, forever. And that all those worshippers we created for her—all those inhabitants of that planet that was hers, ours, and who had come from so far away, undaunted by the knowledge that soon they would start to melt, faster all the time, as the sun came up—were our witnesses."

"Don't ever forget. The moment has arrived to remember forever."

"Look at us."

And Ezra reaches one hand into the interior pocket of his briefcase and takes out a photograph and gives it to me and when I take it a tingling runs through the tips of my fingers, and I look, and there we are: Ezra and me and her. Ezra and I are staring seriously at the camera, but she's laughing. She's laughing without inhibition. She's laughing as if she were the true and undeniable inventor of laughter. The owner of the patent, showing her invention to the world with pride, with all her teeth. Seeing her—and, suddenly, remembering her and remembering the force of her love for us and our love for her—I remember everything.

Then something strange happens. And it's not as if what happened previously isn't strange; but what happens now is stranger still. Then, there inside, in the tower, despite the clear and sunny day rising outside, it starts to snow. And I look at Ezra and Ezra is the Ezra he once was and I don't need to see myself—I feel a vibration across my whole face, as if someone were correcting lines, retouching details—to know that I am who I once was too.

We're young again with all the snow before us.

Ezra smiles.

"Until next time, my friend."

I smile.

And, all of a sudden, a horizontal roar shakes the windows and Ezra and I look at the sky just in time to see the airplane, first in one edge of the sky and suddenly so close, crashing into the tower, into us.

Ezra speaks:

"Remember, Isaac: marvelous moments."

And I felt happy. I felt new. I felt at peace. Everything was disappearing around me and I, at last, was part of that everything. All of a sudden I had an explanation for what had happened. In the final second of my life, I was conscious of everything. Of the multiple, oh so many, variations. Of the infinite encounters across all that time. Of all the possible endings that did or did not happen—a hunting accident, crossing a street and not making it to the other side, a snap in the chest while eating a slice of cake in a museum cafeteria, going down in a fishing boat in an unexpected squall—and of this ending that was happening now.

I thought that, at last, it was time to rest, to die, to travel far away, to ascend into the sky.

The sky is full of the dead because the living, when they die, go into the sky. Or at least that's what—again, science fiction—they teach us and want to make us believe when we're little. We die and we go elsewhere, to live our death in the highest of high places.

And then I understood that death was the most beautiful thing that had happened to me in my life.

Death wasn't a light at the end of a tunnel.

Death was the end of all tunnels.

And my death was so much shorter than my long life.

All of a sudden I was at home; I don't remember getting there. I do remember the roar of the airplane and the fire. And I remember, as well, that there is a part in *Evasion* that talks about falling towers.

I walk to the river and nothing appears to have changed. It's a bright morning, the sunlight reflects of the white surface of the towers. A mime persists, with his deafening silence, in walking against a nonexistent wind. He looks at me and smiles and I think, I'm not sure, that I insult him with words I don't often say, words that are like an exotic taste in my mouth.

I pick up a newspaper someone left on a bench and I discover that today is not today.

Today is a few days before today.

I wonder if this dizziness I feel, this nausea, is the effect of having been projected backward, if this is what it feels like to travel back in time, when the mannequin in the storefront displays, suddenly, a more or less outmoded style.

I return home and go into my library and pick out a book at random and open it to a random page and read: "A hallucination is not, strictly speaking, manufactured in the brain; it is received by the brain."

I look at the cover. I haven't the slightest idea who Philip K. Dick is, but his writing seems a lot like that of Warren Wilbur Zack.

I return to the city a couple days later. I return to the city the morning after being visited by the not-so-young young journalist.

The same day a few days later.

The same date, the same weather.

I wear the same clothes.

Again.

But I've set off multiple variations.

I want to know what happened to me, what is happening to me.

I've made an appointment with a doctor, a specialist.

I can't remember any of what I've done these last two days, other than the phone call, a short conversation with a secretary, scheduling me an appointment for something called "brain mapping," and a furious but resigned exploration of news broadcasts and papers.

There is no news.

It's a clear and normal September and the last measures of summer have taken on that reddish and golden aura that unhurriedly heralds the yellows of autumn.

I get in a taxi and, as usual, almost without thinking, find the name of the driver hanging from back of the front seat. His last name isn't Indian, but European, Spanish actually, with an Anglo-Saxon first name. On the radio a singer repeats over and over "I've got you, babe . . . I got you, babe . . . I got you, babe . . ."

The taxi driver smiles at me in the rearview mirror. "Isaac Goldman, right?" he says. It disturbs me that he knows my name, he says it like he'd guessed it or read my mind. I glance nervously at the thin cardboard folder that contains my medical history that I'm holding against my chest like some sort of protective shield, checking if my name appears on it somewhere, then I remember that the operator at the taxi company asked my name in order to schedule the day and time of the reservation and I relax.

Then the driver says, "Isaac Goldman, the greatest science-fiction writer of his day." And I start to tremble. And the driver keeps talking as we move down tree-lined streets toward the bridge and I confirm that, yes, the towers are still there, that everything appears normal, that the only oddity is this taxi driver who's saying: "My father was a great fan of yours. He read all your stories. And he even recorded videos of the episodes you wrote for that great television series . . . My father was crazy about robots and rockets and stuff like that. That's why he named me *Ray*. My dad wanted me to go into space. But asthma, you know . . . He never got over the frustration and that's why he offered to be one of the first volunteers to try that drug . . . the one that makes you forget undesired, sad, unbearable memories. My father wanted to forget that at one point he'd dreamed of a stellar future for me, a future in the stars. But those were the drug's early days, it was still being developed. He forgot me completely. And now that I think of it . . . That's a lie . . . I've thought about it many times since then: maybe he found everything around him, his whole life, intolerable. Afterward he was totally blank. Like a blank page. We had to hospitalize him. Fortunately, the damages paid by the laboratory were enough. I could even afford to come here and buy this cab . . ."

I wondered what drug this man was talking about. Could I have taken this drug? Could that explain the increasingly deep and dark lagoons in my memory? I don't remember taking it, but maybe not remembering was undeniable proof that I had indeed submitted myself to a now-forgotten treatment to keep from remembering so many things because, when it comes to forgetting unpleasant things, I don't think there's anything more worth forgetting than having reached the point of taking such a drug. Maybe The Incident was just a side effect. A glimmer of rebellion, my brain rattling its chains. Or a sign that I've been medicating myself for too long without remembering my medication or remembering it just long enough—for no more than a few moments—to take another dose. Or maybe my own body is already producing the compound, which it can't forget. I open the folder containing my records, looking for the analysis and conclusions from my last checkup. There's nothing there. No strange names of sophisticated drugs. Just the familiar analgesic for my rheumatism. An old medicine, from a time when medicines felt obliged to explain their purpose, even with their name: Outpainex 600mg.

The taxi driver is still talking: ". . . a Mexican girl. The other day. And it turns out she was the sister of Manolo 'Muñequito' Mantra. You know, the first Mexican astronaut. The tiny one. Like a *muñeco*, a doll. The one who decided to stay on the Moon, remember? The one who sang Mexican songs until his oxygen ran out . . . 'How far I am now from the ground where I was born . . .' the little bastard sang. The Mexican girl also told me that her boyfriend had been torn to shreds by the steel blade of an industrial ventilator and that she was pregnant. And she asked me if I could get her some 'forgetting powders.' Then we went to her hotel and she swam in the pool and I'd never seen anyone swim like that. Let's see if I can describe it: it was like, instead of her swimming in the pool, the pool was swimming in her. Then we went to bed and she cried and told me she wanted to forget so many things, that she even wanted to forget her desire to forget. Then she said something that made an impression, a phrase so lovely that I wrote it down so it wouldn't escape. I have it here. Listen: 'Memory is like the most stupid dog, you throw it a stick and it brings you any old thing.' Isn't that beautiful?"

I tell him yes, and leave him a generous tip.

In the street, sitting on a curb, there's a bum holding a sign that reads: "Unemployed science-fiction writer recently returned from the colonies on Urkh 24. Please, for pity's sake, I need a few drahleks so I can eat and recharge my androids."

It's then that—with the sudden image of my father, imagined after so much time, as if, like him, I were floating just so I could fall— I think something like "Oh, absent God, please send one of your exterminating angels. Send an implacable robot of steel and muscle back from the future, I beg you, program it to erase me from this story forever. Or if not, make the fiercest wolf hatch from an egg and enter me through my mouth and grow inside me and burst out through my chest and bring an end to everything that moves in this worn-out spaceship of my life. Or, better, order the sun to rise at night and sing to me. Sing to me until my dazzled eyes burn with its voice that is yours. Thank you."

"Thank you," I say. And I don't know why. I guess it's one of the automatic reflexes of getting old: when you reach my age, you thank everyone for everything, just in case: thanks, it was nothing, you're welcome, no problem.

They have put me in a metal cylinder.

The assistant left me here inside and has gone to the other side of a transparent panel.

First she looked at me with that mix of admiration and distaste that I've grown accustomed to: I'm so old and yet so functional (I walk, I speak, I eat on my own) that instead of being admired I provoke a kind of mistrust. I suppose they'd like me better if I went around in a wheelchair and needed help using the bathroom. The idea that I've received a rare reward—an almost youthful old age—arouses the same suspicion in young people as Wall Street swindlers or a Vegas cardsharp.

Then, she told me—ordered me—not to move and that, if I do, the whole process would have to start over.

It'll take, they warn, forty-five minutes of absolute stillness, rocked to the music of whirrs and clicks.

She asks me if I have any type of metal implant. I tell her not that I remember, but it's possible that I've somehow forgotten my involvement in some war or traffic accident. The assistant gives me an odd look and keeps on reciting rules and instructions.

She tells me I'm lucky, that this scanner is a latest generation model and that inside it features a small video monitor that allows me to contemplate, in real time, Manhattan's adjacent skyline.

She tells me the engineers added this innovation because of the number of claustrophobic patients who insist they're not claustrophobic until they're *inside* and discover that they always were, that claustrophobia is something else entirely, that it's got nothing to do with an elevator stuck between floors or a jam-packed subway car.

She tells me that I'm going to debut it, that I'm the first one to go in and see.

She tells me this as if it were a special honor, as if they were giving me the key to a city or the scissors to cut the tape at the inauguration of a stadium.

She tells me this as if the possibility of a tumor nesting in my brain were a secondary concern and a bit of a bother, like a guest who drinks too much and, throwing drinks and insults into the air, ruins the party.

She tells me this, I suspect, almost hoping that I've got some rare and terrible disease so that brand new machine will get a chance to bestow on me the privilege of detecting it and thereby, with the digital and digitalized seal of a laser, sign my death warrant. The certificate of the beginning of my end with no need for a second opinion because, the assistant explains, the precision and accuracy of the diagnosis would be 99.9 percent.

The assistant—reappearing now in her more or less futuristic flight-attendant uniform—leaves me alone and there I am, machine at last, robot in part, contemplating the gap-toothed-smile of the Manhattan skyline.

Tzimtzum . . . tzimtzum . . . tzimtzum . . . the machine breaths.

And it's then, just then, that I see it, that I see it happen again. As if it were an old but classic episode of a television series we'll never tire of watching. The repetition of The Incident on that small screen: an airplane (I see that it is an airplane, I have no doubt, it is a big airplane) crashing into one of the towers and the sound of the impact so close, because the tower is nearby, its shadow falling across the building where the doctor's office is located. I hear screams too and crying in the corridors, in the waiting room. And doors opening and closing. The terrifying sound of men and women running, so much more terrifying than the sound of frightened animals running. Human beings never learned to run as they should, I think. Or, our mistake, we've forgotten how, in the name of civilization. I think about that, maybe, to justify my absolute stillness, my almost reflexive obedience to a woman who, no doubt, is running down the stairs right now. I realize, suddenly, that I've been left alone, there inside. And that I should get out. But I don't want to mess everything up and have to start over from the beginning. I've already screwed up so many things in my life to, in addition, screw up my death. So I stay there a while longer, watching, on the small screen, flames bursting from the side of one building. It's then—I expect it, I know it's going to happen, but I don't know how I know—a second airplane strikes the other tower. I stay there a few more minutes. Then, with considerable effort, I pull myself out of the metal cylinder, like a snake shedding its skin, and leave the office.

The building appears to be completely empty. I get in the elevator and—the kind of thing you think about when you don't want to think about what's actually happening—go down to the street wondering why it's called an *elevator* and not a *de-elevator*.

Down below, people are running and screaming. Everyone runs and screams as if chased by one of those huge monsters whose sleep has been interrupted by a nuclear explosion or who has been blown up to the heights of a nightmare by runaway radiations.

People run and scream and the air is full of papers.

Love letters, files, stocks, bills, photos of loved ones whose love is about to be activated more powerfully than ever, with an exquisite and irrepressible sorrow. I can feel stabs of that sorrow spreading through the morning air, encompassing everything like claws caressing faces wet with tears.

Everything floats.

Now yes, now it's real, now it happens, now it's happening, I think.

The air is full of things that are not air but are part of it now.

People fall from above and the ground is strewn with random parts of bodies that'll never be put back together.

Sirens mingle with screams and there I am, hands in pockets, thinking about how much I'd like to have a great deal of time to describe all of it. Millimeter by millimeter. How the view has been totally and forever altered. The way the ground shimmers with millions of shards of glass, shining like diamonds in the blue morning, cracking like the thin ice of a lake under the blades of brave skaters. How millions of postcards suddenly become lies, out-of-date photographs of a place that no longer exists.

I remembered my father, his voice, telling me about the Divine Light that broke into innumerable fragments and fell like a crystal rain across the face of the earth. I remembered my father and felt like I saw everything all at once: the totality of the devastating view and, simultaneously, each of its smallest and most secret details. Something like turning the pages of those books devoted to the classic paintings. First, a double spread with a full reproduction of a painting, full of characters and situations. And next, several pages devoted to specific details. Enlargements. The smile that, close up, seems constructed with the patience of a mosaic. The false proximity that makes us feel like proud masters of ephemeral superpowers that almost give us a glimpse of the artist's first rueful sketch or the inevitable and playfully hidden signature (the dog's paws marking the initials of a patron in the dirt, the maiden's hand pointing to a cloud in the shape of a royal crest). The cracks in the oil, fine as hairs (I bend down to look at what I believe is a wounded bird and, no, it turns out to be the scalp of a head that's nowhere to be seen), like incriminating evidence for the scholars, who will try to explain to us how it was that something like this could happen without our anticipating it, like damning clues for the experts already arriving, already here, already coming to show us everything we always looked at but never saw.

Then I see her.

Then I see you.

And the sight—the sight of you who, without a doubt, see me too, that slight discomfort of eyes meeting—lasts only seconds. Because, then, something blows up. And a new dust cloud and the crush of flaming ruins covers everything. And covers us—me and her and I can't see her anymore—as if it were the curtain running and falling across the stage, without warning, before the actors can bow, before the end of the show.

And when does this show take place?

Because it's clear that something has come to an end. Not with a bang but a bang . . . bang . . .

And so many tears.

Because it's clear that we've entered a new era, that this is the beginning of a new act in History.

This is the Age of Strange Things.

Welcome.

Once, many years ago, I cut out an illustration from a science fiction magazine—I don't remember which one, I'm not sure if it was *Amazing* or *Fantastic* or *Astounding* or *Thrilling* or *Marvel* or *Startling Stories*, it's all the same—that, at the time, I couldn't stop staring at. I brought it everywhere with me. I took it out of my wallet on the subway, or in the bathroom, or when I woke up and couldn't fall back asleep.

I don't remember what the story that went with the drawing was about (it doesn't matter, it probably had nothing to do with it; a lot of the time the illustrations were inserted in the pages of the magazine at random with no attention to what they depicted or to the story being told), but before long I knew every detail by heart and I think, if asked, I could've drawn it with my eyes closed.

The illustration had a caption that said: "The return of Halley's Comet in 1986." And it showed the comet—one of those omen-bearing comets of antiquity, one of those comets that would justify the mass suicide of cultists toward the end of that century—trailing across the dark sky above a city of the future. A city of the future like cities of the future would never be and like they were imagined in times when 1986 was as distant as another planet. Details of tall and spherical buildings and people, ready to embark on their voyage, climbing aboard a rocket and, in the foreground, looking out from a sort of curving balcony, a man and a woman in space suits, holding helmets in their hands, looking up at the heavens, watching the comet as it passed. And I looked at them, and imagined I was the man and she was the woman.

But I told myself that it would be all right if the man were Ezra and not me, if that would make her come back, and make him come back, and I could see them again.

Even if it was only at a distance and for but a brief instant.

As if I were just passing overhead and waving to them from on high

Like a smile of ancient cosmic dust.

Like a passing beam of light in the immense darkness, illuminating their love.

Like a comet that had come back just to see them.

What comes next is the end.

It's not really clear to me how I got home.

Walking?

Did I cross the ash-covered bridge with a crowd of statues come to life, dragging their feet and speaking in clipped phrases and never closing their eyes, with men and women and children who couldn't and didn't want to close them, aware that they were living through and taking part in an event that was plunging now and forever like an impossible-to-remove sword into the stone of the planet's memory?

Did I open the door to my house as the sun was starting to set?

Did I shower to rid myself of a smell that wasn't the smell of death, but the smell of the dead?

Who knows?

Does it matter?

All that matters is that I am calm.

And that it be the terrible and consoling calm that only comes when we accept that History, our History, the History of our History is coming to an end.

It's then that we like to think and feel that, with our departure, everything will end.

Reaching this point, the worst people go to bed every night, crossing their fingers, to dream that the exact moment of their last breath will magically and justly coincide with the universe's last sigh. You know the ones I'm talking about, they tend to appear on the eight o'clock news: those exalted prophets who, from on high, threaten Apocalypse of diverse sign and form. Everyone else—let's call them *normal people*—lack such aspirations and settle for the fantasy that someone will still think of them, that their memory, snuffed out so suddenly, will ignite a spark in the memories of those who survive them and that their faces and actions will live on in the actions of younger faces.

I understand that, for me, this won't be the case. I have lived too much. More than you're supposed to. So much that—without certain adjustments—I would have caused problems with the natural cycles of the system. I would've ended up remembering dead younger than myself. It would've been sad and uncomfortable, so I can't complain.

I'm the only one left to remember me and there's not much time left.

My work, like I said, hasn't been important. My last name has never managed to impose itself onto my work. My last name never mutated into a personalizing and qualifying adjective; so the only thing left of my work are plots, stories, moments that some will remember but won't ever associate with a *Goldman* and much less with an *Isaac* and I suspect that—given what has happened in recent days (days?)—the young journalist who came to visit and question me was nothing but a glimmer of optimism, a desperate illusion of my imagination.

One ghost visiting another.

I'm all that's left, here, under the sky.

Under the vast indifference of a sky that poets and religious people insist on pluralizing (*the skies, the heavens*, they say and recite, romantics, idiots) but that actually is one and indivisible.

That sky that's inside the sky and that stretches all the way up from the horizon.

That place to which, when we were shiny and new, we looked with the peace of knowing it unreachable, happy because we had all the time in the world, never suspecting that—now I know, now I feel it—it is the horizon that comes unhurriedly and inexorably toward us. The horizon that approaches from the horizon and finally reaches us and enters us and, all of a sudden, we are the horizon.

The other night while I was starting to write all of this down—when?—I watched an interview on television with a writer of children's books. Best-sellers about a boy who travels back in time on his bicycle, searching for his mother. Something like that. The man answered questions with his face hidden in darkness, because he said he didn't want to be known or recognized in the street. He insisted that it was his stories, not him, that mattered. At one point he said something unforgettable: "We write to take revenge against reality."

To me those words seemed spot on and true and even undeniable.

But I'm not sure if that's been my case.

For me it had more to do with the fact of writing first in order to feel more or less real later.

But I don't think that is a better option.

Nor do I think that there is one that is better than another.

Everyone—Ezra, myself, Zack, whoever—writes for reasons that are entirely distinct but connected by the same impulse: we can't stop writing and, even when we're not writing, we feel that we are or that we should be writing.

Like a computer at the far reaches of the universe singing its last words that were also its first words.

Like an android that shuts down under the rain in the middle of a monologue about everything he has seen and that no one else will ever see.

Like the last inhabitant of a faraway planet who, surrounded by sunsets, evading himself, can't stop watching us until the last moment of his life.

Like original beings in the genre who sought to recover that lost and broken Divine Light that my father used to talk about. *Tzimtzum*

... *tzimtzum* ... *tzimtzum* ... the sound of the insect of electricity wearing itself out in the cables of machines far more sentient than their creators. Ingenious geniuses who, in the beginning, resigned themselves to being misunderstood because they were aware that it wouldn't be long before they'd be elevated as classic entities, quotable, invoked over and over.

Thus, as they went in a future past, so I wish to go.

Of course, that's not possible.

My role has been different, but it's always been *something*: a humble extra in an extraordinary thing, a shy and fleeting walk-on in the screenplay of a story whose importance isn't entirely understood but, at least, in the end, is felt.

Now it is night, now I write my own ending, which is an open ending.

Of course, the temptation exists to close it, to have it be me who closes it, to balance myself out.

To look for and find the moon rocks, to contemplate for a second their pale and waning phosphorescence. I saw them again not long ago, when I reorganized a closet, and they looked worn out and banal, like just some random terrestrial rock and they barely glowed, as if they'd already gotten used to living here and to not being recognized as anything special, spatial. I thought about taking them one by one and filling my pockets and going to an artificial lake at a nearby reservoir and letting myself sink, like a romantic writer from another century, until my lungs filled with water and my brain ran out of thoughts.

Or maybe a hot bath and a glass of cold wine and slowly draining myself of blood, like an ancient Roman tribune.

Or to burn atop my books like a Viking funeral—the smoke of my pages mingling with the smoke of the towers—before those who'll burn books for the pleasure of burning books arrive.

Or to carefully draft my suicide note (the best I know of is that of an Englishman who simply wrote "This is my last" and, on the next line, "word"), but I don't think anyone would be interested in reading it; my body would be discovered days later and would spoil any patrician or classical intention. And the news of my sacrifice wouldn't cause anybody sorrow or joy. It wouldn't even make anybody think of their own death, learning of mine, by my own hand, writing my own ending, waiting for that other open hand, used for the first and only time, to cut off that last look that no longer sees.

Besides, it seems to me that disappearing would be more a matter of convenience than of cowardice. And convenience isn't a privilege I deserve.

And so no.

My fate is elsewhere and it is an uncertain fate. My final pages have nothing of the solid conclusions that tend to characterize the most popular science fiction: futuristic pages with rarely a doubt regarding what now won't ever come.

Because today—unlike in its early days (will I be able to stop thinking about all of this, my genre and my profession, someday?)—science fiction has no desire to anticipate what will happen here but, instead, what could happen out there, as far from this place as possible.

Or to toy with an alternate almost-present.

Besides, for a while now, readers of this genre seem to have migrated to other territories, to alternate worlds governed by myths more fantastical than scientific. The supposed innovation of recent years—the megalopolis like a sour and spilled Milky Way, outer space supplanted by computer wiring and neon lights and digitalized drugs; the hacker occupying the role of intrepid tamer of meteorites—never really compelled me. All those people in front of screens, barely moving, almost never leaving home and, in the best of cases, watching on their televisions, with nostalgia for what once was (with respect to the parameters of the genre) and (in reference to a possible tomorrow) will never be again: the odyssey of a galactic and colonial spaceship that can't find its way back to earth and, meanwhile, lost, battles against a race of human-made androids who got tired of not being human. And I've never really been convinced by those theories regarding visits from other worlds. It doesn't seem logical. Who would want to come *here*? What for? I don't think anyone has ever been interested in traveling to our world and, if some came, it's easy enough to imagine that they were something akin to mischievous kids. Like boys dressed in black leather jackets riding motorcycles too big for their bodies, popping wheelies (all those reports of commercial airline pilots with too many of those little bottles in the fuel tank), terrorizing and taking advantage of the residents of a small town (all those absurd stories of astral coitus), and ending up crashing on the first tricky curve (oh, the Roswell blues), or more or less clever boys who came down here, to the edge of the galaxy, and built a sand pyramid or two and then went home to their parents when the suns of their planet set. And that's it. Nothing more. I feel it, I don't feel it at all, I don't feel anything anymore: there were never black men with silver pupils, or triangles devouring ships and planes in the Caribbean. Earth isn't hollow and nobody helped us erect sacred temples and their derivatives. No messenger came here to guide or paralyze us and the halo of the Messiah isn't a spacesuit or an energy shield. We don't need a death ray to melt the poles and drown us: we can and are doing it on our own, we don't need the help of extraterrestrials to destroy our planet. The Sun and the Moon were never gods; and why worship an eclipse overhead when eclipses abound here down below, all the time, day after day . . . What time is it? Time to eclipse myself, to turn myself off like a television that's been on for too long with nobody watching or having the remotest control over its programming.

Someone told me that now there even exists a Sci-Fi Channel. But there's no way it could be all that different from the History Channel:

versions of what's to come based on models of what's already been. Or—each and every one of its ingredients perfectly and predictably calculated—one of those channels dedicated to gourmet cooking where short little chefs move around with the pomposity of alchemists.

Later, everything else, you already know it: kindly dragons, wizard teachers, and sexy vampires. As if now young people preferred to inhale the ochre perfume of extinct species instead of the chrome aroma of wonders yet to come. What might come to pass doesn't interest them or makes them feel a kind of mistrust. And it's not that the past has always been better, but at least you can know where it's going and how it ends. The future, they think, is overrated. And even less trustworthy than one of those card sharks shuffling cards like a juggler.

There are exceptions, of course, who rely on and stick to the immobile and monolithic will of the classic and irrefutable: the ending of that movie I saw once, the one with the title that coincides with this year and that's already starting to be dated. That movie with an old and moribund and reborn and evolved astronaut who returns home in order to, maybe, put things in order or, perhaps, to bring about the end of everything, to wipe us off the face of the planet and start again with a better beginning.

But that is and will be another story and I won't be in it and it seems appropriate that my story ends here, in this year, or in something that claims to be the same year in which that movie takes place. In that number that denies us the round numeral with a small and slight irregularity that alters everything forever. The year, yes, when there would supposedly be colonies on the Moon, floating flight attendants, and we'd make contact with a superior and alien intelligence.

And yet nobody appears to have come to our aid. It's possible that we're not alone, but now nothing interests us less than being accompanied, and the fact that there are guidebooks named *Lonely Planet* doesn't seem like a coincidence at all. We've become extraterrestrial terrestrials, and we crash into each other, and on the other side of the river I can still perceive the warm glow of underground fires, the black smoke a different black than the black of the night.

Now—last regressive story, everything set for take off—I'm on my way out.

I go out into the garden and the stars have yet to appear, but it won't be long. I lie down on grass the color of shadow that won't be green again until tomorrow.

I'm still not entirely sure that I write, just before living them—minimal and brief poetic license—certain details. I write now, in what will soon be past, everything I will do in the next few minutes with the certainty that little or nothing can change, that I'm not lying and won't be lying, that I can see the future and write about it without this being part of a science-fiction story.

Because my future is *so* brief.

My future is now shrinking toward the present, like a boomerang coming back to its point of departure.

My future already passed.

My future, like many things, extends until tonight.

That's it.

It's such a small future that the only thing I wish is for the night to close in over it so that later it can open to the immensity of my past.

It's an unusually cold night for this time of year.

It's a night that reminds me a lot of that other night, but without the snow and Ezra and her.

The ground is already covered with dry leaves, I'm naked and I've poured myself a generous glass of whiskey, a couple is arguing next to an open window, a few dogs of distinct breeds sing different parts of a single opera that men never learned to understand, the blue eyes of all the channels of all the televisions broadcasting the same images over and over and the same explosions and the same fallings and the same collapse (nothing makes us more similar, nothing brings us closer together than bad news) and, from the city comes the scent of burned metal and of so many other things that are still burning in that inverted pyramid of smoke that now rises where two steel towers once stood. Just beyond, that metal statue destroyed so many times in so many movies, remains standing, with its arm and torch held aloft, illuminating brutal humans and intelligent apes, as if nothing had happened, as if nothing else could happen.

And I open my arms. Arms open like my father once opened his (Solomon Goldman, my father flying, my father falling, my father suspended and trapped forever in the weightless amber of my memory, in that monster that came aboard like a sidereal cop, inside my body, and left, bursting out of my chest and breaking my heart, and that now wanders the corridors of a defunct spaceship where everyone else is dead) and I look up.

Higher still.

And even higher.

There.

There, appearing now though they are always there.

Here they come.

The light goes out so they can turn on.

The stars, the stars.

How did it go?

How did it all end?

The verses of an ancient poet. I'm sure he was Italian because I remember his words in Italian. But I don't dare think his name for fear that he never existed, for fear of not finding him in my library.

Better like this.

Settling for the image and the language of he who, leaving the Inferno behind—"*E quindi uscimmo a riveder le stelle*"—rediscovers a sky pulsating with stars. Ah, yes, the last lines of the rhymed comfort of a just order based on crimes and sins, where the polarity of acts is easily translated into rewards and punishments. Hell and

Purgatory and overhead, enclosing everything, Heaven: *"A l'alta fantasia qui mancò possa; / ma già volgeva il mio disio e'l velle, / sí come rota ch'igualmente é mossa, / l'amor che move il sole e l'altre stelle."*

The end of the elevated fantasy that no longer has the strength to continue its ascent to the bottom of the sky. Out of breath, almost blind from so much seeing, and yet, it insists, fights on a little further. Because at the finish line, at that goal that is the ending, awaits the revelatory reward of being able to remember your name, her name. Until then, the longing that spins and the will that rolls remain. One and the other lifted up by the impulse of love's inertia, hovering over the red and burning lust of celestial bodies. Not the stars in the sky, I discover now, too late, but the sky in the stars.

I start to count them.

Right to left.

One by one.

They are many, they are so many, they are too many.

I swear I won't get up until I finish counting them, until I've counted all of them, until there are no stars left to count.

II

The Space between This Planet and the Other Planet

The space between this planet and the other planet is small enough for us to be able to watch you from our own forgotten world and, at the same time, big enough so that you, in your unforgettable world, so busy looking at one another, can't know that we're watching you.

That we're always watching you.

And that it's good, that it makes us happy that it is so.

One of the ways—maybe the only way—not to collapse from the pain of realizing that nobody will remember you, not to break when you become aware that from here onward nobody will ever wonder even once what became of your life, is to forget about yourself before anybody else forgets you, that's how you achieve a kind of immortality. You become, in a way, paradoxically, unforgettable.

My case.

And—hey hey hey, fire in the sky and death on earth—here I come and there I go.

Again.

Talking to myself.

Have you ever talked to yourselves in the desert, in that place where your self is the only one you can talk to?

Here I am, somewhere inside nowhere, talking to myself, as if I were that last extraterrestrial who disappears in the pages of my favorite novel.

Now I disappear. Or, better, now I vanish. To vanish is to disappear slowly, without hurry, without drama, without thinking about the fact that you're disappearing.

I am the last of my species.

So, not only do I vanish, but the history of my kind vanishes as well. I guess that's a little dramatic. But I don't get too worked up about it. I'll miss you all so much, but I don't think anyone will really miss me. There won't be anyone left to miss me and I don't think our voyage through this universe has been especially interesting to the inhabitants of other planets.

Perfection isn't interesting.

So here I go—here I go—and here goes the past and the present and the future (though those are temporal categories that we never conceived of or understood in the way you do) of all those who once dreamed of surviving by invading another planet and, all of a sudden, awoke from their dream understanding, too late, that they are the ones who have been invaded.

This is the story of one of the most triumphant failures (I'll use, from now on, the space jargon of earthlings so you understand me better; though I'm actually talking to myself) that ever took place in this or any galaxy.

This is the story (to tell it I'll also use earthly names when it comes to measurements, colors, distances, and even sentiments) of what happened. Or, better yet (again, out of respect for the origin of the readers of these pages, which don't take the form of pages but of light, transparent spheres, out of fondness for your hospitality, no doubt incredulous, but hospitality nonetheless, here I'll invoke the way we figure in your childish astral charts, courtesy of telescopes that will never return home), this is the story, I insist, of something that stopped happening in a place known as Urkh 24.

A place whose true name (in a rushed and imperfect translation battered by the eons, based on our symbols that were never meant to be rendered in your written and read letters) would look and sound more or less like That-Place-Where-The-Most-Disconsolate-Melodies-Can-Be-Heard.

Now I read; but it's as if I were listening. Because I could read all of this with my eyes shut and my mouth open. To read with my teeth, chewing the sand that gets in my open mouth and swallowing the exact memory of the words, which is much more precise. Because I don't even have to follow the curved and straight lines of the letters or make the effort to hold up my book. Better to read remembering and reciting each and every word, as if they were just occurring to me or, better, as if they were being transmitted to me from a faraway planet. A planet that doesn't appear on any maps of the sky because there aren't yet maps that great, maps that encompass that much, maps that look that far.

If someone were to spread a map of the hitherto known universe across the burning sand of this desert, the planet where this message originates—the planet that I've read over and over until I've memorized it—would sit at one of the poles: surrounded by ice once thought and believed eternal and that has begun to melt in the way of certain ideas, certain feelings, certain questions.

And so, suddenly, you ask yourself how you got here and what it is you've come to do, and you don't get any answer.

So—maybe there, who knows—I open the book and close my eyes and read and discover that, for a while now, like I said, I talk to myself and think to myself, in a way that increasingly resembles the manner of speech of certain extraterrestrials in certain books. Slowly and with great care, as if rehearsing an autopsy of words and ideas, as if assimilating them in the very act of learning them, like those heartless blond children who have arrived from a distant star to conquer us, staring at the schoolmaster who, all of a sudden, understands that the hour is approaching of a final exam that nobody has prepared for.

I speak in the liturgical language of faraway beings. I think like beings whom, were we to meet them, we'd worship without hesitation like gods. But—and this is the interesting part—they were the ones who worshipped us, believed in us. When there is nothing left for them to accomplish, having attained absolute perfection, all they have left is the pleasure and comfort of marveling at the unpredictable imperfections of others. All perfection is equal, identical, no surprises. On the other hand, there are so many entertaining and different and oh so interesting ways to make mistakes . . . I remember those movies from when I was a kid, *Ulysses*, *Jason and the Argonauts* . . . The parts I liked best weren't when the adventurers confronted dangers and monsters, but those almost placid and Olympic interludes when the gods were shown contemplating everything from their heavenly abode, playing chess with figurines that represented the heroes and villains, intervening in the action when they deemed it appropriate, enjoying themselves, passing time, passing eternity while, down here, on Earth, men and women sent up their prayers and offered offerings, never suspecting that what the gods wanted wasn't their riches, but their stories, their unpredictable stories.

And that the gods believed in them, that they prayed they would never end.

Now is the moment for prayer and for me to reflect on all of this.

Now. I imagine the space that separates and connects us, as I pray. And my ideas penetrate my prayers that aren't praying or giving thanks to anything: they are merely affirming. The prayers that sustain our religion aren't rigid and fixed structures, rather they allow themselves to be governed by everything we choose to believe in. A dogma that's liquid and intangible in appearance, but immense like the oceans that once were and are no longer, like the immortal memory of those oceans.

We believe in everything and there's nothing to believe in, and maybe, in that absolute and yet impossible mode of preaching and proselytizing resides the beginning of our end. We believe—we believed, I believe, because I am the last of us—in ourselves. Weary gods, we resigned ourselves to being ineffective and idle divinities. And so Time—that true God that isn't late or early, but simply is, in the here and now, opening its arms to what has been and what will be—passed, and we passed along with it. We—a false and deceitful plural that I use to try, in vain, to deny the fact that I am all that's left and that, soon, there will be nothing—who have nothing left now but to watch all of you from the opposite side of the space that separates one planet from the other.

The man who said he loved the desert "because it is clean" was a madman. Or he had the luck of drawing a different desert in the raffle.

The desert—at least this desert, this exceedingly populated desert—is full of trash. Trash that doesn't appear on the maps of the desert, but there it is. Pieces of various wars, wreckage of armored vehicles, tatters of uniforms, bones difficult to identify as human or animal, flags long past their expiration date snapping in the wind, food containers and empty bottles, little pools of burning oil, folding chairs like the ones you sit on at the seashore or the sidelines of a sports field, various oases closed for a change of ownership, loose magazine pages with pictures of naked women, dismantled weapons, a pair of ownerless camels roaming around with the disoriented air of someone who has survived a catastrophic party and now can't remember how to get home, random pieces of the puzzle of a helicopter, a tent with a red cross on the roof and nobody and nothing inside, skinny dogs that seem to waver like mirages . . .

Come and look.

And, yes, the touching need humans have for knowing exactly where they are so they can, almost immediately, get lost. Their incredible, irrepressible desire to believe in almost anything. Where am I? Does it matter? Would you like it if I expressed myself with the obsessive logic of your science fiction novels and buried you under an obsessive onslaught of irreal details in an attempt to gain verisimilitude? Would you be happier if I indicated a point in the sky and said, "There . . . Right there"? Would you rather I filled pages with the dimensions and luminosity of the celestial body where the stardust of my thoughts originates, that stardust, swept by the solar winds, that we're all made of? Would it please you to be almost sadistically subjected to numbers and vectors and quadrants and geologic compositions, and maybe even a broad summary of our history and science?

Sorry, can't help you: millennia ago we renounced certain notions and ideas that we deemed useless. Dead matter. Long ago we decided that the act and effort of remembering made no sense. It was then that, better, we decided not to forget. To know that we know everything, that we've missed nothing, and that, for that reason, it makes no sense to search for it over and over, to store it away and, later, to pray that we don't lose it again. Each of us the perfect museum of our species. And I am the last museum. One of those museums where now, over the loudspeakers, you hear a polite but firm voice informing the visitors that in fifteen minutes the doors will be closing and the lights will be turned off and to, if you please, proceed in an orderly fashion to the exit.

The past and the present are the same for us.

The future doesn't exist.

The future is for cowards and madmen.

Then, of course, we found you.

And nothing was ever the same.

Without names for people or places.

Without geographical coordinates.

Without dates.

Without space or time and the time of war—spasmodic, inconstant—is so different from the linear time of peace or the suspenseful time of truce when everything is known, when there is time to know everything.

It's like this—this total lack of knowledge, this obsessive attention to the details of knowing that nothing is known, that the plan is that there is no plan and let's just see what happens—because this is how high command commands it.

I don't know if it's right.

I don't even know if it's an intelligent strategy.

I'm referring to this absolute lack of any form of orientation.

The idea that if we don't know who we are or where we are it will help to keep the enemy—The Unmaker—and his followers from becoming aware of our existence. Disappearing to make ourselves invisible to them. That's how our immediate superior explains it to us. Someone who confesses, in a whisper, that the method works, that

that very morning he was unable to find his own face in the mirror. I, of course, am not entirely convinced. But failure to obey the rules established and the laws implemented here, so far from home, will be punished.

And yet, we pass our time dreaming of Grynarya, of spending a few days there, at the colony that we established in this land, at the only more or less safe zone in this place. "Grynarya," we sigh and one of my comrades says he was stationed there for a couple weeks and tells me fantastic things and high command says we'll get to go soon enough, during our next period of R&R.

"The exact spot where, in the Bible, it says Paradise was located," my comrade tells me. And I let myself doubt him just as another soldier interrupts our conversation and says, indignant, that, "No no no: it's where Sodomy and Gonorrhea were. And we're here to exterminate all the sinners in Christ's name and . . ."

And—some and others—tell us that we should be proud of Grynarya because it's ours, it's part of our home and a piece of our homeland transplanted into these inhospitable deserts (where I discover that there's no place more fertile for planting ideas and thoughts than a desert; you think so much more in the desert than in cities or in forests or at sea) and that not even the previous expedition to this world, more than ten years ago, could establish or construct a marvel like this.

"Grynarya," we repeat to ourselves over and over in steady voices; but it's the kind of steadiness you only achieve a few meters from the brink of tears.

Grynarya is the Promised Land and the Compromised Land.

Grynarya is mirage and oasis at the same time and we advance and recede, who knows, singing that song from that movie about the fine art of following the Yellow Brick Road.

Grynarya is the way in which I think about *Green Area* every time I hear its name. Only in that way—the sound of *Grynarya* has about it a whiff of the *sci-fi*, combining better with the sensation of feeling more and more like an extraterrestrial—can I bear the idea that all we can do is dream of getting some R&R in that, supposedly safe, Bagdad neighborhood, where every day car-bombs and truck-bombs and man-bombs and woman-bombs and child-bombs of both sexes explode to the scream of "Allah is great."

And that's where we're headed, to the Emerald City.

We're heartless tin men.

We're cowardly lions.

We're brainless scarecrows.

We're munchkins with high, singsong voices.

And Dorothy has stayed home, in black and white. Here there are colors, yes, but it's as if they didn't exist, as if the sun had washed them out until they attained the dazzling and filthy purity of white on white.

We are lost youths in a horizontal landscape furrowed by vertical tornados and, no, we're not looking for the Wizard of Oz. No. The Wizard of Oz is coming for us and the Wizard of Oz is all-powerful, great, and terrible.

Oz is great.

Oz is greater than Allah and—unlike the actual Wizard of Oz—his powers are real.

Oz is The Unmaker.

And nothing would make this Wizard of Oz happier than to test out his powers on us.

And we have *so* few powers, we are *so* weak . . .

That's the way things go around here.

Soon, it won't be possible to protect you from yourselves anymore.

Soon, we won't be able to intervene in your squabbles and conflicts.

Soon, all I'll have left will be to watch the perpetual sunsets of our planet, and these memories (it's so strange to remember everything in the moment it should all begin to be forgotten) will be transformed into an archive of lights and skies and shapes and clouds and stars and colors. Perpetual sunsets that soon will be nightfalls as once they were eternal sunrises or ceaseless middays: here, we don't enjoy or suffer, like you, the repetition of brief days, here it has always been one long day. And I fear that now we are entering not the hour, but the age of nightfall. It's a shame not having a window to, at least, watch all of you as if on a screen . . .

It's a shame.

Soon, we won't be able to watch you anymore, our favorite actors.

"My name is Lieutenant George Clooney," the officer tells us. The man who says he's named Lieutenant George Clooney is, obviously, not George Clooney. Lieutenant George Clooney is very tall, bald, and has an absurdly high voice that gets even higher and more absurd when we fall in and he says:

"Right, I know, I can imagine what you're thinking, maggots . . . You're probably doing all you can not to smile, and that's the right thing to do. Anyone who smiles will be sent out on patrol in the desert with barely any water or ammunition . . . But just to be clear: I am the true George Clooney. The *authentic* George Clooney. And I can prove it quickly and efficiently. Listen up, maggots: George Clooney, that mediocre actor to whom, I rush to clarify, I am not related by blood, was born May 6th, 1961. And, you probably already know this: his middle name is Timothy. A ridiculous name. My name, on the other hand, is George Clooney. And that's it. And I was born on November 1st, 1960. More than six months before George *Timothy* Clooney would arrive to this world. Which means that I was number one, I was here before him, I am the legitimate, certified, genuine, original, accredited, undeniable, and authorized George Clooney, got it?"

And, of course, we all smiled. One of us, even, let slip a chuckle.

And out into the desert we go.

And as you already know: this is the kind of person who is in command, watching out for our well-being.

Let us pray.

Now I pray.

Now I bow my head and pray, facing away from our planet's two suns. The dead sun (it's as if the sky were left with only one eye) and the dying sun that barely warms and illuminates everything down below from so high overhead.

Now I pray, but what I do or what I think isn't exactly praying the way all of you understand it.

I don't pray—we never do—to a god or a higher power.

We pray to it's absence.

And the only thing we ask of that absence is that it endure, that it stay like that, absent, so we can continue to pray to it.

In our prayers we say we don't need it, we pray that it never come, we cry out for its eternal abandonment. We say that everything is fine and that we've been managing everything perfectly without its divine intervention. We explain that we have become our own gods and that we like it that way, that after a miracle like that there's no other miracle we could hope for.

So, in our prayers, just for fun and out of curiosity, we imagine what our god would be like if it appeared and manifested and filled that absence with its presence.

We fervently believe in that absence, which, it's understood, is not exactly nonexistence or a void. It's something else: it's like the faithful memory of something that we don't remember and don't want to remember, it's like the vibration that someone leaves behind in a room when they leave. We kneel down and prostrate ourselves before that mystery that will never be solved and it's good that it is so. That's why each of us had a god all our own, different and unique.

The personal god, the god that lives and resides within you.

That's why we never fought or killed each other in the name of god.

Because that would be an absurdity.

Because there were never two of us who believed in the same thing, in the same divine variable.

Because there were many, so many, too many gods. And they were so different and independent and private that— the territories of the invisible have neither limits nor frontiers—there was always room for all of them.

Now, mine is the only one left.

The holy and imminent absolute absence of my god.

Because it's still here, inside me; but I won't be out here much longer.

We kneel and say an Our Father.

"Who art in Heaven," we say.

"Forever and ever," we say.

The voice of the chaplain, dressed in a combat uniform, reciting that part about "Thy will be done on Earth as it is in Heaven."

No.

It's hard to believe that the will of a higher being and all of that is being respected and obeyed here.

There is no plan.

We don't even know exactly where the hell we are.

We know, yes, that it's a desert and that it's hot and that the unanesthetized light of the sun illuminates and burns everything and ends up evaporating even our shadows.

It's a terrible light.

A blinding light.

A divine light, yes, but also an infernal light.

"Amen," says the Chaplain and his words, almost without vowels, are barely intelligible in his dry mouth.

We get to our feet and look at each other and the landscape is colorless.

It's not even a landscape in black and white.

It's a landscape in white on white.

And white again.

Even more white.

Then comes the, let's call him, the Manager of Chemical Matters to distribute the pills.

As if they were communion wafers.

Today, he says, what we're going to dissolve in our saliva is not what we call Exterminating Fury (the reports from the scouts in the mountains aren't warning of any sudden activity by The Enemy), but what we called Contemplative Joy.

We fall in line and arrive in front of him and open our mouths and an acidic flavor of a complicated name—pure consonants and a dash and a number—settles on the tips of our tongues and drops into our stomachs and bounces back up, lighting up different centers of the brain like someone going through, one by one, without any hurry, turning on the lights inside a house in flames.

Then, the head of the soldier praying next to me—I'm almost certain it was Lieutenant George Clooney, who was already smiling with the false happiness of the artificially enlightened—explodes into hundreds of pieces.

Splinters of flesh and bone.

And for an instant, all those suspended fragments of what once was a face seem beautiful to me. I've also started feeling the effects of the medication, a kind of slow bliss, and suddenly I have all the time in the world to think how happy I am to be *right there*. Fragments floating in slow motion, as if tempted to come back together, like parts of one of those anatomic transparent-plastic models that we're given when we're kids, when nobody knows yet what to give us, when we hope for anything but *that*.

But the illusion lasts less than a second and everything falls to the ground and now nobody will be able to put back together the brainteaser of that broken brain.

A shower of red liquid—we learned months ago not to think of it as blood—covers my face and I'm almost grateful for that red; because it alters the white on white horror of our surroundings.

And we throw ourselves to the ground and start firing at the dunes, at the air, at anything, and the noise of the gunshots mingles with the noise of the voices. Bang, crack, kapow, stuk-stuk-stuk-stuk, swap, kaboom, we all scream in the international language of metal and gunpowder, the Esperanto of war.

I fear that it's going to be another one of those unforgettable days, I say to myself.

Rat-tat-tat.

Yesterday was an unforgettable day.

Yesterday, for a few seconds, I picked up your signal again.

Yesterday I saw all of you again.

And I watched you watching the towers fall.

They say that in the mess hall, in Grynarya, there's a huge enlargement of a photograph showing the towers how they were before that morning in September.

They say that it's strange to eat next to that photograph, that it's like eating next to a picture of Atlantis, a place that no longer exists and that, sooner or later, will grow and grow until it attains the dimensions of a legend whose origins and veracity have become impossible to verify.

They say that—when morale is low—high command recommends repeated viewings of footage of the towers falling, from different angles, so we comprehend why we're here and what it is we're doing.

They say that in the theater for the troops, in Grynarya, they show the fall of the towers as a kind of variety preview before the latest blockbuster, full of special effects and explosions and all of that.

They say that, in the beginning, the troops maintained a respectful silence but that, as the days and weeks passed, they stood up and released howls of vengeance.

They say that now, so many years later, the troops laugh as they watch the fall of the towers.

They say that they watch it like a cartoon. Like one of those Coyote and Roadrunner bits, one of those ACME-brand accidents.

I saw the planes crash into the towers, I saw the towers in flames, I saw the men and women falling from the towers, and I saw the towers fall just as I once saw the sinking of that transatlantic, those men dragging themselves through the trenches, that Russian family shot in front of a soviet wall, that blond actress dying with the telephone in her hand, those earthquakes bringing down churches full of believers, heard someone say for the first time "To be or not to be . . . ," saw all those men marching in front of flags with exotic crosses, that astronomer on his knees in front of a man who claimed to be God's representative on Earth, those heads chopped off by the guillotine, those people singing "All You Need Is Love," that space shuttle exploding in the sky.

I saw the planes crash into the towers, I saw the towers in flames, I saw the men and women falling from the towers, and I saw the towers fall, and it made me so sad to know that, very soon, I'd no longer get to see all those marvelous things.

We fell like towers. Struck down. And there I was, surrounded by dead men, by open-eyed bodies. I closed my eyes to keep from seeing, but that solved nothing: the less I looked at them, hiding inside that dark whiteness that grows behind the eyelids, the more I knew they were looking at me, that they would keep looking at me, that me looking at them was the last thing they had seen. And that they would never let me forget that. All that blood and all those holes and all that blood spilling from all those holes. The holes that shrapnel makes. Hole-riddled bodies, all of a sudden, acquire the texture of comic strips that when enlarged—I remember how much I liked to look at them like that as a kid, magnifying glass in hand—we discover are composed of dots. All those red dots and all that spattered blood and I wonder if the most logical thing wouldn't be for, when somebody dies, the blood to stop flowing, spilling out, turning red. If everything stops, I say to myself, then the blood should stop too.

The blood should stop running.

Today I noticed that my vital fluids are circulating more slowly. I can see it. Our bodies are transparent. Just by looking at our organisms we could tell, perfectly, how they were working. Structures complex in their simplicity. Something you only achieve after millennia of constant evolution. Nothing like your structures, so full of parts that can stop functioning, of unresolvable problems, of impossible-to-predict accidents. Nothing so thrilling and absurd and magic as the notion of the same blood circulating, coming and going, above and below, unceasing, between the opposite planets of the brain and the heart.

We never considered what might go wrong.

We never needed professionals to name the horror of the unknown, wanting, in vain, to make it less horrible.

There was never any fear.

There was never any mystery.

So it was that we perceived how a slight shift in the atmosphere began to affect us.

First, something like a slight cold, then a slight fever.

So it was that, for the first time, we got sick.

So it was that we started to vanish.

So it was that we decided that the moment had come for us to leave our world, to leave Urkh 24, That-Place-Where-The-Most-Disconsolate-Melodies-Can-Be-Heard.

So it was that we searched and found you.

So it was that we began to watch you.

So it was that we became fans of you.

So it was that we got hooked on Earth-Fiction.

Later, in Grynarya, they say that the thermal readings and satellite images reported that everyone fired into the air and that the air filled with holes that immediately filled with air and that then we fired more bullets into that air that entered those bodies.

They say that the first person to fire was Lieutenant George Clooney, who lost his mind, that he'd been under observation for a while, that his recent coded reports were nothing but lines from *Ocean's Eleven*, and that as soon as he got back to Bagdad he was to be relieved of duty.

Friendly fire, they say.

Friend fire.

Fire that is the best friend you've ever had, my friend.

Fire that, when it enters your body, makes you feel a cold you've never felt and will never feel again because this fire, once inside you, is the last thing you feel before feeling nothing, before no longer feeling anything.

And so, they say, tired of firing into the air, we started firing at each other, at friends who we barely knew but with whom we shared fire and uniform and flag and this is the kind of thing that happens when too much time has passed without seeing the enemy who is always there, but invisible: you fire into the air and at anything in the air or on the ground.

And, as they strap me to a stretcher and lift me into a helicopter, they say—to me, whom they don't blame for anything because I acted in self-defense; to me, whom they admire for my marksmanship—that I was the only one who lived to tell the tale.

And, of course, they're lying.

They say all of this suspecting that I don't believe them, but to believe is an order and I shall obey.

So I nod and I don't say that Lieutenant George Clooney (who, of course, was completely crazy) was the first to fall and that we were all struck by a black wind, that came out of nowhere and blew over us and extinguished our fire and made us burn like we'd never burned before.

We start to go extinct sweetly, as if falling asleep. Some of us, even, adopt the custom of going to die on the mountain where we built the spaceships for the invasion, the spaceships that never lifted off, bound for Earth, and that now were almost part of the landscape, as if they'd always been there, from the beginning of time until the end of time.

And, reaching this point, I always loved that oh so human, oh so primitive, oh so childish custom of wondering "What time is it?" or "What day is it." And immediately responding with the most absurd of abstractions. With numbers.

And feeling oh so satisfied.

Four days later, I wake up in a military hospital in the Green Area in Bagdad (enough with the whole Grynarya thing) and this is as far as my attempt to pass all this off as a science-fiction novel—as something that took place on another, faraway planet—goes.

Now I'm someone else.

I've changed.

I'm far from home, indeed.

And, in a way, on another planet.

But it's another planet that is on this planet.

Here I am.

There you are. There you were. We found you. All of you. Living in a world with conditions ideal for our survival and, at the same time, so different from our own. So much more fun.

"THEY'RE CALLED LIBERTY FRIES, BITCH!!!" screams the soldier in the bed next to mine. The soldier who is strangling the poor nurse who had the bad idea of offering him french fries with his hamburger.

The soldier is missing his legs and he's hanging off the poor girl's neck. The soldier's arms are covered with tattoos and the nurse's face is starting to acquire that same blue-ink color when three military police officers come in and hit him over the head one and two and three times until the poor lunatic falls back and lets her go and drops from the bed to the floor, but still doesn't lose consciousness though he's completely lost his mind. They stick him with a couple syringes and wheel him out on a stretcher, like a giant baby, while, in sweet voices so he stops crying, they explain to him that the thing with liberty fries is no longer current. They tell him that they're called french fries again and that the French are our friends again and that everything is fine and then, outside, something—a car, a woman, a child, all three at once—blows up.

Everything blows up.

So much funnier . . . And, yes, we were brought up with the contemplation of our endless sunsets. We learned to chart stories and myths in the patterns of their colors. Calm and gentle fables where almost nothing happened. Just a slight shift, a soft burst of violet on yellow lasting several centuries. But with you it was so different, so much happened in your stories. And the things that happened were so absurd that, suddenly, we could talk or think of nothing else.

And, yes, of course, we were still vanishing.

In the bed on the other side of me, there's a soldier named Kowalski.

I've always wondered why there's always a soldier with the last name Kowalski. In books, in movies, in television shows, in real life. I wonder if all those Kowalskis might belong to the same family or a secret brotherhood. A hidden and occultist tribe dedicated exclusively to the production of Kowalski-brand soldiers. Pilots, marines, Special

Forces, whatever you want and whatever you need. For high in the sky or the depths of the oceans or the most impenetrable jungles: we've got a Kowalski for you.

The fact that the soldier in the bed next to mine is named Kowalski, also, calms me. Because—statistically speaking—Kowalskis don't end well; while those in their vicinity almost always live to tell the tale, to recollect with cup or glass in hand, years later, in a bar or at a party or alone in front of a mirror, the great guy who was Seymour or Mark or Johnny or even Jerzy Kowalski.

And—I have to say it—this Kowalski is my second Kowalski. My first Kowalski wasn't a classic Kowalski. The classic Kowalski is the one who dies in your arms asking you, when you make it home, to visit his girlfriend and his mother and deliver them a bloodstained letter or a broken watch or a kiss. The classic Kowalski is, also, the one who falls, wounded, and orders you—because his rank is higher than yours—to "Go on alone, don't worry about me."

But this war is strange, different.

All wars have become different and strange since Vietnam, because in one way or another all wars still are Vietnam, someone said that once, and they were right.

Which means that the Kowalskis are no longer what they were.

Which brings me back to my first Kowalski: we found him wandering among the dunes, his uniform in tatters, blond hair and blue eyes and an idiot smile and repeating over and over: "Draw me a sheep . . . Draw me a sheep . . ."

What is essential is not invisible to the eyes. What is essential is what is visible. What is essential is to never stop watching. Ever. And so, before long, we took the liberty of interfering, of making certain modifications.

And, reaching this point, maybe I should ask your forgiveness.

But it wouldn't be sincere.

We would do it all again.

Again and again.

How do you put it?

Ah, yes: "The show must go on."

This Kowalski—my second Kowalski, here in the hospital—isn't in great shape either: hands bandaged, face red with burns and blisters, pupils white.

"Chemical weapons?" I ask.

Kowalski lets out a sigh that wants to—but can't—be a chuckle. "Chemical weapons" has become, at this point, like saying "Mission accomplished."

"No. Mirage. Or I think that's what it was . . ." he answers.

I don't need to ask for an explanation. Kowalski wants to talk. It's not easy for him. The words come out intermittently. His sentences are short. But, still, he has a story and he needs to share it with someone, to pass it along before it's too late. To give it up the way someone gives up a puppy so it can live somewhere else. And he barks but doesn't bite:

"We were out there . . . Somewhere in the desert . . . No idea what we were doing . . . Not knowing what we're doing is what we're the best at doing . . . You know . . . A small patrol . . . About ten men . . . Two vehicles . . . Then we saw something . . . At first we thought it was a group of Bedouins . . . Or something like that . . . Sand people . . . About twenty of them . . . We told them to put their hands up . . . But nothing . . . They came up to us slowly . . . And suddenly we saw . . . And here comes the really funny part. They weren't men . . . I mean, yes, they were men, so to speak . . . But they were made of snow . . . No, they weren't *snowmen* . . . They were *men* of snow . . . There in the sun . . . Not melting . . . We all saw them . . . And we looked at each other and couldn't believe it . . . We got up close to them . . . I took off my gloves and touched them . . . They were cold

. . . They were cold like snow . . . And they seemed to give off a faint glow . . . And it was like they were buzzing . . . We lost our shit . . . All of us . . . We took off our uniforms . . . Started to play . . . Like kids . . . Snowball fight . . . We took the men of snow apart . . . Some of us tasted the snow . . . And it was the best snow we'd ever eaten . . . Or drank . . . Later, back at base, nobody believed us . . . They put us under observation . . . We started getting sick . . . High levels of radiation, apparently . . . Don't worry . . . They've already determined that it's not contagious . . . But I'm the last one left . . . I'm sure I don't have much time . . . But, if you asked me if I'd do it again . . . Or if it was worth it . . . Well . . ."

"Well," is the last word that Kowalski says. All of a sudden the room is full of nurses and doctors.

"He's fried! Like liberty fries!" the soldier in the other bed starts shouting.

That soldier isn't named Kowalski.

I don't remember his name.

And, yes, the obvious question for all of us—who had everything, wanted for nothing—was what was it that attracted us to you, what seduced us?

And the answer is easy.

The answer is that you had something we never had.

The answer is that substance you call snow. We couldn't stop staring at the snow the way all of you can't stop staring at a painting, a sculpture, a work of art.

The snow, the snow, the snow . . .

They've sent us to guard a museum, but they've made it clear that, in the event of looting, we shouldn't intervene. Only open fire in self-defense, a crackling voice tells us, a voice that walks and talks. A walkie-talkie voice.

It's a strange order.

It's another strange order to be added to an increasingly long list of strange orders.

There are four of us. Two teams. Snipers.

My good marksmanship has led to this promotion and I don't entirely understand what it entails. But my comrades look at me with respect, as if they were looking into the infallible eye of a machine. There exists, it seems, an instantaneous sniper mystique that consists, primarily, in speaking little and in monosyllables. And we move in twos. Sniper and spotter. The latter aims the eye and the former aims the bullet. The former pulls the trigger as soon as the latter provides the perfect criteria for hitting the target: atmospheric conditions, distance to the target, possible last minute variables.

Sometimes we switch roles.

Or switch partners with some other team.

So we don't get bored.

So there we are, it's night and, all of a sudden, we start to hear a rising hum approaching from the horizon. The glow of torches lights up the night and hundreds of people advance down the avenue toward where we're stationed. We ready our weapons, but the mob passes by and goes up the museum stairs and tears down the doors and goes inside shouting. It seems like the end of one of those movies where the hunter becomes the hunted. We watch the scene through infrared goggles, but we don't need them because, from our position, we can clearly see and track the movement of the torches along the stairs and hallways of the museum. "Pac Man," someone says, the other sniper's spotter. I don't know him, I don't know his name, but—though it's characteristic newbie humor, a humor that soon disappears—I have to admit that he's right: little lights running around behind windows and, every so often, one of the windows explodes and someone falls into the emptiness and someone else laughs from a balcony watching them fall. Soon, a column of smoke begins to rise from one of the internal courtyards and we can hear gunshots and, this really is strange, dance music. It's clear that they're having an unforgettable party inside. We report what's happening to the command center, but they tell us not to worry, that everything is fine and under control. *Under* and *control* are the two words I've heard the most since I got here, the two sounds whose meaning I've seen embodied the least in the reality of this time and space.

But, I suppose, it doesn't matter.

I suppose that this thing about *under* and *control* is a personal issue, my problem. And that also, in a way, it's under control.

At sunrise, the museum invaders start to emerge. They've got the look of people who have spent not one night but multiple millennia shut inside. Like they'd turned, in a few short hours, into museum pieces. Into museum pieces that aren't particularly valuable, but still worthy of being exhibited.

The first ones to emerge are still holding torches, now gone out, useless, but they refuse to put them down. They've become an extension of their arms. We watch them run away.

Then, around midday, the whole thing gets even stranger.

I see a man emerge dressed in the golden robes of an ancient king, martial and ominous, his friends bowing before him and not, it doesn't seem to me, in jest or mockery.

I see another man emerge, without any pants and with a scroll hanging out of his ass.

I see another emerge carrying two mummies, one over each shoulder, that crumble as soon as the sun touches them. The mummies turn to dust when the light strikes them and the man tries to hold on, to wrap his arms around them; but, like the sand of the desert, the sand of the mummies slips through his fingers.

Dear mother, wherever you are: today I saw something I never thought I'd see in my life. Today I saw dust turn to dust.

Really.

I see things—too many things—that I don't want to see and know I'll never forget. If I live to tell all this, in a few years, I'll wake up from a nightmare screaming and in bed next to someone who, I hope, will love me for who I am and not for who I might have been. Someone who will ask me what I was dreaming and I'll answer, like a person getting up in front of the class to recite the lesson: "I dreamed what I always dream: mummies crumbling under the blinding sun of Iraq."

But now, no doubt, a lot more has to happen before that.

And, all of a sudden, one of the museum walls is coming down and a tractor pushes out through the hole, dragging an enormous statue behind it: the effigy of a god with the head of a man and the body of a lion and the wings of an eagle, passing right in front of my position. One of those ancient and combo-mix gods. Gods greater and more powerful than men because they were able to take the best parts of the best animals for their own bodies. And it looks at me. And I think I see, in its eyes of blind stone, an infinite sadness.

The man driving the tractor sees me look at it and looks at me and smiles the whitest of smiles and blows me a kiss with his hand and shouts: "Allah is great!"

Soon I will cross the desert. Soon I will make the pilgrimage to the mountain of the spaceships. Soon . . .

Desert nights are full of sounds. In the darkness, the white desert sounds like a green jungle. In the darkness, you hear all the noises made by all the desert animals invisible by day. At night, all the desert animals come out to see us. And to talk among themselves about what they see.

There are four of us.

Two sniper teams.

Two snipers and two spotters who can become two spotters and two snipers.

Names do not interest us.

We don't need them. Our gear is already too heavy to weigh it down with first and last names.

We are, yes, the best of the best.

We've heard what people say about others and we've heard what people say about us.

We are only deployed on big occasions.

So, they summoned us to a meeting in a Bagdad basement.

They showed us maps and photographs. Blurry photographs, but still, I knew I was on the right path.

They told us our mission was to take out The Unmaker.

"Deactivate him."

They told us that The Unmaker was responsible for all of it. For the towers and for everything else.

One of the spotters or snipers interrupted and said that he thought that the person responsible was someone else, that guy who sent messages from a cave and . . . First, they ordered him to be quiet. Then they explained to him—to all of us—that no, that wasn't the case. That that other man was nothing but a façade. A curtain. One of the many curtains concealing the individual who was truly responsible for all of it. Someone who called himself The Unmaker.

Then they made us listen to some recordings. Sounds and noises. And a voice reciting a countdown in a too-perfect English.

"That's him," they told us.

Then they put us on a helicopter.

And dropped us out in the desert.

Here we are.

You don't know, you're not aware, of how lucky you are and have always been.

You don't know what an immense privilege it is to have stories to tell.

Those first nights in that desert, we told each other our stories. They all started the same, we coincided on our first words, modifying that introduction of meetings for alcoholics or addicts or whatever: "I'm Special Forces and I haven't the slightest idea what I'm doing here and . . ."

To begin with, under the first moon, we all lied.

We all claimed that we signed up just days after the towers came down, riding the crest of a frenzied wave of patriotism. But by the second night we were already telling different stories. In war, almost immediately, you tell the truth and dispense with lies, because nobody wants to die lying, in the name of a lie invented in offices on the other side of the world. There's nothing more instantly superstitious than a soldier in combat. Soon, everything is omens and signs and portents and conjurations that, you think, can only be neutralized by telling the truth or what you think is the truth.

So, surrounded by the possibility of death, we take turns telling the stories of our lives.

"Well . . . I was always intrigued by those theories of gods as extraterrestrial astronauts. The pyramids. You know . . . So it occurred to me that it was the quickest and easiest way to come see all of that. The ruins. I never had enough money. And the truth is, I didn't think all of this would last so long. Or that Egypt was closer," says Sniper 1.

The three of us look at him the way you look at something you don't entirely understand.

"Ah . . . Well, my grandpa worked on building the atomic bomb. They say my father died aglow, radioactive, and that he thought he was an extraterrestrial, that he'd been replaced by a being from another planet, like in that old movie . . . the one where those pods came from space and turned into human replicas, remember? One day they came and took him away and we never saw him again," says Spotter 2.

"I was born in New Mexico . . . You know, near that site where the flying saucers supposedly crashed . . . and, hey, have you noticed that we're all into science fiction?" says Spotter 1.

He says it in a very thin voice, the voice of the boy he once was and, in a way, still is: the boy who not long ago promised himself, that when he was grownup, he would get a job where he could say things like "Alpha-Tango-Foxtrot" all the time.

I say nothing. I could tell them who my father supposedly is, which book is my favorite.

I say that now it's time to get some sleep

And before I finish saying it, we are accosted and taken prisoner and our hands are tied and we're led away in a line, walking into the night and, I'm sorry, I can't offer more details to anyone who's wondering how we didn't see them coming. I'll just say that what you can't see in the jungle you can see even less in the desert, because in the desert there's nothing to see. And yet, at the same time, in the desert, the desert is always watching. You feel its eyes stabbing into your back and your profile and between your eyes and you have no idea where to look. Mecca is always shifting location; and I wonder how the men who hunted us down with no need for bullets and gunshots, who took us out with the kind of perfect marksmanship that doesn't even need to aim and pull a trigger, locate it and prostrate themselves and pray. I have no doubt that they know and recognize the exact position of that most sacred of places with the same precision and speed with which they can pinpoint the exact spot of their heartbeat. I suppose it must be some kind of reflex, sixth sense, magic without the trick. I suppose that they let go and look into the eyes of the desert and the desert looks back and winks, indicating the exact location of that all-important site.

And there's something nice, comforting, about being taken: our captors—unlike us—seem to know perfectly well where they are and where they're going and the truth is I feel envy but, also, comfort and calm, and I even appreciate the exhaustion of the march. At last, we have a direction, somewhere we're going.

Hours later, we stop beside what appears to be an empty swimming pool, surrounded by sand dunes.

And in the bottom of the swimming pool is an open drain and they make us go down it and descend toward the center of the Earth.

I climb the mountain. There, on the summit, await the spaceships and the remains of all those who . . .

They show me the headless bodies of my comrades. If there is anything worse than being shown a head without a body, it's being shown a body without a head. And now they show me three headless bodies. And there's nothing worse than knowing that it's them, but not knowing who's who, which is which.

For some reason, they haven't decapitated me. I have survived again. I am becoming a professional survivor. Maybe, it occurs to me, my three comrades, whose last names I never knew, were all named Kowalski.

They've taken all my gear.

I feel so light.

They make me kneel.

They remove the blindfold from my eyes.

Facing me, on a kind of throne, is a man dressed in a black tunic and black mask. He looks like the Lawrence of Arabia version of Darth Vader or something like that.

"Where did you get this?" he asks me and, from his voice, I know that it's The Unmaker.

The Unmaker rises and walks toward me. He walks very strangely. As if on a diagonal current of air. Like a cross between a crab and a gazelle. As if he were floating and as if the air around him were made of little lights, as if he were surrounded by an army of fireflies.

"Where did you get this?" The Unmaker asks again. And he shows me my copy of *Evasion*. And he holds it with the tips of his fingers, in the same reverential way that other people hold bibles, photos of children, or programs for horse races with notes in the margins. Nobody ever held a science fiction novel that way, I think.

And when I'm just about to answer, I realize it's a rhetorical question, and the answer is something that I can't understand, something The Unmaker knows—or at least senses—perfectly well.

Then, without waiting for my reply, The Unmaker begins to speak: "I've been waiting for you. I knew you'd come sooner or later. I've been anxiously awaiting your arrival. And I'm very happy that you're here . . . You're the chosen one. Or, at least, you're the chosen one in this variation of this world. And it's good that it is so . . . It gives me joy, it makes me happy. I was getting so sick of this variable, of the role I've been assigned this time . . . For some strange reason, I'm given the most extreme . . . let's call them *fates*. And I can't forget them. I remember all of them. Comings and goings and arrivals and departures. While my friend gets almost-normal situations, boring and pleasantly domestic. Maybe it's because his father was a rabbi. Maybe that subtracts a few points in karma's circles. Or maybe it's because my friend was always a kind of passive observer. I saw him again not long ago (though it's hard for me to understand time now) and he's still pretty much the same. Uncomprehending. Not wanting to comprehend. Just wanting. Pure feeling and no logic. I suppose that's why things have gone better for him than for me. So little happened in his *real* life that very little happens in these post-lives either. He is barely aware that he's being turned on and off and then starting over from the beginning again. Whereas I am so aware of this immortality of deaths . . . Over and over. A perpetual *(to be continued . . .)*. And her, watching, as if she were reading us, as if she were writing us, as if she were discarding some versions in favor of others. She, who hasn't stopped watching us since that night we went to her house and built all those men of snow and a whole planet in her front yard and . . . Why'd we do it? For love, yes. But also to do *something important.* Together. Because we felt that there, that night, in the snow, our brief childhood was coming to an end, so that a long, too-long old age could begin. The time of our lives is poorly plotted. The speed of humanity doesn't match the speed of things very well and . . . I hate this desert. I hate so many things . . . Maybe that's where the difference lies: my fuel has always been fury in the face of the incomprehensible. Fury in the face of the inexplicable nature of her disappearance and, for that reason, I'm given horrible fates, I end up in the worst places . . . And, I guess, that's the punishment for my sins: I, who wanted to build a planet of snow, end up on a planet of burning sand . . . Still, it doesn't seem entirely fair . . . This war. This absurd war. This *other* absurd war in which man is no longer wolf to man. No: now man is extraterrestrial to man and maybe it would all make more sense if we treated these ridiculous missions as interplanetary voyages, as if we were confronting aliens and not foreigners . . . After all, look at yourself: your uniform already sort of resembles a spacesuit . . . Such suits are needed to go to war, to the outermost space that exists in our world. There's no gravity here, we float, drifting through the air and the air is unbreathable and . . . Do you understand anything I'm saying? I suppose not. And I'm sorry, but I don't think there's enough time to explain it. It's a little complex. Have you heard people talk about the theory of multiple universes and multiple minds, about quantum and wave mechanics, about the false vacuum, about the relative state of all things in this world? I suppose so, because I see that you're interested in science fiction. And, after all, a good part of the most revolutionary scientific concepts find their origin in religious texts and ancient folklore. So it's not a new idea: the original multiverses are the dwellings of different deities . . . And I, without wanting to, have become a kind of deity. Let's just say that

here and now and for the age I am, I should be dead. But that I could
have been other. I could have been others. A comic book illustrator
of invulnerable superheroes, whose only vulnerability is exposure to
fragments of their home-planet—there's nothing more fatal for them
than the radiations of their past, light years away—and who hide their
powers behind the masks of bumbling and innocuous humans. Or a
science-fiction writer writing under a pseudonym, hiding behind the
façade of a government employee while imagining stories in which a
police force rules multiple planets with a strict code under the motto
of 'Supervise, but do not execute, preserve, but do not dominate.' Or
someone who died years ago, too young, of a heart attack. Someone
who smoked too much and who worked for a while for the military
and the Pentagon, but subsequently dedicated himself to the field of
physics and postulated revolutionary theories. Theories that nobody
entirely believed. So I was isolated. Me and my theories. And soon my
family was also a family more theoretical than practical. Movable. A
wife who dies of cancer, a daughter who commits suicide and leaves a
note explaining that she was going to look for me in another dimension, and a son who specialized in composing beautiful and depressing
songs: lyrics so sad and melodies with that false and mechanical joy
of music boxes. A boy who found my body lying on the kitchen floor
and, when he tried to resuscitate me, to bring me back, embraced me
for the first time; because I would never let him embrace me and I had
never embraced him. In a way, here and now, you are the son I never
had. Which is why I ask and beg and order you, my son, to embrace
me not to resuscitate me, but (nobody will stop you, I've left instructions for my followers to take their own lives right here, beside us)
to embrace me, and then, with that sword you see there, to kill me."

I am here now, way up high. Overhead, the sky contracts
and expands and, just this once, it seems to be snowing.

Behind and down below are the ruins, the smoke, the fire in the entrails of the Earth like the tongue of a dying dragon.

I am the lone survivor.

I am the only one—my comrades are dead, the monarch's subjects self-immolated to be an inseparable part of his end—who came out alive from the drain of the empty swimming pool and climbed the ladder and here I am, sitting on the edge of the diving board.

In The Unmaker's bunker I found one of those latest generation mobile phones. Satellite. The telephonic equivalent of a Swiss Army knife. Buttons and letters so small, an object so light and tiny . . . I felt like the clumsiest of giants turning it on. Great technological advances are smaller and smaller in size and, inevitably, seem to strive to resemble complex toys as closely as possible. The best of both worlds, I guess: extreme sophistication with childish inspiration.

What was it that my mother sang to me as a lullaby? Yes: "Having read the book, I'd love to turn you on . . ." And after, the sound of the beginning of the end of the world. A sound that comes from nowhere because, all of a sudden, it seems to be everywhere, right here too.

I think I've input my position correctly. But the coordinates are vague, barely an approximate, disorienting. It's hard to believe that high command—or more or less high command—will deem it worthwhile to put a whole operation in motion to rescue one man, someone who lived to tell the tale of a secret mission that, no doubt, nobody wants told anyway.

And, besides, what I have to tell is implausible, complicated, uncomfortable.

It's hard to imagine that someone would be all that excited to transcribe my words, to put in writing how I obeyed The Unmaker's order or plea and cut off his head with a single blow of that sword. Actually, I didn't cut off his head: I raised the sword and brought it down—The Unmaker was on his knees offering me his bare neck—and I couldn't be certain that the blade had cut anything; because in that instant, the precise moment of impact, the room was flooded with light and, after, there was neither body nor head. His body—though I never saw him die—vanished, as if someone had suddenly opened a door and let in one of those winds that erases and sweeps away everything. Better, I suppose, for that same wind to erase me too, for no traces or loose ends to be left, for my file to be lost forever and, with any luck, turn me into some kind of urban legend. A barracks and regiment legend. A rumor tiptoeing through the mess halls and bars and offices of military bases. A ghost story and the ghost will be me because, now, sitting on this diving board, I am a ghost already. The ghost of the ghost swimming pool in the middle of a haunted desert.

Better to forget me, decorate me, and move on.

Yes, here I am.

Yes, I knock three times on the wood of the diving board, but no one asks "who's there?"

"To travel, to get out of my shitty hometown, to see the world," is the standard answer soldiers tend to recall, laughing nervously as everything blows up around them, unable to believe that at one time they were dumb enough to say *that*, whenever someone asked why they had joined the military, why they had gone to war.

They also recall that at one point they lied to themselves and to others and even kind of believed the lie that goes "I wanted to defend my country."

But it's harder and harder for them to remember it and—when they're already long gone, when the air they breathe seems clad in the lead casings of bullets and everything tastes like gunpowder, after they struck out and left behind everything they could no longer bear to face, because nothing was more frightening than the dead-end peace of becoming replicas of their parents—all they can think about is going home to that place they left and swore they'd never return to.

To return home to those sweeping small-town landscapes where nothing happens but the calm contentment of knowing exactly what tomorrow will bring, because it won't be all that different from what yesterday and today brought. To walk those short streets you know down to the last stone and, worst case, to arrive in a coffin wrapped in a flag, to be buried in the cemetery beside the drive-in movie theater, one of the last drive-ins in the universe where, every so often, they show old movies with radioactive monsters and giant women and robots who paralyze Earth as soldiers point and scream and shoot with useless weapons and, when I was a kid, I always wanted to work as one of those actors who runs away and turns back and looks up and screams and is squashed by a giant paw or struck down by a deadly bolt of lightning.

To rest in peace.

Rocked to the cacophony of those old movies.

Anything would be better than getting lost forever in the desert.

That is not my case, those were not my reasons.

I don't have a home.

I don't have an X on the map to return to and dig up a treasure that was always buried there.

I've spent a long time wandering and running.

So much time that I don't remember where the starting line was.

I remember, it seems, only what's essential; as if someone decided how far back I should remember, as if someone had assigned me an exact quantity of memories: limited but enough to keep me moving.

I remember, yes, the pistol shot that sent me out to track down two men I'd never met. I remember, yes, the photocopies of a strange book in my mother's even stranger library.

My mother—once an all-out hippie known, under one of those absurd Aquarian aliases, as Mothership Rainbow—crashed years ago into the asteroid of one of those illnesses with two last names.

My mother—like many of her lysergic friends—was a devout consumer of science-fiction novels (especially the trilogies, tetralogies, pentalogies . . .) and wanted to name me Sandworm and, luckily, the employee at the civil registry refused to do it.

In any case, my mother managed to infect me with her passion for those books that launched you into orbit, those books that sometimes were like a trip.

I never knew my father, but before she died my mother showed me a photograph and gave me a letter he had left. The photograph showed a round man with a black and white beard and a shy smile surrounded by dogs. The man had the unmistakable air of someone for whom every day is Sunday. The caption—the photograph was cut out of the newspaper, it was an obituary—stated that it was "W. W. Zack, explorer of impossible possible worlds." And then I felt something strange happen: the letters seemed to slide across the page, like they were dancing. And that man wasn't named, as far as I could tell, W. W. Zack anymore, but Philip K. Dick.

My mother said that she barely knew him, that he spent just one night at her house in the early 80s, that they drank a couple bottles of Californian wine while discussing the arrival of benign extraterrestrials, guided by minds of the young, all together now, sliding down the highway in spaceships designed through hours and hours of transcendental meditation. But the only one who arrived was me, that's where I come from, my mother smiled a smile full of freckles.

I opened the letter and inside there were just a couple lines, written in a twisted handwriting, down toward the bottom, as if they were trying to hide away in the deepest depths of the page: "The key is in *Evasion*." And two names: "Isaac Goldman & Ezra Leventhal."

And that was it.

It wasn't a great inheritance, but it was something.

A sign.

A star to be guided by.

Something pointing in some direction.

My mother told me that Zack (Dick?) had shown up on the run from the FBI, or something like that, looking for a woman, some other woman, but that he found her and seemed to make due for the time being. He told her that the woman he was looking for was a "strange woman." Someone had told him she might be living nearby, in a suburb called Sad Songs. And Zack talked about *Evasion* the whole time. And my mother realized that Zack *really was* running from someone or something. That he wasn't lying or hallucinating. Zack wasn't running from one of his many ex-wives, but from something that he had discovered and that, he thought, nobody else could understand.

Zack talked about his idea of reality ("Reality is that which, when you stop believing in it, doesn't go away") all the time and about things that to my mother were completely irreal: about androids that weren't aware they were androids, about Disneyland as "an evolving organism," about the message he had found in a fortune cookie from a Chinese restaurant ("Deeds done in secret have a way of becoming found out," the little roll of paper said) about Parmenides who "taught that the only things that are real are things which never change" and about Heraclitus who insisted that "everything changes," about the many applications of the *I Ching*, about "the many truths that tend to be considered science fiction," about the supposed "plot coincidences" between his novels and parts of the Bible, and, again and again, about the morning when a strange young woman—the woman he said he was looking for—had knocked on his door:

"Days before her arrival I'd had two wisdom teeth removed. I couldn't write from the pain, so I called a nearby drugstore and asked them to send me painkillers. The strongest they had. A half hour later, the doorbell rang and I opened the door and there she was. A woman who was young, but who seemed far older than her years. There are people like that: people who seem to have been living for far too long inside the mausoleums of their own secret grandeur. I saw that she wore a shining gold necklace in the center of which was a gleaming gold fish. I don't know why I asked her what it meant and she answered that it was a symbol by which ancient Christians recognized each other. All of a sudden, I stopped feeling pain and, as I stared at the gold fish, I experienced what I later learned is called *anamnesis*—a Greek word meaning, literally, 'loss of forgetfulness.' I remembered everything. I didn't just remember it, I saw it too: I saw flaming gothic sunsets over lands that couldn't be of our Earth, I heard conversations in a nameless language, I wondered if that was the voice of God talking to Himself, and I remembered the words of Xenophanes of Colophon: 'God is one, supreme among gods and men, and not like mortals in body or mind. The whole of god sees, the whole perceives, the whole hears. But without effort he sets in motion all things by mind and thought. He always abides in the same place, not moved at all, nor is it fitting that he should move from one place to another.' Maybe, the key lies in, one of these nights, jumping the fences of Disneyland and replacing all the robot birds with real birds. Maybe then . . . But it is her I must find. After she left, there I was, in front of the open door, not knowing what had happened, as if I'd been singled out by the finger of a lightning bolt of absolute knowledge . . . I called the drugstore and they told me that nobody worked there who fit my description of the woman. I thought I saw her once in New York. I followed her out to Sad Songs. I lost her trail. I found you. Everything means something. And all I want is to recover that unique and definitive moment. To remember everything again so that there's nothing left to forget."

And I have forgotten so many things since coming here.

Even my name.

I hope it's not Kowalski.

Maybe that's why I've forgotten it.

I'll never forget you, my children. You've never met me,
but I've never stopped loving you.

The screen of the mobile phone gives me access to so many things . . .

I could call some friends—acquaintances more than friends—but
I don't remember their numbers.

The only phone number I have (scribbled on the last page of *Evasion*, in the copy he gave me that afternoon when I invaded his house
with my questions) is Isaac Goldman's and I dial it and it takes a long
time for anyone to answer.

And it's the young voice of a woman (I don't dare say that it's the
voice of a young woman) who tells me that Mr. Goldman disappeared
some time ago.

I ask when he died.

"I said he disappeared, not that he died," the young voice of the
woman says.

She asks me if I'm a relative.

I answer that, in a way, yes.

And there's not much else to say, to talk about.

The young voice of the woman explains that she's busy, cooking
and looking after her children and she hangs up and it's as if I, from
where I am, were talking to someone from another planet, to a native
of a place where people still cook and look after children.

I see that the battery of the mobile phone is almost dead, that
soon it will be nothing but a piece of metal and plastic. An object as
sophisticated as it is useless. An instant fossil.

So I decide to enter a corner of the web and track myself down,
locate myself.

I go to one of those sites that allows you to—live and direct—go
up in the skies, to contemplate the world from outside, a view once
the exclusive privilege of astronauts and angels, to orbit high overhead

until you position yourself above more or less the exact spot where you are down below.

And, then, the descent.

Not too fast and not too slow.

Experiencing the cold acceleration, the warm slap entering the atmosphere and continuing down, closer and closer, over the desert, here I go and here I come and, suddenly, there I am.

Closer and closer: a man surrounded by the sand dunes of the night.

Sitting on the diving board of an empty swimming pool.

I descend toward myself, guided by the faint yet clear light of the screen of the mobile phone and, suddenly, on the screen of the mobile phone I see the screen of a mobile phone wherein the screen of a mobile phone can be seen.

I've abducted myself.

I've swapped this no man's land—this empty space—for the planet of another.

I am infinite and I begin and end in myself.

I am the universe.

I've come home.

Welcome.

We wanted so badly to travel . . . We wanted so badly to meet you . . . We could've done so quickly and easily. We could've done it with the power of our minds alone. Projecting ourselves like light beams through space and appearing beside you without prior warning. And defeating you almost without you even realizing you'd been defeated.

But it didn't seem appropriate.

It didn't seem right.

You—who'd dreamed so long of the day of our arrival—
deserved far better.

Something much more science fiction.

That's why we built the spaceships.

We made them big and ominous and elegant and we were
so happy imagining you detecting them first with the
myopic pupils of your orbiting telescopes, then with
your scatterbrained radar screens, and then, finally,
seeing us come down from the sky and drift gracefully
over your cities.

Our spaceships—like the flying saucers in your movies—always settling above historical monuments and
tourist sanctuaries. We wanted so badly to make all your
fantasies come true . . . We had made so many plans: to
assume a menacing or absurd or sensual appearance.

Or all three at the same time.

Tentacles, huge skulls housing megabrains, beautiful
women wrapped in sexy diaphanous-metal outfits . . .
Like a costume party. And we even considered destroying
something in a ridiculous way. Knocking over the Tower of
Pisa or crashing into a pyramid, silly things like that.
Then, afterward, we would show ourselves as we really are
and reveal our true intentions. To invade, yes. To conquer, also. To subject you, of course. But, also, to make
you participants in our perfection, which, with your
help, would never be boring again. Because inside of you
there would always be something unpredictable, a nucleus
of surprise, a potential explosion of the catastrophic.

And, together, we would be happy.

But it hasn't been possible.

It's late now, now it's too late.

Here comes the last of my sunsets: a fury of colors, a chaos of clouds, shapes shifting across a sky that can't stay still.

One of your poets, a poet in the trenches of a war that we followed with such pleasure and that caused us such anguish, once wrote that "soldiers are dreamers."

We were never soldiers, but, yes, we were dreamers.

And you were the dreams we dreamed.

Now, the dream ends and I ready myself to fall asleep forever.

That's it.

It's off now.

No battery left.

Out.

Off.

K.O.

I close the mobile phone and open the book, and books never lose their charge, books always function, books are always ready to be read . . . Unplugged machines that connect instantaneously to our brains and possess us and invade us. Maybe, now that I think of it, books are extraterrestrial organisms. Beings that abduct us and take us to other worlds, better worlds, worlds much better written than our own.

. . . and it's worth pointing out, once more, that now I think and even write with terrestrial terminology. It's been so many years (and it's clear that our years are not the same as terrestrial years, and that they're not even called years) of watching and learning? that, seeing the situation I've ended up in, it makes more sense and is so much more poetic?, ironic?, poetic and ironic? to express myself this way. After all, this isn't a message for my own kind because there are none of them left, but for the others, the ones I've made my own.

Those distant beings I've watched from here, so closely; for in the end it is the eye of the watcher that determines the reality of distances.

And it's clear that in the resigned and final calm of my disheartened eyes (that are not eyes, that are not called eyes) also pulses and resides the impossible hope, the absurd dream that someone, some summer night, with fireworks bursting in the sky, will experience the strange sensation of feeling that they're being watched from far far away, and they will look up and, without seeing me, will watch me watch them for the last time.

Again, I open *Evasion*.

The light is almost gone.

No nights are darker and yet more luminous than desert nights.

There's no light on the ground, but there's so much light in the sky . . .

The stars shine brighter and better in desert.

Out here there's no Earthly glow to dull the glow of space.

And so you can read by starlight.

I open the book to the last page and—though it's not necessary, because I could remember every word without having to see it—read, I read with my eyes wide open:

In a way, our wild yet shy and secret love for you was, also, a kind of betrayal. We didn't get here in time, we missed our moment. And it's because we like to watch you so much . . . And in that way—without being able to stop watching you as I now watch the eternal sunsets of Urkh 24, of That-Place-Where-The-Most-Disconsolate-Melodies-Can-Be-Heard—time passed and time escaped us like water through our fingers, like sand in an hourglass. Please, forgive us, even though you never knew of our faults and our failure.

And don't ever forget us though you never got to know us.

In a way, we were always there, at your side, worshiping you.

It would've been wonderful to meet and speak and exchange stories.

We had so much to tell each other.

That's why I'm recording these thoughts, these last ideas of the last of my kind to disappear, to vanish.

These are the memories of someone who—though they're no longer here, though they're already becoming part of the incommensurable matter of oblivion—will never forget you and will remember you forever.

The last of The Faraways.

Always faithful.

Semper Fi.

III

The Other Planet

And so, sometimes, this planet becomes another planet.

Thus, we travel from one planet to another without having to cross space.

It is just a matter of crossing time and not letting it be time that crosses us, that crosses us out, that erases us from the map.

It's not easy, no simple thing to achieve.

And yet, I could do it.

But—not to confuse you—I'm not especially happy about that.

I didn't choose it.

They chose me.

If there is anybody out there, please, stay tuned.

We'll keep reporting.

But I know that there's nobody here and nobody out there.

There's nothing left.

End of the World News.

And yet I—and nobody is further away from everything than I am—keep transmitting.

Ghosts, echoes, reflections, traces of voices and landscapes.

I can't help it, it wasn't part of any equation; yet, somehow, I remain turned on, broadcasting all shows at the same time, all episodes of all seasons, trying to find the only one that interests me.

But it's no easy task.

There are many, too many chapters.

And the one I'm looking for is neither the most interesting nor the most successful.

But it's my favorite.

In that episode, I appear and they appear and it is just one scene. But it is, for me, the best possible scene, the most important moment of my life, of our lives.

Someday—I swear—I'll find it, I'll be able catch it, I'll get to replay it.

Over and over.

Until the end of the world, until the ending of all the ends of the world.

Welcome to the ends of the world.

The first end of the world—the first of the many ends of your world, which is also, in part, my world—took place in the very instant of its beginning.

Which is to say: nothing happened.

More a Big Crack than a Big Bang.

Or better yet: a Big Pfff.

Something like the snap of fingers in a dark bedroom. Just a quick pop of pure energy that found nothing to burn and feed on and grow into a raging blaze, happy to live and to burn. So, merely, an order to be disobeyed; because you simply cannot obey it, no matter how badly you want to.

Thus, the curtain that is opened or raised to reveal nothing but an empty stage without props or actors, barely illuminated by a small lamp that someone forgot and won't even come back to find, because it doesn't matter, because nothing matters, because it doesn't matter to anybody: not a single ticket has been sold for this dysfunctional function that doesn't and won't start when all of you don't show up.

There are no seats left because there is no theater.

The second end of this world was duly recorded. The second end of the world that I've heard of had at its center the small island of Santorini—Aegean Sea, about one hundred fifty kilometers from

Crete—christened thusly in honor of Saint Irene of Thessaloniki, who burned, ecstatic, at the stake in the year 304 AD for refusing to renounce her Christian faith. The Greek nationalists refer to the place as Thera, in homage to the first Spartan commander to come ashore after the great disaster.

It's approximately the year 1500 BC—I'm using, so you can understand better, this banal and inexact temporal notation—when the inhabitants of the island who didn't refer to it as Santorini or Thera but, indistinctly as Kalliste (the most beautiful island of all the islands) or Strongili (better known as "the circular island") wake up to a roar that seems to burst from the throat of a thousand sea lions.

The island's volcano has opened its eye.

Some of them run to the beach and there they see it: a wave that comes rushing toward them as if driven by the love of a mother who longs to drown her children in an embrace. And the great wave drowns them and embraces them and never lets go. And not satisfied with that, the great wave completely covers the island (they'd never seen anything like this, but it's not like they had much time to think about what a terrible marvel it was either) and then recedes in search of a new destination, and in that way goes on to sink, one by one, all the islands in the Aegean. And when it finishes with them, the wave continues on its way toward new seas and new lands and new civilizations. That wave is like a razor slitting the throat of the world from one side to the other and, somewhere, in this version of the story of History, that same wave, so many years later, keeps rolling around, always on the prowl, ready to wipe out with its foam any sign of solidity, of solid ground.

That wave is the same wave that shakes my bed night after night and turns me into a raft that someday, with any luck, will run aground and turn into an island where one solitary palm tree will grow. And there I am, writing messages like this one, waiting for the tide to bring me a bottle I can slip them into.

Here it goes, here I go.

Then—I miss my island so much—I wake up so the nightmare can continue.

The whole world is made of mud and is surrounded by the water that the ice cubes become as they melt in my glass.

Another whiskey double for me, please, and there's nothing more unsettling than the light on in an empty kitchen, in the middle of the night, and someone rummaging through cupboards, trying to remember where she hid that bottle that now she can't find anywhere.

The third end of this world that I've managed to tune in (now, all alone, I pick up glimmers of the old transmissions of ancient transmitters, of those who preceded me in this task) took place at some point during the Roman Empire.

The gods—angry or happy over one of those oh so capricious and childish matters that tend to make the gods angry or happy—descended from the heights, all together, all at once. So many gods on the surface of a planet that, weighed down by such divine weight, shifted in its orbit and got too close to the Moon and . . .

. . . forgive me, but I'm going to pour myself another drink. A long and deep drink. A drink almost as deep as my thirst and, of course, *almost* being the operative word here, because nobody drinks to feel satisfied. You drink to be able to keep on drinking. Everyone gets a turn (though there's nobody left to take a turn) and here I am taking my turn, like a glove, like a costume you take off and let fall to the side at a party, in a room on the top floor, in a house that isn't yours. And suddenly you're cold and, so, another drink to warm you up and to keep you here a little longer, to dream more dreams of glasses full of floating ice cubes. To dream of drinking down one of those long and tall drinks in a glass made to accommodate about a fourth of the bottle.

Now I enter—soon I will enter—markets empty of people but full of bottles to empty. I empty bottles—I've found that alcohol lets me feel, at least for a while, that I feel nothing but what I feel—just so I, the perfect excuse, can fill them with messages that read "I empty bottles just so I, the perfect excuse, can fill them with messages and . . ."

. . . the fourth end of the world took place when the Knight Templar Enric Coriolis de Vallvidrera returned home—near the Pyrenees, on a rocky hillside, in a place where centuries later the luminous scepter of a very tall communications tower would rise—from the Crusades clutching a piece of wood that, he'd been told, originally belonged to the supposed cross that a supposed Messiah had been nailed to.

The piece of wood was, in reality, the abode of toxic and exotic spores. A virus as old as the world.

Enric de Vallvidrera falls ill—fevers and deliriums slipping through the rusted cracks of his suddenly softened and disarmed armor—and infects first his family and then the village at the base of his castle. Soon the virus is traveling in the coughs of travelers and before long, when it clings to the wings of birds and the backs of fish, the die is cast.

A disease doesn't differentiate between the Old World and the New.

The rules of the game don't change.

The board is the same.

And the game has ended.

And everyone loses.

The fifth end of the world . . . I don't remember which was the fifth end of the world. Something to do with a mass suicide, with a multitude of deranged prophets.

But it doesn't really matter anyway.

What I refer to here are the ends of the world that I've *seen*, of which I'm certain. But there are many I know nothing about, that are like a whisper at the end of a hallway of a last supper whose invitation never came, and yet, I know that it's taking place, so near and so far. Like an echo of an echo of an echo.

The sixth end of the world was cooked up over a low flame in the laboratories of the talented mad scientists of the Third Reich. Flashes and lightning bolts and electrodes and bubbling beakers and griffins in the form of swastikas and the scenography of sloping rooftops and, just like that, a race of supermen. Giant Aryans nearly three meters tall. Invincible soldiers.

First the Tristan series and then the Siegfried series.

And, the ones and the others, magnificent.

Spotless boots, perfect uniforms, and Cyclopes'-sized monocles that, perfectly synchronized, march on Washington D. C. and throw the wheelchair-bound President Roosevelt down the White House stairs. Soon, bored, having conquered the entire world and eliminated all the inevitably inferior races one by one, the Tristans and the Siegfrieds return from all points around the globe and march on Berlin and execute the pathetic and oh so imperfect Adolf Hitler, throwing him in a cauldron of bubbling lava.

Soon, almost immediately, there's nothing left for them to do. And the Tristans and Siegfrieds languish and die out listening to Wagner operas in empty palaces; because the talented mad scientists of the Third Reich forgot to create Isoldes and Kriemhilds.

And this is a joke, this didn't happen, I just happened to think it up right now and I swear if there were someone to apologize to, I'd apologize.

And even invite them to have a drink.

Two.

Three.

The seventh end of the world—and in the twentieth century, the successive ends of the world take place more and more frequently, as if the planet wanted to test all possible goodbyes, as if it didn't know which bonbons were still in the box—took place that morning in Los Alamos, New Mexico. Trinity Site. Heavy dark sunglasses and the desert sand and the buzz of the cameras recording all of it; because man has learned how to record historical events and it's this power to record them that, in a way, compels him to provoke them, so he can have something to record.

And so, Earth has become a dangerous place and Robert Oppenheimer and company (who know him as "Oppie" and who hear him say something about being the destroyer of worlds, something extracted from a sacred and exotic text); and the massive explosion that was thought to be controlled but wasn't; and the joke-hypotheses of the catastrophist Enrico Fermi turned out to be true but not at all funny.

The atomic explosion ignites the nitrogen in the air and in the oceans, and the atmosphere is stripped bare like a woman tearing off her dress all at once—one of those dresses that functions more to undress than it does to dress whoever's wearing it—after a whole night spent dancing fast and fiery dances knowing, fiercely happy, that everyone is watching her and can't stop watching at her.

Just like they can't stop watching that mushroom shaped cloud that climbs into the skies and grows and grows until it blots out the light of the sun with its light of a thousand suns.

The eighth and ninth end of the world are a lot alike.

An American satellite that suddenly decides to drop from the sky and that the Russians confuse for a missile coming straight at Moscow.

And that makes the rapid and ephemeral art of pressing red buttons after shouting into red telephones easy and at the same time oh so complex.

Before or after that, President John Fitzgerald Kennedy survives the assassination attempt in Dallas and reassumes his duties somewhat changed and erratic. And one night—on a guided and unscheduled visit to the Oval Office, to impress a young university student—he gives the incendiary and terminal and burning order and forgets to turn it off, to cancel it.

The tenth end of the world that I know of . . .

I should stop here to clarify that not all the ends of the world I've heard about (a voice describing them to me that sounds like a wind blowing in reverse, like those supposed inverted satanic messages on old LPs from back in the sixties) are so spectacular and histrionic.

There are other ends of the world—or, even though all finality implicitly carries the will and destiny to attain and obtain an end, should I say *endings?*—that are almost secrets: accidents, blunders, tumbles down the stairway of History.

Ends—like the previous ones—that I learned of, like I said, reviewing my operator's files, my antenna picking up lost waves and tuning them in.

Ends suspended by the action—sometimes subtle and almost secret, other times bumbling and rushed—of those who occupied my role before me.

I didn't meet any of them personally, but I knew their existence to be undeniable, because I couldn't be the only one, because, half closing my eyes, I detected their presence everywhere, their secret as desperate as my own.

Like when I saw that painting that hangs now—or that once hung—in the living room of my house in Sad Songs; and more details about this coming soon.

Now, again, another of those ends of the world (ends, like I said, more private, almost domestic) shows a boy of about eight playing with one of those introductory toy sets to the marvelous world of chemistry. You know the kind: small and oh so fragile test tubes, a rudimentary microscope, a harmless burner, and multiple little beakers containing supposedly innocuous substances to which the boy adds a small piece of chewing gum, of the gum he's chewing, combined with the reactants in his saliva and . . .

In another, a deranged rabbi, interned at a psychiatric hospital in Manhattan, discovers, after years and years of research, the exact way to reunite the loose and broken fragments of the vessel that once contained the divine presence of God and he starts to levitate, to float up into the heavens and . . . I don't really know what happens next. The image is lost. All I know is that his story doesn't end well, that they say he committed suicide, falling from on high, or that they threw him out a window, who knows . . .

Another one takes place at a rural airport. A passenger who has already checked his bags doesn't appear at the gate of departure and an employee calls him over the loudspeaker—the passenger's last name is complicated, packed full of consonants—and he reads it poorly and, without knowing it, pronounces the name of He-Who-Awaits-On-The-Other-Side-Of-All-Things-And-Whose-Name-Must-Never-Be-Pronounced because, to do so, would free him and—to the joy of Phineas Elsinore Darlingskill—he would come here from his dwelling in a golden hole in time and space to bring about an end of everything and . . .

The last of the most personal and domestic ends of the world I remember has as protagonist a man who is brushing his teeth in front of the bathroom mirror. His wife has left him, she's taken his little daughter with her, and he's just been fired from his job. It hasn't been a good day. All of a sudden, the toothbrush breaks inside his mouth with a snap. Too much. He can't take it. The man goes out onto his apartment balcony and jumps off and dies unaware that he is the person responsible for his time, that someone like him is born only every so often, and that the lives of all humanity depended on him. Around him, as the man is dying in the street, everyone starts jumping out of windows. Some of them, from lower floors throw themselves off again and again until, finally, a blow to the head brings an end to their suicidal zeal. Others throw themselves down stairways of subway stations or jump hilariously over ship rails or open the doors to airplanes in mid-flight. All of them, in one way or another, fall and fall and keep on falling. People falling from on high, people who one morning find themselves in a lawless world and, as their last and only comfort, embrace the Law of Gravity.

There's another variation of the end of the world that is the one that, I suppose, will produce the most pleasure in readers of techno-thrillers, gun collectors, and people addicted to the insomnia of war games in which the white of day melts into the black of night and, when all is said and done, they end up inhabiting that timeless and space-less gray that is the unmistakable and mistaken color of paranoia.

This particular end-of-world scenario takes place in the final and hottest days of a Cold War that has gone on past its thaw date. The Wall hasn't come down and now there won't be time for it to come down and in the White House a man sighs and sweats and descends into the depths of a bunker where other men await him with tense faces and perfectly ironed uniforms and an acute agitation that they barely conceal under grave voices. Screens and files with seals that read TOP SECRET and so much information. American satellites have stopped broadcasting and are now—wounded and fallen—classified as missing in action. Satellites with supposedly clever names like OLD BLUE EYES or SPACEY LOOK or STAR STRUCK. Then, details and movements of Russian satellites that, all of a sudden, seem to have taken over the frequencies of the MIA satellites, coloring the white noise with inverted and Cyrillic letters. Satellites named VODKA or MISKIN or TOVARICH. And the concise summary of everything that's been happening, assimilated by the president like a movie projected in fast forward, with the supposedly fun but oh so sad rhythm of vertiginous, silent slapstick. Like one of those short films where everyone falls down and gets up and does it again just for the pleasure of running into another wall, into another cake that comes flying into their smiles.

And so, the fall of Afghanistan, the homemade atomic bomb blowing up in a Beirut apartment, the fundamentalist groups howling that Allah is great and fighting to earn the reward of heavenly virgins (because there can't be *that* many virgins up there), India attacking Pakistan and Pakistan counterattacking and the sky furrowed with nuclear contrails and those red and violet sunsets so similar to the sunsets of another planet, to the colors of certain paintings.

Then, Iran launches Soviet- and American-made missiles at Iraq—or was it the other way around?—while Africa devolves into machete-blow border wars and the ground is strewn with arms and legs and heads.

Meanwhile, a group of Mexican narcotraffickers under the command of Moises Mantra, having invested a great deal of their earnings in high caliber weapons, amid blood and fire cross the border at El Paso, resolved to retake the Promised Land of Texas and California.

And an American pilot aboard a bomber decides the voice that he's been hearing in his head for weeks—and that the pills don't silence—is the voice of God telling him that he is the Avatar of the Last Days, and he fires on a flotilla of Russian submarines docked in the port of La Guayra, Venezuela. Several large Caribbean cruise ships disappear en route to Miami and fail to respond to calls and no one even considers the whole Bermuda Triangle thing anymore and confirmation comes in that, near Curaçao, wreckage belonging to the

S. S. Sunflower has been spotted. On the round conference table the lights blink and the dates extend across the screen, and the president recalls his youth, his days of training to be an astronaut, the first time he looked down, from the surface of the Moon, at the face of this planet, ready to fall out of orbit, to be forever and irrevocably altered. The president wonders why it has fallen on him, he says to himself that maybe it would have been better not to survive the two assassination attempts, and in the end he convinces himself that there's no turning back now. All he wants is to put an end to all of it. To rest. To rest in peace. The president breaks the seal of a metal folder and reads and types numbers and letters into a computer. Then he presses ENTER and shuts his eyes and, in a low voice, recites the prayer of a countdown.

Happy?

Had enough?

Having fun?

Want some more?

But in the episode that repeats now—so that nobody *sees* it but me, my memory like an immense vault or archive where everything that happened is stored, so that what might have happened does not happen—we depart and travel and arrive to Sad Songs.

To one of those shiny-new residential neighborhoods in the suburbs of a big city.

All the houses are new and impeccable and virtually identical. And all that distinguishes one from the next are the different last names on the mailboxes, the kinds of toys on the front lawn, the various plant and flower species, the styles of furniture in the living and dining rooms visible from the street, the many breeds and models of dogs and automobiles.

We pull up and the moving truck is already parked in front of our new home and the movers are removing boxes and carrying them into the house through the kitchen door.

I go inside and light a cigarette and look out the window. More than lighting the cigarette, I burn the cigarette: I fully submerge it in the lighter's flame, which consumes half of it before dwindling to a little ember. I smoke it in a couple deep drags. For a while now, I've been smoking cigarettes the way I take shots of whiskey. Sucking them down in one or two swallows, mouth wide open, like a swimmer who, all of a sudden, decides to drown.

My husband doesn't like to see me drink.

He doesn't like to see me smoke either.

And yet—apart from the minor detail of being convinced that his wife is completely and totally and absolutely mad—my husband still likes to see me. I don't think it has anything to do with love.

At least not anymore.

No, my husband looks at me like a trophy won on the most unforgettable day of his life. A day that will probably never come again. But, luckily, he's got the trophy there to prove that it happened.

The trophy like an unnecessary reminder of something unforgettable but, at the same time, like an object that is indispensable when it comes to convincing incredulous second and third parties, all those people who come up and talk to him at social events and business meetings.

And, yes, I already perceive them preparing the invasion, peering over the fences and hedges of neighboring houses: looking out to see who the new neighbors are, whether they have kids, whether they make more money or have more expensive jewelry, whether their bomb shelter is equipped with more and better conveniences.

Here they come, they'll be here soon.

Welcoming us with dishes of food wrapped in tinfoil, inviting us to the dance on Saturday at the social club, asking me if I want to join the church choir or to take riding lessons or to participate in reading groups or to tell them what my secret for staying so young is or . . . The rites of the natives who are actually colonists; because none of them were born here, because until recently there was nothing here but hills and forests and wild animals—deer and wild boars—that, every so often, approach trash cans in search of food and get caught in the headlights of a car that, drunk, is coming home after a party where V went up to the children's room to kiss W in secret (the children will tell their parents—moving in the slow motion of a hangover—this the next morning at breakfast, their parents will yell at them that they dreamed the whole thing), X unexpectedly burst into tears, Y got naked and jumped in the pool, and Z started shrieking that it was time to drop The Bomb "over there and there and there too."

The unmistakable sensation of being on another planet.

The sensation that's been with me almost all my life and will accompany me throughout eternity.

Now, here, it's the early 60s.

My favorite time period.

I live all times at the same time; but this is my favorite, the one I tune in most often, the time where I feel most comfortable when it comes to talking about my life, my lives.

The period when everything becomes slightly more tolerable for me, and there are times when I'm almost sure I hear, in the background, the laugh track of the watchers watching me from afar.

But now they're all gone, almost all gone.

And yet I can't stop acting and transmitting.

Like right now, here again, coming back, toward the end of 1962.

I hear my husband's voice telling one of the men to "be careful; that's a very fragile device." I think that he's referring to me, but no: the man—I decide his name is Kowalski—is carrying, as if it were a huge, overweight infant, our television in his arms. He sets it on top of a little table, plugs it in, and turns it on. The image isn't good, but there's not much to see: a man holds a few papers and looks at the camera and says that no agreement has yet been reached with the Russian Premier Nikita Khrushchev regarding the missiles in Cuba and the turning back of the soviet ships, which are still advancing toward the port of Havana. "The situation is more and more tense," says the news anchor, who anticipates that "in a few hours President Kennedy will address the nation and . . ."

It never fails, the same thing always happens: someone just has to say the word *Kennedy* for me to see, vividly, far clearer than on television, his head blown to bits, a few months later, on a September day in Dallas. The problem is that someone is always saying *Kennedy*, and the image of his head bursting apart always gives me an explosive headache. And I don't have any problem with the name Kennedy. I never forget it. Now that I think of it, I tend not to forget names that start with the letter K. Kennedy, Kowalski . . .

And there are even days—days when I'm particularly receptive— that I can see his brother shot down too, not long after, and his son falling from the sky so many years later.

The man who plugged in and turned on the device looks up at me and looks back at the screen and looks at me again. "Welcome to the end of the world," he says.

And I smile.

Later, maybe, it's one of many possibilities, it depends on me, on my desire to modify History (I'm alone, a camera with almost nobody on the other side watching what I record, I can move around and focus on whatever I like, I'm the last and the only one still functioning, the rest shut down when their operators shut down), that stranger and I will go down into the basement without my husband noticing and he'll make love to me, or something like that; I don't think that is really making love, maybe unmaking it. In any case, a sudden and fatal cancer that begins right here—the expansive wave of my orgasm—will erase that man's satisfied smile within a couple months.

And I smile back at him because I think he's welcoming me to this end of the world known as Sad Songs and, no, better not to go down into the basement with him, poor guy.

Then, two men enter the house carrying the painting. I don't see them, they carry the painting and are hidden by the painting. I just see their legs poking out beneath the frame.

I see the painting.

The painting is one of those paintings that, every time it enters a room—or every time you enter a room where that painting is—you can't help but look at.

Look at it.

The painting is called *Yellow and Blue (Yellow, Blue on Orange)* and it's dated 1955 and its painter is Mark Rothko.

The painting is precisely that: what its title says.

And so that's why I say (it was as if I'd called to it and it'd obeyed from the first day I saw it) *called* and not *titled*.

Because the painting is yellow and blue.

And yellow and blue on orange.

Some catalogues—in some of the many dimensional wrinkles—claim that the painting hangs in the Carnegie Museum of Art in the city of Pittsburgh and that it was acquired with funds from the Fellows Fund, the Women's Committee, the Acquisition Fund, and the Patrons Art Fund in 1974.

But no.

Here and now it hangs in my house, in Sad Songs, in the early 60s.

And I stare at it.

I haven't been able to stop staring at it since I saw it for the first time.

I saw the Mark Rothko painting for the first time in a gallery in Manhattan.

On Park Avenue, I think.

I'm not sure of the exact place.

I don't remember the date either, but it doesn't matter.

Dates don't matter anymore.

Dates are the first thing forgotten or ignored where I find myself now.

Now, time has become something else.

Time—all time—is all times at the same time.

Time is matter and material out of which I extract multiple variations and use the one that suits me best as I continue my search, as I try over and over to replay my favorite episode.

There are no limits; there is no control.

Now—like I said—I'm alone.

And, for that reason, I can live anything I want. The most unimaginable possibilities. Not what could have happened but what could *never* have happened. Ways to kill time while I keep trying to go back and bring them back—myself and the two of them, together again—to that night.

To hang that night on the wall like my favorite painting.

So that everyone sees it.

And to make it so that night never ends, so it never goes off air, living and surviving, forever, together in the eternity of those few hours.

It's not easy.

Sometimes it seems that I'm about to make it happen.

Sometimes I'm able to reunite them somewhere else, in some other moment.

But the magic—the illusion—doesn't last.

Reality—though, like time, reality doesn't matter one bit—ruins everything. Reality resists modification.

It's not easy to rewrite the past without the help of my operators. And my operators are gone. The one for whom I work is still there, on the other side. Sometimes I can even hear the echo of his slow and heavy breathing; but he barely pays any attention to me now.

He doesn't watch me watching anymore.

So the variables are unstable, suddenly, there are issues with the signal, impossible to keep the two of them aloft and everything vanishes into thin air.

And something happens. Something takes them away long before I can put myself into the scene.

Sometimes I manage—for a few seconds—to see them separately. And for them to see me.

And the truth is that I don't really like how they look at me in those moments: they see me but don't believe in me, they look at me thinking "I can't be seeing what I'm seeing right now."

They look at me and think the exact same thing I thought when I saw the Mark Rothko painting for the first time.

"I can't be seeing what I'm seeing right now," I thought when I saw the Mark Rothko painting in the gallery window.

And I went into the art gallery and there were more Mark Rothko paintings. And there were several people looking at them and smoking and, yes, those were the days when you were still permitted to smoke in public and private spaces.

And the paintings all depicted—with variations in color, going from blazes of light to glimmers of near absolute darkness—landscapes I had already seen, that I couldn't stop seeing.

The eternal twilight of another planet that—for reasons of convenience—I have christened Urkh 24 or, if you like, That-Place-Where-The-Most-Disconsolate-Melodies-Can-Be-Heard.

The planet from where they watch me so that I make them see.

Central studios or something like that.

The place where a science-fiction novel called *Evasion* takes place.

A fiction of the *based on real events* variety.

Real events as the basis for small fictions that, every so often, I insert into what was, the way you thread pearls on a necklace or affix diamonds to the hilt of a sword.

In one of these variations, I see the Mark Rothko painting and read an interview with Mark Rothko where he talks about the "lights that come to me from very far away" and "divine visions" and "ecstasies" and "multiforms" and "breaths of life in blocks of color" and "look at the paintings from only a half meter away to feel as if they envelope you, like a landscape." And I understand—though he doesn't know it the way I know it, the privilege of being the last one left—that Mark Rothko is just like me. That he doesn't entirely understand what happens to him and what it is that makes him, again and again, paint those colors that are skies, the skies of Urkh 24, of That-Place-Where-The-Most-Disconsolate-Melodies-Can-Be-Heard. Interplanetary postcards digging their fingernails into his brain, ever more exhausted from painting such bright colors on such huge canvases where, little by little, night starts to fall and it begins to get dark.

And, so, I'm the one who opens the door to his studio one night—I'm there to explain to him what's happening to him, I'm there to tell him everything—and I find Mark Rothko's body, a still-fresh suicide, both arms cut by the blade of a razor. Everything is red, red is the color and painters are lousy transmitters, they can't cope well with the bombardment of colors. It happened to that other painter who cut off one ear (I'm no good with painters' names) and it happened to Mark Rothko (the only painter's name I'm sure of).

Writers are better. They suffer imbalances too. Like Zack (Or was it Dick?) or Nostradamus (Or was it Stradivarius?) or so many others who traded ink for liquor to try to sedate everything that happens inside their heads, which, though they don't know it, actually happens somewhere else. And yet, writers last longer than painters.

But no—me in Mark Rothko's studio, on 69th Street, I think, in New York, in an old garage with a cupola and, in its center, a skylight that could be opened with pulleys—that is *not* what happened.

That's just a sketch—a sketch for a never-painted painting—of something that could've been but that I break and toss into the fireplace.

What *did* happen is that I saw that painting and I knew for sure that I wasn't alone, that I wasn't unique (though it's possible that I have been unique as far as my endurance and ability are concerned), and I asked the gallery employee's permission and phoned my husband. My wealthy husband—I never call him *Jeff*, which is what he wants to be called, what he wants me to call him—and I said: "Jefferson Franklin Washington Darlingskill, I already know what I want you to give me for our next anniversary."

And I kept looking at that painting with the same eyes that—years later, barely a second for me, a blink—I look again . . .

. . . and see Isaac Goldman, looking at me. And he and I are the only two people not looking up, at the towers in flames and the people throwing themselves into the void and falling all around us, on that corner of a city called Manhattan, on September 11ᵗʰ, 2001.

Another end of the world.

This is, really, the beginning of an end more than an end itself.

This is what puts in drive the heavy and slow machinery of this Apocalypse.

A—yes, now yes—Big Bang that everyone hears and sees far and wide on television broadcasts across the planet. Red-hot antennas—antennas different from the kind of antenna that I am—and there he is: Isaac Goldman looks at me unable to believe that it's me and I look at him with the eyes of someone who believes in too many things. With the eyes of someone who, from so much believing, no longer even needs to activate that verb: *to believe.*

I look at him and he looks at me and we look at each other. We're frozen in each other's eyes. He more than I, because it's been so long since he's seen me. Everything seems to have stopped for us.

Klaatu barada nikto.

Ha ha ha.

I look at him and contemplate that street corner where everyone is screaming screams that have lost all will to be words and are nothing but noise. The voices have become something purely animal. The sound of horror leaping from mouth to mouth and lending potency and identity to all those who fall from the heights of the two white buildings where the red brushstrokes of flames burst forth. Soon, they will fall. The towers. First one and then the other—taking turns bowing, as if dancing a final minuet—and nobody dares think about that now. They can't even imagine it.

But I saw it.

I saw it already.

I've seen so many things . . .

I've seen this street corner before and I'll see it again.

I see it *right now* before and during and after.

Past and present and future all at the same time, like three television shows broadcasting simultaneously, in a single timeslot, twenty-four hours a day, nonstop.

I, right now, am standing here.

I was here before.

I will be here.

I was and am here, one morning many years ago, and I will still be here when everyone is gone.

I'll see the empty streets fade away.

I'll feel in the soles of my feet the exact instant when the power plants cease to function. The moment when their security systems no longer detect the human presence that keeps them running.

I'll breathe the radiation-scented air that'll contaminate the radiating plants that are abandoned but that—at the last glorious second, a mere seven days without having someone to tend to and water and cool their nucleuses—will open like fragrant venomous flowers.

I'll perceive how the water levels in Manhattan basements will rise and how the legendary albino alligators will swim up from the sewers to take over, now phosphorescent and atomic, the subway's flooded tunnels and stations.

I'll breathe in the seeds of plants and trees traveling on the wind to plant themselves in the cracks in the pavement and the concrete that—with the running and crawling of the seasons—will be covered by the shadows of fantastical elms, by the branches of trees pushing through walls and tangling in horizontal jungles.

I'll hear the final moans of so many buildings saying "this is as far as I go" and "no more" and "what's the point of going on like this, empty?"

I'll see the skyscrapers on their knees, the gargoyles on their cornices sinking their claws into the pavement of broken streets where wild animals run with no respect for blinded stoplights and speed limits.

I'll perceive the satisfied delight of that artificial hole, of that invisible and concave ruin that—finally, after so many negotiations and models and advances and retreats—nobody will dare to fill with anything. And, so, nothing but water and mud and plants with thick and serrated leaves and at last reaching the category of crater and almost-natural wonder. And I wonder if, with time, I might not build myself a home there and live as the last specimen of the species . . . Or maybe it would be better, a few millennia from now, to install myself in one of the displays of the Museum of Natural History. And put myself on exhibit for the nothingness.

I'll feel the quivering and impressionistic multiplication of abstract larvae and figurative insects nesting in works of art and I'll witness the collapse of once-modern museums that'll have attained the paradoxical condition of being antiquities themselves.

I'll record the fall of those mausoleums of memory, sinking into their own basements, in the same way that I now record the fall of the towers under a sky empty of eagles and falcons, of all those birds that one day will reign here again, nesting in the collapsed girders of bridges that nobody will cross anymore.

There's nothing sadder than a bridge that's there, suspended, leading nowhere.

And I am a bridge.

Come on over to this side and consider yourselves welcome to the beginning of the end of my world.

A sad beginning that—if all goes well—will function as the eternal and invulnerable bridge to the happiest of endings.

But it's well known that the right and the privilege of a happy ending require, beforehand, in general, certain explanations.

And some bridges require a toll before we're allowed to cross them.

And the explanations that precede happy endings tend to be unhappy explanations and, sometimes, the impulse to cross a bridge just to throw ourselves off the middle.

I'll take the risk, try to resist that impulse.

It won't be the first time.

It won't be the last.

There we go.

There I am, there I'll remain, there she is.

A strange girl whose parents regard her strangely.

A girl who doesn't really understand what's happening to her, but who does understand that the thing she doesn't understand happens only to her.

Sudden trances, recurrent dreams in which she gets in and out of swimming pools and each swimming pool is a world unto itself and there are so many swimming pools in the world. Migraines like earthquakes where everything seems to burn with strange colors that don't figure in the pages of the books that teach the names of normal colors. These strange colors—these *other* colors—have no name, they don't answer when you call because you don't know what to call them.

And yet, that strange girl attempts to explain them and get them out of her head in order to put them on a page in a combination of colors that everybody knows.

She can't.

There's no way.

They don't come out of her.

The strange colors stay inside her and scream her awake in the night and the strange girl wakes up screaming, eyes rolling and speaking in tongues.

One night the house goes up in flames and the investigators say that it was arson and the strange girl's parents look at the strange girl in an even stranger way than before.

One day the strange girl goes out walking without any clothes on.

One afternoon the strange girl neglects her normal little brother and he almost drowns in the bathtub.

Medications and treatments and electric currents and "natural remedies" at houses in the outskirts of the city, and the strange girl gets even stranger, almost stranger than all the strange colors.

And the strange girl turns into a strange adolescent.

It doesn't matter that, in addition to being strange, she's the most beautiful young woman many people have ever seen. The word has gotten out and nobody dares ask her to dances, let alone court her. "Damaged goods," someone says. And the hate of the other girls, the normal girls, the girls who take comfort in their shared ugliness or their own graceless charms and say that only someone truly crazy could be that beautiful.

The strange young woman who, at parties, removes her shoes and sits on the edges of swimming pools and, sometimes, jumps in with all her clothes on and from that point on is known as "the girl who fell in the pool that one night," because nobody can believe that she jumped in on purpose, because they'd rather think that she tripped, that she was drunk.

The strange young woman becomes the one who doesn't dance at dances and the one who lets herself be groped in the bushes by boys who, in the shadows, suddenly shy, recoil in fear, impotent confronted by her smile and naked beauty.

The strange young woman discovers that orgasms (like alcohol) calm, for a while, all those colors blazing in her head and so she becomes a serial masturbator. If the orgasm is a little death, then each of those orgasms is like a little suicide; and the strange young woman commits suicide so many times a day that before long she doesn't even have to touch herself to die.

And, all the time, from when she gets up until she goes to bed so she can keep on committing suicide, the strange young woman thinks that maybe the best thing would be to experience a great death.

To go.

To not be strange anymore because—therein lies its greatness, it makes all of us small—death normalizes everyone.

And, maybe like that, dead, everyone'll finally love her.

The strange young woman was me, and before long I realize that, if I'm going to commit suicide, a small death won't do. No, I want a great death, suicide on a grand scale.

So I decide to do my research and I go to the library and—coincidences do not exist, but we believe in them to keep from going mad when we learn that everything is connected to everything, so we don't realize that there are organisms whose sole function in the universe is the serial production of earthly coincidences—a book someone left out on a table catches my eye.

A title that could be the title of the story of my life: *The Colors That Come From Space*. Its author is Phineas Elsinore Darlingskill. Or, at least, that's the name of the writer and title of the book that I transmit now. I've never heard anyone mention him. I start reading and I don't stop until I get to the end. The novel—a short novel—tells the story of a family driven mad by beings that arrive through a tear in the fabric of the universe. The book is written in a pompous and precious style, overflowing with adjectives. But—and this is what interests me most—it's written by someone who seems to believe in what they're writing, by someone who, at the same time, seems a prisoner of fevers and visions like mine.

A few inquiries put me on Darlingskill's trail and it's easy for me to join his circle of acolytes. The doors of his mansion a couple hours outside New York are always open. They are somewhat absurd individuals. People even lonelier than me, because they're alone for reasons far more banal than mine: they're alone because they don't dare let themselves feel accompanied, they don't feel confident they can bear such responsibility. For that reason, they prefer to dress up in absurd uniforms, shave their heads "like Ancient Egyptian priests," burn scented powders, execute childish magical waves of their hands, and convince themselves of anything to the point of autohypnosis.

It wouldn't make much sense to go in-depth here regarding my conversations with Darlingskill. It would be like transcribing the fantastical conversation between a cat and a lioness. We belong to the same race, yes, but we are so different: Darlingskill envies my colors and I envy his envy, because it's the envy of someone with the genius to imagine—with no need to suffer—what I experience perfectly.

For Darlingskill, I am like a saint. A virgin. A vestal. One of those sibyls in labyrinthine caves, sitting inside a golden cage, awaiting the trembling questions of Caesars and emperors. My chromatic hallucinations are my stigmas and, in a way, for Darlingskill, the definitive proof that his imagined cosmogony might have about it a glimmer of reality and, so, he feels he's been elevated from more or less popular novelist to singular prophet and distinguished oracle. The proud host who will help open the door to a new age. A kind of guide of mystic tourism.

Darlingskill explains to me that, most likely, I am a bridge to another universe, that I've been chosen to bring visions from one world to another, that sooner or later the true meaning of my visions will be revealed to me, my mission communicated.

And, of course, Darlingskill is a complete crackpot, but this time, for once, he is right.

But Phineas Elsinore Darlingskill doesn't have long left in "this thankless dimension." Darlingskill falls ill, his family comes to collect him and take him back to Manhattan. He's hospitalized with no hope of being discharged and he dies a few days later, the night I meet Isaac Goldman and Ezra Leventhal and Jefferson Franklin Washington Darlingskill.

And, ah, I find that I like this almost telegraphic summary—dry, concise, without frills—of my oh so distant past.

I like that my strange story can be told in a simple and functional language, like that of someone reporting her activities with just the right words, not wasting any time, because soon she'll have to return to the battlefront.

I recount all of this in the language of science fiction: a style simple by mandate, because it knows it must convince people of complex ideas, believable words for unbelievable situations.

Now, like then, this way of expressing myself calms and relaxes me like, in a way, it relieved me back then to be surrounded by all those aspiring writers discussing with naïve solemnity things far more delirious than my own deliriums.

And I could, yes, try to explain the intensity of the love that I felt for Isaac Goldman and Ezra Leventhal.

But it would be in vain.

Certain nerve endings, certain emotional circuits no longer function.

Material fatigue.

Isaac was right when he said that science fiction and love never went well together. Or maybe they do: because in one way or another we're all abducted by love, by that extraterrestrial and always different force whose language we try, in vain, to understand. But that's not all. Love—that benign tumor, but tumor nonetheless—was cut out of me a long time ago, that night when I changed forever, when I became what I am now.

So don't expect passionate words from me, unbridled emotions, descriptions of bodies on top of bodies.

Instead, it would be much easier for me to offer you a detailed portrait of what was done and what was said in those meetings of young fans of the still-young world of science fiction. I could, even, briefly illuminate you regarding the almost visible sexual currents that ran through those environs, contaminated by the smoke of first cigarettes and the fizz of soft drinks, where real women were the occasional girlfriends and imagined women were innocent lunar damsels or mercurial Amazonian princesses or dedicated laboratory assistants (whose primary function was to scream or be taken prisoner so the hero could rescue them) or naughty little sisters with short hair and rude manners who later turned into almost-incestuous beauties.

I could, also, attempt to chronicle the temperamental doctrinarian and aesthetic crises and to create an explanatory diagram of the glut of political factions in which—postulating different possibilities regarding how and by whom other planets should be colonized—the ideological differences and persecutions of the coming decades would ferment.

But I can't say anything about what I felt when I was with Isaac and Ezra, because long ago I resolved not to feel anything about it. To feel it would be to distract myself from my ultimate goal, to lose myself in the past instead of concentrating on the future. To remember that love would endanger my aspirations to make it immortal.

So how to go about telling this story without pausing too long on them, without staying with them forever.

The answer is easy: Jefferson Franklin Washington Darlingskill.

Much later, on this side of things, one autumn morning, I will find my dead husband, stretched out across the floor of our house in Sad Songs. Face down, one arm outstretched and one leg bent upward, as if he were a swimmer run aground. I won't feel sorrow, but I will feel pity for that miserable man, who loved me desperately for so many years, convinced that his was an unrequited love. Someone whose only oddity—the only aftertaste of what he could've been, something like those useless appendages that remain almost hidden, just hinting at another direction a particular organism might have evolved in—will be that of swallowing too many uppers and complex vitamins in order to make it to the end of the century when "it'll be possible to transplant a man's essence into a machine and thereby allow him to live forever."

He'll tell it to me everyday (yellow pill and blue pill and yellow and blue and orange) for years. And I won't say anything. I'll just look at him in silence, the way you look at something unimportant yet interesting.

I can see myself: I look at the Jefferson Franklin Washington Darlingskill that is and I think of the Jefferson Franklin Washington Darlingskill that could have been.

I think—my mission, the mission that his uncle could never have imagined, the mission that I carried out with great success, the efficient neutralization of one of many possible ends of the world—of the Jefferson Franklin Washington Darlingskill that never was.

Jefferson Franklin Washington Darlingskill ceased to be who he could've been on the same night that I became who I am now.

Jefferson Franklin Washington Darlingskill asks to speak in what is the largest meeting of science fictions fans to date. The Futurians, The Cosmics, The Futuristics, The Dimensionals, The Astronomicos, The Futurexicos, and The Faraways Isaac Goldman and Ezra Leventhal who, from a corner of the school gymnasium, watch Jefferson Franklin Washington Darlingskill with embarrassed resignation.

Everyone is there.

And there I am.

I, who have become an unsettling presence for the science fiction fans. "What's a girl like that doing here? What does she want with us? What can we do to make her never leave and get her to look at us?" they all seem to be asking themselves.

I can't provide the answer to those questions because it's one of those answers that would just provoke more questions.

I'm there because I have nowhere else to be.

I'm there, bombarded by inexplicable colors, by sudden explosions of yellow and blue (and yellow and blue on orange). There's a Mark Rothko painting inside my head. A Mark Rothko who doesn't paint like the Mark Rothko of that time, dedicated only to small figurative and slightly surrealist paintings.

I am there because, not finding an explanation for what's happening to me anywhere—my parents have filed me in front of successive specialists who classify me with different shapes and sizes of psychosis, like those stickers stuck on the sides of travel trunks—it soothes me a little to hear those young men proposing and imagining variations of the future with the true passion of early Christians. My parents don't complain much about my new activities. They don't really like it that I associate with people like Isaac Goldman and Ezra Leventhal (my parents are Jews from the city's upper class), but they fantasize that "something happens" with Jefferson Franklin Washington Darlingskill: an excellent match who might, perhaps, domesticate their lunatic daughter and transform her into a respectable society lady in whom any oddity will be quickly rewritten and understood as an admirable exotic feature.

And my parents—may they rest in peace—will see all their fantasies come true, like everything related to their daughter, for all the wrong reasons. But it's well known that it's impolite to ask for too many explanations about wishes granted.

So that's where everything begins.

Jefferson Franklin Washington Darlingskill asks to speak in the name of The Faraways (Isaac and Ezra look at the floor, embarrassed, as if searching for something they dropped but dare not pick up) and pulls out a pile of carefully typeset pages from his inside jacket pocket and starts to read.

And what Jefferson Franklin Washington Darlingskill reads— which starts off as a kind of elegy to his uncle Phineas Elsinore Darlingskill—takes a quick detour into something that sounds very much like a messianic delirium. The coded autobiography, barely dressed up as fiction, of a shy and tormented boy who, really, is convinced that he's a superior being destined to rule the universe.

First there are a few scattered chuckles, but, then, the gym fills with bursts of laughter and boos and shouts demanding the expulsion of the speaker. Someone yells that he's a racist. Someone else accuses him, simply, of being "fat and worthless." Jefferson Franklin

Washington Darlingskill starts to stammer and get red in the face and his eyes fill with tears. Isaac and Ezra take him by the arms and lead him away, almost dragging him, and it's then that, from the door, Jefferson Franklin Washington Darlingskill screams: "You'll see! You'll see! Laugh now but soon you'll be begging for mercy. Who wants to write little stories when you can start a religion? Who wants to be a writer when you can be God?"

Then it happens.

Then: all the colors at the same time.

Then—I can't know it then, but I'll never menstruate again or bleed in any way, all bacteria and viruses will die upon entering my organism, from that moment on, it's not that I become immortal, but, yes unbreakable, my blood could be used to produce a vaccine for all the ills of this world, but no one ever asked me for it—it's as if I were struck by a lightning bolt. It's as if I dove into the sea, riding an animal that held the whole world in its jaws. A wild but not exactly fierce animal. An animal whose dangerousness—whose degree of mortal threat—was a direct consequence of the audacity or lack of awareness of the person who risked putting his hand between its fangs. I wanted to grip the hide of its currents, to let go, to sink, to be devoured and drown and decompose slowly until I was reincarnated as one of its waves.

And only then learn to swim.

And I faint.

And I regain consciousness.

And then I turn on.

Then—after so many sporadic tests, brief rehearsals, episodes that the neurologists and psychiatrists of my planet couldn't explain—I start transmitting.

I've been activated.

The next morning I show up at Jefferson Franklin Washington Darlingskill's house and ask him to marry me.

I tell him I've realized that I love him, that last night I understood his greatness, that I can't live without him.

And like that—obeying instructions—I transform myself into a secret and nameless heroine, into the strange young woman who has prevented one of the many ends of the world and, along the way, into the little Jewish girl who wrote the Bible.

And the name of the Bible is *Evasion*.

And the time has come to try and offer some explanations. It's not going to be easy, there won't be any of that much-appreciated final and clinical cleanness of certain detective mysteries here. There won't be anything resembling those enigmas solved by a somewhat absurd detective who gathers all the suspects together in a train car or a library to explain to them step by step and second by second, what it was they did or didn't do. And the guilty, there all along, with a cold smile and a warm cup in hand, waiting, polite and chivalrous, the moment of the accusation, knowing that we'll never witness the moment of his arrest or entrance into the jail or his exit through the door where convicted bodies are sent, because these things aren't shown, it's not proper.

This won't be the case here.

Interplanetary plots aren't endowed with the dubious structure of terrestrial plots, even though they also take place in hermetic environments, in pressurized chambers, in rooms always sealed from inside.

There are too many factors to attend to, sudden atmospheric shifts, mechanical flaws, different cultures, suns that don't necessarily illuminate and cast light across the surface where the corpus delicti lies or where the weightless bodies of those who live to tell the tale walk oh so slowly and, befuddled, discover that they never really know what happened, much less the best way to explain the inexplicable.

Isaac Goldman and Ezra Leventhal can't comprehend what's happened, how I could have left them behind, and—they read about it in the society pages of the *New York Times*—why I'm going to marry Jefferson Franklin Washington Darlingskill in what's already being considered "next spring's big wedding."

So, the night of the winter's final snowstorm, they come to my house and they work all night.

Men of snow and a whole snow planet.

A planet that includes all three of us and excludes the confusion of my sudden rejection of their love, and I watch them from my window without being able to say anything to them. Without explaining to them that it's been decided—very far away, so nearby—that Isaac's sadness and Ezra's fury will be far less complicated for our world than the hate of Jefferson Franklin Washington Darlingskill.

That's where I come in.

And here I am to give explanations, closer to a victim than a detective, and so aware that, strictly speaking, the parameters of detective fiction, as I've already noted, don't apply here, nothing is resolved, no guilty party is found guilty.

Which is maybe why, I decide, it's better not to aim for the clarity of a closed ending, but to repeat, again and again, so that even the children understand, that simple magical line: the key that opens the lock of all the fairytales.

Once upon a time . . .

Once upon a time there were two young men named Isaac Goldman and Ezra Leventhal and I think I've already told you too much about them.

You've already watched them and listened to them.

You've already seen and heard the things I make them do, the words I make them say.

Once upon a time there was a young man named Jefferson Franklin Washington Darlingskill who one night, many years ago, is humiliated in public (everyone laughs at him, Isaac and Ezra and I laugh at him too), at a meeting of science-fiction fans, and he leaves swearing that he'll have his revenge. He leaves an insulted mortal and promises to return a vengeful deity.

And he's true to his word.

Somewhere else, in another corridor of a reality that never was, there is a great deal of bibliography and documentaries about his life and work. But none of those books or films would be able to cover the final chapter of his life because there was no time to write it or film it. The final chapter of Jefferson Franklin Washington Darlingskill's life would also be the final chapter of all our lives.

Jefferson Franklin Washington Darlingskill leaves the meeting and—by means of a generous bribe—manages to get the essay he was unable to finish reading that night published, not as fiction but as nonfiction, in the pages of *Tantalizing Episodes*. It's the first of several writings that proclaim the good and strange news of a system that puts him at its heart and makes him the master of a "Supreme Power," a power that he alone can teach, to all those who bow before his greatness and proclaim themselves his humble and devout disciples. There are many members of the sci-fi community who write off the whole thing as "a demented revision of Freud." But there are many others who begin to pay attention to and believe in Jefferson Franklin Washington Darlingskill and his teachings, which combine faith in the terrestrial superman as vehicle to attain the power of the stars and the ability to create and destroy entire universes, provided that you ask his permission and get his blessing first.

Jefferson Franklin Washington Darlingskill collects his writings in a book (whose dedication reads "For those who laughed at me: I'll be the one laughing soon") that becomes a best-seller (few things are more attractive than a book written by a lunatic), and soon indoctrination centers sprout up all over the world. Sanctuaries that impart his methods and teachings and technologies and submit new members to absurd initiation rites that they rarely ever discuss, because they're forced to take vows of absolute silence, because the rest of the vulgar mortals have no cause to participate in the "Great Secret." There are, yes, rumors of machines that only function via psychic powers, of regressions in time, of complex hierarchies and rankings that go up to "Maximum Wisdom," which "can't be explained to the uninitiated, because they'd never be able to understand it," and of being one with Jefferson Franklin Washington Darlingskill, who rarely leaves his mansion in the Nevada desert. All of it in exchange for generous donations to the cause. Soon, an array of Hollywood actors join the movement and say they've understood everything with perfect smiles and pupils fixed and dilated from the passion of their love for the "Absolute Master." Soon, in addition, the Cosmic Church of Jefferson Franklin Washington Darlingskill comes under investigation by governmental organizations. But they can't do anything, they don't find anything. And then something terrible happens: the president of the United States survives an assassination attempt in which his wife and daughter die. An aide and member of the Church of Jefferson Franklin Washington Darlingskill puts the president in touch with his master. And there's nothing more fragile and malleable than a man wrecked by pain. The president declares himself "purified" by Jefferson Franklin Washington Darlingskill, whom he names Secretary of State and Advisor of Mystical and Spiritual Matters, and together, one unforgettable summer morning, they press all the buttons and fire all the missiles and bring about the end of our world as we know it.

But none of that happens.

I prevent it.

I am science nonfiction.

I obey orders and, the morning after that night when everyone laughed at him, I run to Jefferson Franklin Washington Darlingskill's house and fall to my knees before him and tell him that I am his, that I've realized I love him.

Jefferson Franklin Washington Darlingskill accepts with delight and, soon, he takes over his father's store, opens various subsidiary branches around the country and becomes an admired businessman.

I become the admired businessman's enviable wife for whom the years seem not to pass. His trophy. His reward. The strange woman who mistreats him with painful delicacy, who will never give him a child, who barely lets him touch her, who drinks too much, and who always refuses to call him Jeff.

The strange woman who now has almost nothing in common with that strange girl and with that strange young woman; because being that strange for that long changes someone. Children are much stronger than we think. By comparison, adults are merely tough. As they get older adults realize that they're not as strong as they once were. So they get tough. Or—like me—they focus all their attention on just one thing. It doesn't matter if that thing is strange because, after all, we live in the Age of Strange Things. What matters is to not think of other things, of other strange things.

And that's all.

Sometimes, Jefferson Franklin Washington Darlingskill—a good man, an oh so sad man—seems to be listening to voices that arrive from remote rooms, in temples that he never got to build, and he talks in his sleep about ceremonies and subjects and secret messages and absolute powers and gods who are waiting for him to call and order them to cross over to this side.

Once upon a time there was a strange young woman who decides not to obey the orders that come to her from somewhere, from so far away, and she scandalizes everyone by going to live with Isaac Goldman *and* Ezra Leventhal.

She loves both of them, they both love her, why choose just one? why can't they both love her? why can't the three of them adopt a single pseudonym and—who is it? where does he or she live? is it a man? is it a woman?—secure their place as the most brilliant and original science fiction writer of all time?

Later, the young woman isn't entirely sure what happens.

Maybe Isaac and Ezra start to hate each other.

Maybe they can't maintain balance and harmony.

Maybe they die on Omaha Beach, Normandy.

Maybe it's a baby that dies and which one of them was that baby's father.

Maybe I die, far away from them, and with time Isaac and Ezra turn into two gray old men, feeding pigeons and playing chess in Washington Square, thinking about me all the time and talking about anything but me, because talking about me hurts.

Maybe . . .

In any case, each and every one of the options that I manage with true difficulty to tune in aren't any good, all of them end badly. A way of warning me that it's better to stay where I am, to not alter the order of the movements that they have established for me from so far away.

Once upon a time there was a planet that—for reasons of narrative functionality—I've given the name Urkh 24 or, if you like, That-Place-Where-The-Most-Disconsolate-Melodies-Can-Be-Heard.

A planet inhabited by superior beings. Beings that have reached the zenith of their evolution, who no longer have anywhere to go, who are so bored of everything being so perfect.

At some point something happens on that planet: a shift in the composition of its "atmospheric nutrients" or something like that. Or a virus. Or, simply, sooner or later what happens to any place where everything functions perfectly, where no one wants for anything.

Entropy.

End of the line.

Then the inhabitants of Urkh 24 or That-Place-Where-The-Most-Disconsolate-Melodies-Can-Be-Heard begin to search for a planet with characteristics similar to their own. A planet where they could take refuge and start over.

Then the inhabitants of Urkh 24 or That-Place-Where-The-Most-Disconsolate-Melodies-Can-Be-Heard discover our planet.

And, over the years, they proceed to pick out human beings to function as antennas, to transmit everything that happens here.

They create a secret species.

Strange men and strange women and that strange young woman I once was and still am.

Every native of Urkh 24 or That-Place-Where-The-Most-Disconsolate-Melodies-Can-Be-Heard—operators or employers or watchers or readers or directors or editors; call them whatever you like—has one at their disposal.

And they care for them.

They keep them from breaking down.

They're so proud of them.

Sometimes they break, commit suicide.

Or end up in a room with padded walls.

Or enter boring monasteries where nothing ever happens.

But there are so many of us . . .

There's always a new model, a new story.

And they start observing us with our own eyes.

Carefully.

All the time.

They can't stop watching us.

We're so entertaining.

And so, hooked, addicted to our stories, they postpone the invasion of Earth.

They don't want to interrupt our activities.

They don't ever want it to end.

Every so often, they help us, save us, correct plot lines, and, manipulating us like stringless puppets, prevent so many ends of the world.

And so, in the end, they forget to initiate that end of the world in which they would be the ultimate and decisive protagonists—charged with uttering the last words in the script.

So they never come.

They stay at home.

Watching us.

The spaceships they've built never lift off and are left atop a mountain and before long become part of the landscape, metal geological formations covered in rust, with branches and roots wrapping all around them.

They're so intent on watching us and saving us that they forget about themselves.

They evade themselves, yes.

And soon, they begin to die.

And so, protecting us from ourselves, they go extinct.

And as they die, the observer they've chosen here—the camera, the antenna, the viewfinder; whatever you like—also dies.

Some of them close up like those demented flowers that only open at night, to give off their scent when almost everyone is asleep.

And—even though I close my sad eyes to not know how it will all end—I like to believe, it's not hard for me to think, they died happy.

Once upon a time there was a native of Urkh 24 or That-Place-Where-The-Most-Disconsolate-Melodies-Can-Be-Heard.

Mine.

Or, better, the one to whom I belong.

The last native of Urkh 24 or That-Place-Where-The-Most-Disconsolate-Melodies-Can-Be-Heard.

The last and true Faraway.

The protagonist of *Evasion*.

He has not died yet.

But it won't be long.

Of course, it is still a great deal of earth time that he has left (and that I have left), but it's not too much for what I want and need to do.

I don't feel that close to him anymore and—I think this is proof of his quiet and drawn-out death—I can see more clearly, from here, the planet from which he watches us. It's not like at some point point, throughout all these years, I have felt him close to me. I never saw him, never heard his voice, which I imagined across so many pages. But I would experience a certain excitement—a characteristic vibration, an intensification of certain tastes and smells and sounds and textures and sights—every time I looked at and transmitted something that, I suppose, gave him a special pleasure.

But not anymore.

Now it's almost as if he weren't there.

Now there's nothing but my perception of something slowly fading away and a ceaseless succession of sunsets.

The days are always different on other planets. The texture and even the shape of the days—their colors and light—change depending on the composition of the air and the look of the clouds and even the mood of the people who inhabit and work them.

The nights, on the other hand, are the same everywhere.

The nights obey the same design and identical style of a single unknown creator.

And yet, the nights—so like the nights on Earth—are what I miss most of my other planet.

That planet where I was born and to which I'll never return, but that travels with me now everywhere I go.

That planet where I never was but always am.

That planet with a sky like a swimming pool, dark and deep. Bottomless. A sky that's this sky—because every sky is *the sky*—but that in a way, through the pure power of distance, is also another sky. A place in which to sink until you reach the bottom.

Illuminated by the diffuse light of that sky—little by little, page by page, without any hurry—I wrote *Evasion*. In cars, on trains, on ferries, in funiculars ascending a mountain, at parties. Portrait of a woman writing. Elsewhere. Never at home. So, in places of perpetual motion, the most motionless book ever written. And so—large envelopes, ordinary stamps, without return address—I made my book-in-transit reach the two of them.

I knew—all the time, at all times—where to find Isaac and Ezra; because it was I who put them wherever they were, I who tried, little by little, to bring them together, without my operator noticing or now, on his way out, without him caring all that much.

Maybe it was his way of repaying me.

Maybe he liked how I wrote.

Who knows.

Evasion was the way to tell Isaac and Ezra that I hadn't forgotten them, that I was with them, that I was still doing everything I could to bring us back together, to keep us together forever, until the end of the world and beyond.

The last end of this world—the ending of its ends—will occur within the next 7,590 million years and it won't be a result of variations or adjustments in the script of its history.

There won't be anyone left to deal with such things.

Or that's what I hope.

I hope I'm not still here, waiting.

I hope that by then my operator has taken his last breath—end of transmission—and that I have achieved my goal long before.

And that at that point I'm enjoying—that being's energy which is, at the same time, the energy that keeps me *functioning*—the just deserts of a deserved and endless rest where even the idea of time will have ceased to exist.

Does the idea of an end even make sense if there's nobody left to verify it as such? if there's nobody there to think or mutter to himself that "ah, everything came to an end, this is as far as we go?"

Yesterday I read—as bombs exploded in a hitherto-peaceful city, and the canals overflowed with the rising tide of an expansive wave, and the fragile *palazzos* sank into the turbid and ancient water—that when all is said and done, this planet will be yanked out of orbit by a red and swollen Sun. And that then it'll plummet in an interminable spiral trajectory, first breaking into pieces and then vanishing in languid sighs of vapor, leaving behind no trace of its existence.

Other specialists in Apocalypse insist that no, that it won't be like that, that what will happen is the Sun will go out with a click, like a door closing for the last time; and then it'll be night, night without day, and a cold for which warmth will be like an impossible legend.

Who knows, who cares, it's all the same.

What's the point of an end if there aren't any witnesses? An end without audience is nothing, it's not an end.

But before this grand finale without audience, another end will take place.

The strange end of the Age of Strange Things.

The end of the species.

The end of the end of this world, *our* world, the how it all ended, the what happened to make everything stop happening.

The end that they could no longer stop or keep from *ending*.

As with all the best endings—with endings that *are true*, with *true* endings—nobody saw it coming, nobody could have predicted it.

No one heard the grave voice of an oracle, there were no ominous signs at the bottom of a coffee cup or among the tarot cards, no scientist predicted that it would happen because—simply and complexly—it happened all at once.

And this was what happened.

So many years of so much invisible electricity energizing the air transformed—one unforgettable winter morning—into a colossal spark that provoked a definitive short circuit in the privileged brains of men and women.

There was a sound like the sound of a book slamming shut, like a slap in the face of humanity.

The sound of cancel your bets and forget that your number might be up.

A sound like an orchestra crashing against the highest place, in the finale of a final song at the end of a record, a day in the life.

A sound like the sky falling from the bottom of the heavens and crashing into the ground.

A sound that, really, ends up being impossible to describe—and so you have to take refuge in imprecise or overly absurd similes—because it's a sound that sounds for the first and last time.

Debut and farewell and bow and curtain.

Many classes of animal—excluding cetaceans and simians—will be saved from the invisible holocaust, thanks to their unsophisticated intellects. For a few seconds—saturated with waves from mobile phones, from television channels, from satellites falling out of orbit, and with accelerated particles—the oxygen burst into flame like a household appliance and entered through lungs and touched hearts and minds and that was that. Across the world, men and women and children and whales and dolphins—suddenly fossilized from inside—collapsed in houses and parks and cars and on beaches and airplanes and boats and in gymnasiums and schools and marine depths, never to rise again.

And slowly they were devoured by the survivors.

I can see them here and now as if I were there, because I will be there, the lone witness, living to tell the tale.

I raise my glass and drink a toast to them and I won't say here the number of the day and year that this thing will happen that causes everything to cease happening.

I'll just say that it won't be long now.

But that, before then, I will endeavor to alter that ending.

Not to *prevent* the end.

I'm not that strong or powerful.

But maybe I can trade it in for, yes, a better ending.

An ending that won't cease to be the end of all the news in this world, but that, if everything goes well, will, at least, be a happy ending.

This is not my last transmission from the planet of the monsters.

But it won't be long now.

And, with the nearness of the end, I understand that this is not a science-fiction story.

It's not a science-fiction story because the only thing this story does is look back, remember, fabricate memories in the memory machine.

No: actually, this is a love story.

It might not be the greatest love story, but it is, yes, without a doubt, the longest love story.

A story of love that—if you put an ear to the cold ground, against the glacial earth, against the pillow next to you where for too many nights no head has rested—is still breathing and waiting for someone to drag it up from the subterranean darkness and bring it back to the surface.

One of those romances that obeys one of the most frequented and feared precepts of the gothic-romance genre, in that barely-futuristic nineteenth century, where the future was nothing more than a nightmare of lunar craters or centers of the Earth or dead creatures resuscitated piece by piece with the aid of lightning bolts: this is a story of love buried prematurely, a story of love buried alive.

And sometimes I wish this story, if it were a book, had more pages.

Many more pages than *Evasion*.

That it had more than a thousand pages.

Three thousand, maybe.

One of those great sagas where, when we come to the end, when we walk through the door of the last page, we find that we know more about its heroes than we do about ourselves, but that, in a way, those heroes are also us.

But *writing long* is like reading, while *writing short* is like writing. And what interested me here—what still interests me, because I haven't finished, because I am nearing the end, because I could touch it with my hand if I wanted, but I don't want to—was to put it in writing; but I'm not exactly a writer nor is all of this is, exactly, writing to be read.

I don't express myself here with the same techniques and tools that many stories are written with.

I express myself not in the primitive calligraphy of human beings, but in the sparkling language, the clairvoyant braille of the stars.

Thus, to lift this story up into the heavens and fix it there, as if hung by nails of light, to be read in the same way the constellations were once read, with the childish naïveté of people who needed to see human forms and figures overhead to not get lost, terrified, in the abstract expressionism of the cosmos.

But long ago I realized that it was too great an ambition, an impossible desire.

So that's why I've chosen—not to settle but to aspire to perfection—to focus on one perfect and all-powerful instant.

On the indivisible nucleus.

On the Big Bang of our story.

There they are.

Isaac Goldman and Ezra Leventhal.

My love for them and their love for me.

It's a winter night and it's that precise instant when the snow stops, after hours and hours of white falling from the black.

Isaac Goldman and Ezra Leventhal are young and bursting with energy and the disciplined sound of their shovels, up and down, in the snow, is the sound of a new and ephemeral music. Notes that don't take long to melt, yes, but that then—in a then that I want now to turn into an always—compose the only possible melody, the rhythm of the working of the universe.

Everything is dark but, from my window, looking out from behind the curtain, I can make out the glow of their smiles and the warmth of the vapor rising from their mouths and the sparkle of their eyes that repudiates even their lids' intermittent interruption.

Isaac Goldman and Ezra Leventhal, splendid and resplendent and united by that rare pleasure of a common cause that they felt before but now know to be an inescapable fate.

And both the one and the other love me so much, at the same time, with the same love, that it wouldn't even matter to them if I chose the one or the other, because they feel that they are unique and united, inseparable.

The one begins where the other ends so that the other has neither beginning nor end.

The one and the other orbit around me, the gravity of my body pulling them and sending them in perfect circles, in timed intervals of light and dark, in precise seasons. And the one and the other know that they're so lucky to love each other and to love me that they don't even really think about the total eclipse of my betrayal, as incomprehensible to them as it was necessary for me, out of love for them and out of love for everything in this world that contains them.

My ambition—like I said—is too great.

I couldn't save a planet because—contrary to that cliché of the genre—someone from another planet cannot save a planet that never was and never will be theirs.

Sure, I was born here, nearby; but I'll die so far away . . .

And, sure, I could've done something, at some point, for the survival of this rare and random race of which I was conceived; but there was nothing I could've done to alter the fate of those who chose me.

And yet, I think, maybe I can allow myself the modest gesture of saving them, the two of them.

Isaac and Ezra.

And so, with what little strength I have left—with the wavering and dwindling energy that still reaches me from my adoptive planet—I begin to tell different ends of the world.

To tell them and to discard them, to turn them off like lamps in an empty house with too many rooms.

To empty my memory and to make room in space.

In that way, inserting slight corrections here and there as I traverse this empty earth, bursting with ruins and antiquities.

To advance and retreat.

To write and delete.

To correct and insert.

Small transcendent modifications in the fabric of History. Some are unwanted (but, like I said, I was always really bad at remembering names, so I renamed many without thinking twice), others are mischievous and poetic ways of administering justice (all those awards my favorite movie never won), and others are unforeseen and secondary outcomes, collateral effects of altering proven facts just for the pleasure of contradicting or improving them.

To force the experiment to bend more toward fiction than science.

To give the future back the grace and excitement it had when any possibility could be projected onto it and to tear away the gray and boring and poorly cut clothes that it always wore in end times. Times when nobody thought about the future anymore, when no one looked up at the sky because all their heads were bent, focusing on their own bodies (mankind, tired of not finding anything or anyone in space, had devoted itself to exploring its own interior space, making aliens of itself, shifting and mutating its own bodies with surgeries and magic remedies and DNA cocktails) or, at best, on the nearby exterior of a blistering and lifeless landscape, whipped by sudden whirlwinds and sand fevers and swollen oceans and wintery summers. Every so often, yes, some incomprehensible best-seller about the incomprehensibility of time, penned by a disabled genius with a mechanical voice, or some kind of televised evangelical sermon about the improbable marvels of the cosmos, delivered by some photogenic astronaut, or some movie featuring a kind but hideous extraterrestrial who only wants to go home, or absurd men with light sabers, made them think about all of that again for exactly as long as it took them to watch the movie or read and discard the book, all of them outside and unaware of the intimate epic of my intent: the secret challenge to recreate a small and private universe.

And I lack the advantage of knowing I'll be done in six days and rest on the seventh.

And it's so much harder to correct something when it didn't turn out right than it is to invent something when you don't know how it will turn out.

To test and discard varying quantities of so many ingredients and elements and maybe then, some day, to find a way to bring them back together as close as they were on that snowy night, under my window.

Isaac Goldman and Ezra Leventhal—who have heard of my problems, of my madness, of my entrances and exits from institutions, of the electricity that's been sent running through my atomized brain—building me a gigantic planet. An enormous snowball. Shoveling and piling and working all night until the sphere is almost as tall as my house and, when they're finished, standing beside it are a legion of perfect men of snow—I'm not talking about the classic snowman assembled from three snowballs, but a multitude of statues—that are always the two of them, there, on their feet, watching over that world that they've offered me and that will infuriate my father and will end up flooding my mother's flowerbeds and taking several days to melt and sparking the neighbors' curiosity and even getting photographed for the front page of the newspaper in that town where some people will come to theorize that such an inexplicable phenomenon and sudden apparition could only be the work of extraterrestrials.

But none of that matters.

All of that happened after.

The important thing is the two of them.

Their love of my love.

The cold air of a night that stretches pleasantly on and on and that—though they don't know it—will condemn them to appear again and again.

Sometimes separate.

Sometimes together.

Sometimes they aren't even there and all I manage is to *evoke* the snow and the men of snow and the planet of snow.

One time that giant snowball appeared at a reception in Buckingham Palace.

One time, the men of snow were formed, in the most frozen of silences, on a beach in Patagonia.

Other times, both of them alone.

The one here and the other there.

Isaac and Ezra.

In mountains and cities, in deserts and jungles.

And even at the bottom of the sea.

Sometimes I manage to bring them together.

But I can't keep them there long. Something happens, a failure in the program. Like I said before: reality or one of many possible realities resists bringing them back together, letting them be in the same place.

And everything comes to an end far too quickly.

And then it starts over again

It doesn't matter.

I don't have all the time in the world, but I do have all the time in the end of the world (sometimes I need a little help, sometimes

I invoke a dreaming soldier or a final insomniac twilight) to pull Ezra Leventhal out of the hell of being Ezra Leventhal and pull Isaac Goldman out of the purgatory of being Isaac Goldman and to bring the two of them to my strange paradise, to the heaven of my consciousness.

And there, at last, make them aware that, after so many failed attempts, they've crossed through the gates of the bottom of the sky, that place where I've been waiting for them for so long.

Like that, again and again, until I achieve the perfect harmony and acoustics of completely returning them to the fullness of that moment. The closest thing to immortality ever felt by someone who knows that time doesn't stop, that it runs and sometimes trips and falls so that it can get back up and run even faster and . . .

Like that, again and again, until the materialization of my memory is perfect, complete, finished, and precise and even better than my always-faithful memory of what happened.

To find a way to bring the broken pieces of the divine light back together, to pull them out of the shadows into which they've fallen, to recreate that perfect night of a day in the life.

A night that lasts forever and, in it, Isaac Goldman and Ezra Leventhal create a world for me.

A world for me to make my own.

A world far beyond that other version of life that is death.

There, the living ghost of electricity whispering in the cold skin stretched across the bones of our craniums. Happy, because, even underneath the sadness of our faces, our skulls ceaseless smile, showing their teeth to that cold warm-hearted sphere that grows and grows and keeps on growing. And that soon will be so big that it'll be seen and applauded by aliens from another planet who, in that moment, will abort any plan for invasion; because they'll know themselves defenseless and inferior in the face of that unfathomable force, confronting that secret weapon that beats in the heart and the mind of my earthly and terrestrial guardians.

And, there and then, now, forever, the last and final end of the world will take place.

Nothing will be left, nothing else will happen after that, after that night.

I won't commit the hubris of saying that it'll be an act of compassion—because it might be nothing but an act of absolute egoism—but I can assure you it'll be a beautiful and emotional final act. And that everything will be all right, everything will be all right, everything will be all right, everything will be all right, everything will be all right, everything will be all right, everything will be all right forever.

There they were, are, there they'll remain, like constellations that make us strain our eyes, staring up at them, being generous and imaginative, to pick them out and convince ourselves that they couldn't be called anything else or be arranged in a different way; to be sure that, yes, they have *that* form and *that* is what they mean.

There they were, are, there they'll remain, with me, transformed into pure energy that I, in a final frenzy, before melting down and shutting down from the effort—devout host of this twilight zone—will transmit to every corner of the universe, to the bottom of the sky. In the glorious white and black of the night and the snow after centuries and centuries of colors. To and from precisely there. The bottom of the sky like the bottom of the biggest and most infinite of swimming pools. What ancient Hellenistic astrologers referred to as *Imum Coeli*. Some said hell was there. Others, heaven. Or they pointed to it as our exact point of origin as well as the precise location where our lives will end. All at the same time. Beginning and ending. The totality of every variation. All possible selves. One me looking at a Rothko painting and another me staring at a Chagall. Diving and falling. Over and over until . . . I'm convinced, then, that there must be a swimming pool that's mine, the best of all, the swimming pool where I swim like I never swam and whose waters hide all the explanations of all the mysteries and forgotten things and, so, I, from there . . .

With a little bit of luck, someone will catch this mysterious beam—this last sigh of my final and eternal signal—and will know how to decode its pulses and convert them into a faithful and incorruptible image.

And will see the three of us.

The two of them looking at me and me looking at them.

And, overcome with feeling, they'll think that we must have been a great culture that enjoyed the most beautiful and impassioned of endings.

And they'll see the three of us—together at last, together forever, together in the end—and think "they went extinct, yes, but they went extinct in the highest and most sublime moment of feeling; they went extinct burning with love and not drowning in hate."

They'll see me—with eyes that'll be Isaac and Ezra's eyes—the way the two of them saw me.

And they'll see the two of them—with eyes that'll be my eyes—the way I saw them.

They'll see the two of them, now and forever, as clearly as I saw them from my window: looking up at me, on that clear night, in the snow, on another planet, on our planet, on a planet that will be ours and only ours.

They'll see the two of them suspended forever in the time and space of my love.

I'll remember them like this.

Like this I remember them.

BLACK HOLES, COLORED LIGHTS,
AND MARVELOUS MOMENTS:
Explanation and Acknowledgements

First of all: this is not a novel *of* science fiction.
It is—it was and it will be—a novel *with* science fiction.

In the end: one of the books I've read and reread most isn't a novel *of* science fiction but a novel *with* science fiction.

And it's a book written by one of the writers I've read and reread—that exquisite activity that's an even better combination of amnesia and sudden recollection than reading something for the first time because it's like finding yourself back in the company of an old friend instead of with a stranger—the most, and that writer's name is Kurt Vonnegut.

And one of the books by Kurt Vonnegut that I have reread most is called *Slaughterhouse-Five*. And one of the paragraphs I reread most from one of the novels I reread most written by one of the writers I reread most—Kurt Vonnegut—is one that goes like this:

> They were little things. [. . .] Billy couldn't read Tralfama-
> dorian, of course, but he could at least see how the books

were laid out—in brief symbols separated by stars. [. . .] Each clump of symbols is a brief, urgent message—describing a situation, a scene. We Tralfamadorians read them all at once, not one after the other. There isn't any particular relationship between the messages, except that the author has chosen them carefully, so that, when seen all at once, they produce an image that is beautiful and surprising and deep. There is no beginning, no middle, no end, no suspense, no moral, no causes, no effects. What we love in our books are the depths of many marvelous moments seen all at one time.

I like to think that this paragraph—which isn't just a great idea marvelously expressed but, also, a perfect and concise explication of Kurt Vonnegut's work and intentions—contains, distant in time yet nearby in feelings of admiration and gratitude, the origin of *The Bottom of the Sky*.

I like to think of *The Bottom of the Sky* as a clump of simultaneously broadcast messages, like a storyline that wants nothing but to be a succession of marvelous moments seen all at the same time.

And now that I think of it: it was Kurt Vonnegut who in an interview said something about how all writers had the obligation, at least once in their career, to destroy a world.

In *The Bottom of the Sky* I destroy two.

Multiple times.

Mission accomplished, I hope.

And while I was writing the last pages of *The Bottom of the Sky* I read *Cheever: A Life* by Blake Bailey.

John Cheever is the other writer who—along with Kurt Vonnegut—tends to appear, since my first book, since *Historia argentina*

[Argentine History] in 1991, as a protective figure and extraterrestrial friend in each and every one of my books. The one and the other appear again in *The Bottom of the Sky*, but what surprised me most—around page 575 of Bailey's Cheever biography—was to discover that Cheever, after the success of *Falconer* and his living canonization with *The Stories of John Cheever*, didn't really know how to go on, what would come next. And that then—depressed and without map or compass—he started clipping newspaper articles about the possibility of life on other planets and fantasizing about writing "a novel about cosmic loneliness."

As you know, Cheever didn't write that novel, but a perfect novella called *Oh What a Paradise It Seems* where you can't catch even a whiff of other worlds. But, on page 24 of the original edition, at the beginning of chapter 3, he makes the comment, as if in passing, that the narrator of the story is speaking to us from a more or less faraway future, as he prepares to fire a rifle into the heart of a man consciously or unconsciously responsible for multiple planetary catastrophes.

At times when I'm in a really good mood (like right now) I like to think of *The Bottom of the Sky* as a novel about cosmic loneliness that, I hope, makes good and satisfying company. I like to think of *The Bottom of the Sky* as one of those novels that—like *Slaughterhouse-Five* and *Oh What a Paradise It Seems*—seem so small on the outside, but once you're inside . . .

And the thing from the beginning, I insist: this is not a novel of science fiction but, yes, it is fed by science fiction and by my love for a genre that, as a reader, I came to young and that I won't leave until the end. As a writer—you who follow me already know this—I have traveled to Urkh 24 several times, where I went for the first time in the short alien-matrimonial story *"La forma de la locura"* ["The Shape of Madness"], in 1994, in the disappeared *Trabajos manuals* [Manual

Labors]. And I'm reminded, all of a sudden, of *Caras extrañas* [Strange Faces], that now unfindable alien-Gardelian serial for the young supplement of *Pagina/12*. And I've even written a couple stories that can be considered laterally sci-fi. And already in *Historia argentina*—and later in *La velocidad de las cosas* [The Speed of Things]—there's an invitation to stroll through a foundation devoted to the maintenance and preservation of the last specimen of the extinct species of writers. And the viral illuminati in *Vidas de santos* [Lives of Saints], the seismic androids in *Mantra*, and the space/time bicycles in *Kensington Gardens* . . .

But again what interests me here is the same thing that interested me in my other novels: to work with different genres not by approaching them, but by bringing them into my territory. Thus, the rock-and-roll novel in *Esperanto*, the foreigner-trip-in-Mexico novel in *Mantra*, and the coming-of-age novel in *Kensington Gardens*. And thus the futuristic novel (even though, really, it's a futuristic novel that's more preoccupied and occupied with the past than with the future) in *The Bottom of the Sky*.

Thus, a novel whose working and work-in-progress alias was *Tsunami* and its original and mysterious premise—initial note in a notebook—was, merely, "woman devastates three men like a tsunami / *love story* / SADNESS!!!"

Thus, a novel that was written slowly over the course of several years that, now, seen with perspective, seems to me much more nonfiction than fiction. Too many things happened and at full speed. Many good and very happy things, a few very sad things. Something that—though inevitable and impossible to edit and correct—remains partially true: it isn't bad, every so often, for what happens on this planet to be imposed over what happens on that planet where writers spend much of their lives.

I worked a lot too. And I moved. To another world. A better world than the one I inhabited; which doesn't imply that the voyage hasn't been exhausting. And don't ever forget it: when a writer moves, his library *also* moves. And, in case someone is interested, the twilight landscape that the dying extraterrestrial from Urkh 24 ceaselessly watches is none other than the sunsets of Vallvidrera with views of Montserrat out the circular and oh so *2001: A Space Odyssey* window of my study where I am writing all of this.

Thus, a novel in which I worried a great deal about finding a certain "language" to tell it in, knowing that, in general, science fiction doesn't care as much about style (apart from the honorable exceptions of Philip K. Dick and J. G. Ballard and a few others) as it does about the plot, about the "idea," about the "future" it proposes.

And if there's something that always bothered me about classic science fiction it's that hardwired need to explain absolutely everything (even that which is known to be unexplainable, mysterious, that which is better left as pure and unattainable mystery), with that didactic and almost fundamentalist zeal, with those irrepressible desires to lead the way and to be right and to win, wanting so badly to get first place in a race to the future that, of course, has no finish line.

The Bottom of the Sky, I think, concerns itself with something else. Not so much with making the implausible seem plausible but— Cheever again, in an interview—to work with "moments" and not "plots." It seems to me that, in his day, Stanley Kubrick—too bad he was weighed down by Arthur C. Clarke—opted, fortunately, for the same approach.

To put it another way and availing myself of another particular cinematographic gaze: on the planet where *The Bottom of the Sky* takes place, the rockets and space shuttles don't take off from the flat fields of a place called Cape Canaveral, but from the sinuous slopes of a place known as Mulholland Drive.

"I don't work with plots. I work with intuition, apprehension, dreams, concepts," John Cheever explained to a reporter from *The Paris Review*.

Ditto.

So *The Bottom of the Sky* has traveled a great deal and has tried on too many spacesuits before feeling comfortable and satisfied with the one it wears now, with the one it floats in now. *The Bottom of the Sky* had—at some point—many many more pages and was for a while a novel with a much more historic and encyclopedic personality (a more or less close relative of *The Amazing Adventures of Kavalier & Clay*, to offer an example); but there was something that didn't agree with me there that, though I enjoyed reading it, I wasn't interested in writing.* Nor—going to the other extreme on the spectrum—was I interested in having *The Bottom of the Sky* evoke the certain inexplicable alien strangeness of several novels by Haruki Murakami where nothing gets explained. So there were various failures to launch before, finally, taking off and understanding where this novel should go.

And now I'm *so* happy to have arrived . . .

"*Writing long* is like reading, while *writing short* is like writing," someone says near the end of *The Bottom of the Sky*; but I'm the one who says to say it.

And it doesn't seem a coincidence to me that the most constant and powerful part of the process of the writing of *The Bottom of the*

---

* Somewhere, in another dimension much like our own, there's another novel called *The Bottom of the Sky*—I read it because I wrote it, I made it disappear— where, among many other things, it records in detail the composition of each and every one of the sci-fi fan clubs in 1930s New York; it details various missions and military movements during the Iraq war and offers profuse descriptions of the life in Bagdad's Green Zone (Green Area, *Grynarya*); you can read a complete version of *Evasion* and it follows Mark Rothko's career step by step as well as list- ing the necessary requirements for joining a popular religious-freak organization.

Sky—which, for a while, shared space with the writing of another now-finished novel and with three others in different stages of development—coincided with the period of time beginning with the death of Kurt Vonnegut and ending with the death of J. G. Ballard, with the death of David Foster Wallace in between.

May they rest in peace.

And now—when at last, coming back, I land and remove the space suit—my gratitude to all those who watched over my vital signs while I floated so far from home but confident that they were near and dear to this book.

In the launch tower: Juan Ignacio Boido (head reader), Jonathan Letham (who recommended specialized bibliography and told me the anecdote that triggered this novel), Francisco "Paco" Porrúa (who ceded books from his Barcelona library) and Juan Sasturain (who brought me books in Guadalajara from his library in Buenos Aires).

Always orbiting nearby: Carlos Alberdi, Eduardo Becerra, Ignacio Echevarría, Nelly Fresán, Alfredo Garófano, Norma Elizabeth Mastrorilli, Alan Pauls, Guillermo Saccomanno, Enrique Vila-Matas, the Villaseñor family.

In the control room: Agencia Carmen Balcells and Gloria Gutierrez and Javier Martín, Marta Borrell, Mónica Carmona, Marta Díaz, Andreu Jaume, Claudio López Lamadrid, and Editorial Mondadori. And my foreign editors and translators, for the patience they've had with me and, I hope, they patience they'll have with me again.

In the outer space: Dante Alighieri, J. G. Ballard, John Banville, Donald Barthelme, Franco Battiato (those verses of "Milky Way" where you hear *"Noi / provinciali dell'Orsa Minor / alla conquista degli spazi interstellari / e vestiti di grigio chiaro / per non disperdersi"* I always found very moving), Blake Bailey, The Beatles ("A Day in the Life," *that sound*, one more time) Ray Bradbury, Adolfo Bioy Casares for the Morelian projections and reflections ("the sky of the consciousness," "it will be an act of mercy") that are here activated, Jarvis Cocker (and his "Quantum Theory"), Leonard "The Little Jew Who Wrote the Bible" Cohen, Lloyd Cole (*Love Story* in general and the particular version of "Traffic" that appears in *Cleaning Out the Ashtrays*), Philip K. Dick ("How to Build a Universe That Doesn't Fall Apart Two Days Later"), Bob Dylan ("The ghost of 'lectricity howls in the bones of her face," of course, and the novelty of *non-stop*, as I write these lines, from *Together Through Life*, another of those B. D. albums that—in his oh so *sci-fi* way—it is impossible to know when it was recorded, impossible to tell if it comes from the future or the past), Mark Oliver "Eels" Everett (and his father), Denis Johnson, "Big Sky" by The Kinks (for obvious reasons), Stanley Kubrick (for still more obvious reasons), David Kyle, David Lynch, Robert R. McCammon, Norman Mailer, Héctor Germán Oesterheld, Michael Ondaatje, Pink Floyd (*Wish You Were Here* could be considered the head album of *The Bottom of the Sky* and it always seemed to me the perfect soundtrack for a private and domestic science fiction film), John Prine (that one verse from "Lake Marie"), Mark Rothko, Rod Sterling, Cordwainer Smith (Paul Myron Anthony Linebarger), Theodore Sturgeon, "Dream Operator" by Talking Heads (something like the equivalent to "Lara's Theme" in *The Bottom of the Sky*: "Her Theme"), James Tiptree Jr. (Alice B. Sheldon), François Truffaut (and everything is said), John Updike and his *Toward the End of Time*, David Foster Wallace, Dennis Wilson and "Time" on his *Pacific Ocean Blue*, Warren Zevon and "The Vast Indifference of Heaven."

And beyond winks and blinks and flickers more or less fleeting and maybe imperceptible if you don't have a good telescope to capture that not-dead but, yes, somewhat-crepuscular starlight of childhood readings—when the future was The Future—that distortedly arrives to this book.

The first part of *The Bottom of the Sky* admiringly resuscitates a line (the one about the dog of time) and some circumstances from *Tokyo Doesn't Want Us Anymore* by Ray Loriga, plays with a Marcel Proust quote, and abducts and rewrites a couple scenes that originally appear in *The Wapshot Scandal* by John Cheever and *God Bless You, Mr. Rosewater* by Kurt Vonnegut.

The second part of *The Bottom of the Sky*, on the other hand, references a story of mine—*"La usurpación de los cuerpos"* ["The Usurpation of Bodies"]—written by Miguel Ángel Oeste (thanks, Miguel Ángel) for *FreakCiones: 6 peliculas, 6 mutaciones* (Centro de Ediciones de la Diputación Provincial de Málaga, España, 2007) and included later in the French edition of *La velocidad de las cosas* (*La vitesse des choses*, Les Éditions Passage Du Nord/Ouest, 2008).

The third part of *The Bottom of the Sky* winks at and modifies my favorite line from *Distant Star* by Roberto Bolaño.

I'm grateful too for the information—utilized or not, but always nutritious and inspiring—contained in the books *Imperial Life in the Emerald City* by Rajiv Chandrasekaran, *The Encyclopedia of Science Fiction* by John Clute and Peter Nicholls, *Ghost Wars* by Steve Coll, *L. Ron Hubbard: Messiah or Madman?* by Bent Coydon and L. Ron Hubbard Jr., *The Shifting Realities of Philip K. Dick* by Philip K. Dick and edited by Lawrence Sutin, *The Dreams Our Stuff Is Made Of: How Science Fiction Conquered the World* by Thomas M. Dish, *The Futurians* by Damon Knight, *Medea* edited by Harlan Ellison, *Strange Angel: The Otherworldly Life of Rocket Scientist John Whiteside Parsons* by George Pendle, *The Way The Future Was* by Frederik Pohl, *Murasaki* edited by Robert Silverberg, *Divine Invasions* by Lawrence Sutin, *The Bradbury Chronicles* by Sam Weller, *Only Apparently Real* by Paul Williams, *The Looming Tower* by Lawrence Wright, and *The Twilight Zone Companion* by Marc Scott Zicree.

And, more than thank you and, after all, always at my side, traveling *across the universe*: Ana and Daniel.

And greetings to all of you, out there.

We're not alone, thanks for coming back to be with me, and we'll see each other soon, I hope, in another world that's in this one.

R. F.
Vallvidrera, Barcelona
May 1ˢᵗ, 2009

Rodrigo Fresán is the author of ten works of fiction, including *Kensington Gardens*, *Mantra*, and *The Invented Part*. A self-professed "referential maniac," his works incorporate many elements from science fiction (Philip K. Dick in particular) alongside pop culture and literary references. According to Jonathan Lethem, "he's a kaleidoscopic, open-hearted, shamelessly polymathic storyteller, the kind who brings a blast of oxygen into the room." In 2017, he received the Prix Roger Caillois awarded by PEN Club France every year to both a French and a Latin American writer.

Will Vanderhyden received an MA in Literary Translation Studies from the University of Rochester. He has translated fiction by Carlos Labbé, Edgardo Cozarinsky, Alfredo Bryce Echenique, Juan Marsé, Rafael Sánchez Ferlosio, Rodrigo Fresán, and Elvio Gandolfo. He received NEA and Lannan fellowships to translate another of Fresán's novels, *The Invented Part*.

**OPEN
LETTER**

**OPEN
LETTER**